The awnshegh was larger than Richard had expected. It stood nearly seven feet tall and the cephalothorax stretched out nine feet behind it. The old tales said it had once been a goblin, but the upper part of its body, the head and arms, were all that resembled a humanoid. The face was still goblin-like, with small eyes, and a wide, flat nose, and fangs projecting from a big, cruel mouth. Pointed ears rose nearly to the top of its head which seemed small when compared to the wide shoulders and long arms. From the creature's fingers extended long claws, good for fighting, but little else.

Richard had no need to exaggerate the fear that went with his carefully rehearsed first words, but he did not get a chance to use them immediately. Tal-Qazar spoke first.

BIRTHRIGHT™ BOOKS

BIRTHRIGHT™

BOOKS

The Spider's Test

Dixie Lee McKeone

THE SPIDER'S TEST

©1996 TSR, Inc.
All Rights Reserved.

First Printing: September 1996
Printed in the United States of America.
Library of Congress Catalog Card Number: 95-62246

9 8 7 6 5 4 3 2 1

ISBN: 0-7869-0512-3
3115XXX1501

TSR, Inc.   TSR Ltd.
201 Sheridan Springs Road   120 Church End, Cherry Hinton
Lake Geneva, WI 53147   Cambridge CB1 3LB
United States of America   United Kingdom

RIVERVALE FORT

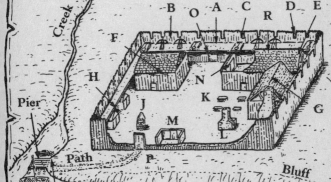

Fire Trenches

Creek

B O A C R D E

F

H

N

K

J

M L

G

Pier

Path P

Bluff

Washout Maesil River

A	Catwalk	J	Well
B	Ballista	K	Outside Tables
C	Catapult	L	Outside Hearth
D	Arrow Slits	M	Smokehouse
E	First Building	N	Stable Doors
F	Second Building	O	East Gate
G	Cooking and Dining Hall	P	West Gate
H	Storage Sheds	R	Roof Tiles
			(just being laid)

1″ = 60′

one

The rays of the early morning sun fell on the top branches of the ancient grove of trees. Below the thick upper canopy of leaves the light that filtered down dimmed, as if shrinking from the scene below. The upper branches that reached for the sun and light grew from giant trees whose boles were host to a ramshackle town built fifty feet above the ground. From a distance, the settlement known as the Web resembled the cruel trap of a giant arachnid. An interlacing of thick strands that created long walkways looped between the trees. Wooden slats provided the flooring for a network of raised walkways. Many had the additional support of giant spider silk ladders suspended from the higher limbs.

Berkerig raced down the rickety spiral stairs that encircled several trees and provided access from the ground. He trotted past the shabby, ill-fitting doors of dwellings that had been carved into the trees. Occasionally he dodged around crooked walls with inadequate shingling and thatching. Rays of light and the black smoke of sputtering torches seeped through the cracks and gaps.

"You be late," Subdug—one of his drinking cronies from the night before—chided him as he ran along a tree limb to another ladder.

Berkerig didn't pause to answer. Subdug was right, he was late taking up his station at the entrance to the Adytum, the residence of Tal-Qazar, the Spider King, one of the powerful beings that the elves had named awnshegh. If Tal-Qazar called for Berkerig and the lieutenant was not within hearing, death would be the reward for his tardiness.

As the sun rose, a few of the goblins inhabiting the Web were already gathering. They waited on the ground, staring up at the huge construction in the center, watching the entrance to the awnshegh's dwelling with wide, frightened eyes. The evening before, a rumor had flown through the Web; the inhabitants were to gather at sunrise. They had not been told why.

Berkerig ignored the rank and file as he raced up the hundred foot ladder-path to the Adytum, the center of horror in the heart of a primordial forest of menace and fear. At first glance the Adytum appeared to be some sort of massive chrysalis or cocoon, all of its fifty by seventy foot length and breadth woven from arachnid strands.

Rumor said the Spider King had attached the huge cable-thick foundation strands himself, but if he had, the work had been done centuries before any living goblin's memory. Then awnshegh's arachnid minions, ranging in size from giants, five feet or more in length, to tiny, barely visible creatures, had completed the construction. Six thick strands connected the Adytum to six large trees, which had long since been strangled of their life. The larger spiders had added supporting strands for the walls and ceilings and a succession of their smaller cousins had filled it in until the thick walls of webbing kept out the wind and rain.

Berkerig reached his station at the left of the entrance and stood panting. To the right, Gosfak stood with his spear in hand, and skewed his eyes toward his fellow lieutenant. Their rank was the highest in the Spiderfell, but with it came the responsibility of passing along the orders of the awnshegh. The job became more perilous with each passing year, as Tal-Qazar grew less and less sane. The Spider King had been born more than twelve hundred and eighty years before, and even with his power, his brain seemed to be aging. He often gave orders even his lieutenants could not understand, and they were faced with having to translate their master's cryptic commands. To fail in understanding, or to ask for an explanation, was likely to bring on Tal-Qazar's rage. He usually killed the offending lieutenant. Berkerig's position was an assurance of a short life. Still, he would live longer than if he had refused the "promotion."

Berkerig stared straight ahead, not daring to peer inside the Adytum. No creature except the awnshegh and the spiders who repaired rents in the interior ever saw the inside of the Adytum and lived. The exterior seemed to be alive with trapped birds and insects. A decoration of skulls, rib cages and assorted bones of the Spider's dead enemies decorated the entrance. The thick accumulation of elf, human, and often goblin bones had widened until it stretched twenty feet on each side and reached twenty feet above the nine foot opening.

The goblins stood on the ground, looking up when they saw movement within the shadowy entrance. They fell silent as their master appeared. He ignored his lieutenants as he paused at the top of the long spider silk ladder that led to the ground.

Tal-Qazar resembled a humanoid from the waist up, with a strong, muscular chest, shoulders and arms. His flat face favored his ancestry, with the large, pointed ears, wide mouth and long, sharp teeth of a goblin. His abdomen extended back into a spider's thorax, giving him a seven foot length and eight six foot long spider legs ended in clawed pedipalps.

He descended with slow majesty, intimidating his subjects as he looked out over the mass of goblins and spiders that waited below. Where his eyes raked the crowds, the goblins trembled, unsure of his mood and what infraction of his uncertain laws had brought him out of his solitude. He had covered only a third of the distance when he suddenly leaped, dropping lightly to a landing on the latticework just ten feet above their heads. He glared down at the assembled group with eyes glowing red with rage.

"Two days ago the wind brought the stink of elves on the Maesil," he said. His voice seemed soft, but it carried across the assembled group and echoed off the trees. None of the goblins believed in the heightened sense of smell the awnshegh claimed, but none were foolish enough to show doubt. Somehow he had learned of what had passed on the river. Through one of his spider spies or a loose-tongued member of their group.

"Why have I not been brought their bodies to decorate the Adytum?" He glared at two of the large goblins who had been guarding the western arm of the forest. The dark woods of the Spiderfell extended to the banks of the Maesil, a wide, navigable river that snaked through many of the lands of southwestern Cerilia.

The goblins who stood between the two guards and the awnshegh sidled away quickly, leaving a wide space around the offenders. The first, Adgrad, a huge brute with a jagged scar twisting his face, backed up three steps, causing the assembly to hastily step back. They fell over each other in their haste to escape the wrath of the Spider.

"Nasty, tr-tricky creatures, smart thinking," Adgrad stuttered. "In boats, sailing qu-quick up the river. We run fast, threw spears, but they was too far out o' reach."

"T-too far, way too far," Hugrit, the second guard agreed, his small black eyes stretched with terror.

"I wanted those elves," the Spider snarled. With a lightning movement he brought up his tail and a thick, sticky strand lashed out from the spinnerets, wrapping itself first around Adgrad, then Hugrit.

The Spider roared, then turned, and with three gigantic leaps he reached the top of the ladder and entered the Adytum. He did not stay to see the thousands of small spiders descending from the trees, spinning their way down to the ground. He did turn to see them cover the bodies of the useless goblins that had allowed the elves to escape. In seconds the offenders were covered with crawling arachnids. Their screams were stifled as the small creatures invaded their mouths, noses and covered their eyes.

In minutes the clothing and the armor shifted as the bodies inside were consumed. He turned and entered his dwelling, knowing the grisly decorations that trimmed the entrance to the Adytum would soon be increased by another set of skeletons.

Berkerig and Gosfak trembled as they watched the scene below. They traded nervous glances. Tal-Qazar was in a bad mood. It would be a bad day, and they would be fortunate to see the sunset.

Inside the Adytum, Tal-Qazar crouched in his favorite spot and grinned. He had accomplished several goals that morning: the goblins of the Spiderfell would put more effort into killing the elves; since he never allowed the spiders of the forest to attack the goblins, he had sated the appetites of some of his pets; and two more skeletons would be added to the trophies around his entrance.

The Spider rose and paced, trying to bring order to his thoughts. As the centuries passed he had discovered the strange, debilitating effects of rage. After a spate of uncontrollable anger his thoughts seemed to take on a life apart, racing in all directions like a colony of ants when their nest was disturbed. The disorder had begun several centuries before and seemed to be growing with the years. His struggles to bring back clear and focused thought became harder with passing time.

"I am Tal-Qazar, Tal-Qazar, a goblin, goblin, goblin, goblin. I am Tal-Qazar, Tal-Qazar." He forced the litany to the forefront of his consciousness, working to regain control of his mind.

"I am Tal-Qazar, goblin king, ruler of this land," he muttered to himself. "This is my land. I rule here. Before I gained my powers I was an elf—an elf who— *no, not an elf!*" He roared aloud.

His enemies had invented that false tale. It passed from mouth to mouth, bringing laughter to those he hated and he had been consumed by rage for years after first hearing it. He hated elves beyond all other creatures. He had been a goblin—he *was* a goblin, though the monstrous body that enclosed his spirit bore almost no resemblance to his original shape.

He was Tal-Qazar.

His people had lived in the forest known as the Spiderfell for many centuries. They were a strong and powerful nation of sorcerers, and he had been their leader, the most powerful of all—all the goblins, he thought and scratched at the soft floor, tearing holes in the intricate webbing that protected him from the wind and weather. He roared in frustration at the damage and then ignored it. The forest was filled with spiders who would race to repair it.

He had been a sorcerer, hadn't he? He tried to pull back the memories. They shied away like leaves on a fast-moving current when it splits to pass a boulder in the center of a stream bed.

He had been a sorcerer. His obsession had been his hatred for the miserable elves that fled north when they were driven out of the forests of the Erebannien. They had tried to take his land from him, but he and his people killed them by the thousands. The Deretha had driven them out. What had happened to the Deretha?

Sudden fear and rage filled his mind. Were they also coming to his land? He tore at the floor again, rushed to the entrance and shouted at his two lieutenants who stood ready to pass on his orders.

"Increase the patrols!" he shouted to them. "The Deretha may even now be on the march!"

He watched as they stared at him with impassive faces and moved away to do his bidding. He returned to the dryness and warmth of his shelter and resumed his pacing. If the Deretha attacked . . . Deretha? Why had that ancient term entered his head? For centuries the Deretha had called themselves Anuireans and lived all around the Spiderfell. They feared it and him. He had already forgotten the orders to his lieutenants.

Yes, the puny humans that now called themselves Anuireans feared him even when Michael Roele had made them into an empire. This Roele had ruled them for many years . . . didn't he die? Didn't he challenge the Gorgon and lose? Yes. Ginmark had brought Tal-Qazar the news. That had been long ago. More than fifty lieutenants had succeeded Ginmark. War and upheaval had followed the emperor's death for more than half a century, but much of that time had been lost in the Spider's foggy memory.

He paced, his eight legs moving with arachnid speed as he wandered the cavernous, tent-like dwelling. He fumed over not being able to remember Michael Roele's death clearly, because he had been an enemy Tal-Qazar had hated almost as much as the elves. The Spider would have liked to savor it again. He probed his memories and the clearest were of the battle of Mount Deismaar. That, he remembered, had been a glorious time, at least in the beginning. . . .

While Tal-Qazar savored his memories of the battle of Mount Deismaar, Berkerig and Gosfak obediently trotted down the spider ladder until they were beyond Tal-Qazar's keen hearing.

"Who is Deretha?" Gosfak asked.

Berkerig, who was the ranking lieutenant because he had managed to survive in his position for four months, shrugged.

"Haukag!" he shouted to one of the junior lieutenants. "Add another fifty to the perimeter patrols." He decided the additional number should be enough. Berkerig had never heard the name Deretha. Who ever he was, he couldn't be much of a threat. . . .

TWO

Richard Endier strolled along the shop-lined streets of Moerel, a river town on the banks of the Maesil in northwest Diemed. He inspected the new civic improvements and gave them the full benefit of his consideration. He was not convinced he liked the cobblestone paving and wondered at its attraction. As he thought about it, he began to see the point. During the rainy months, feet, hooves and cart wheels would not sink in the mud, but he found walking on the stones rather uncomfortable. Berdig, the ranger he had met in an inn the night before, had told him the sharp edges would wear away in time. According to Berdig, most of the streets in the City of Anuire, the capital of Avanil, were similarly paved. The much smaller, poorer town of Moerel had only a few hundred feet of its main thoroughfare so far completed.

Richard strolled a full ten yards along the cobblestones before he had experienced all he wanted of the benefits of modern urban living. Through the thin soles of his boots he felt every sharp edge and decided he would never risk the feet of *his* horse on this modern wonder.

The discomfort reaching him through his well-worn foot gear reminded him that he was due at the cobbler's that afternoon to pick up his new boots, which he looked forward to with almost giddy anticipation. He had run a trap line along the Maesil during the past fall and winter, working in the cold water until his hands hurt, but the beaver and river otter pelts had brought in enough for the new boots with a bit left over to pay for new soles on the old ones.

On his return journey he walked along the shadowed street and finally understood why the townies found cobblestone paving such a big improvement. The tall, half-timbered buildings that housed shops all had dwellings above and the upper floors cantilevered out over the street, generally depriving most of the street of sunlight. The structures huddled together as if seeking the company or security of their neighbors, and beneath their overhangs, the moisture never seemed to dry.

The cobblestone pavement fronted the shops that carried costly wares and were patronized by the rich. Closer to the river the buildings were shabbier and less complex. They catered to the river travelers: the farmers and hunters who used the square by the wharves to trade.

When Richard left the pavement he dodged the ruts and muddy potholes. After two hundred yards he stepped out into the late afternoon autumn sunlight of the market square. For most of the year it was a barren field with the river and the wharves to the west, and the town proper to the north. The hulks of sheds and warehouses hemmed it in on the south. Through the winter, spring and early summer a small weekly market provided the town with its needs, but in the autumn, the farmers for many miles around brought in their crops. They packed the field with colorful produce. Some wore bright clothing obviously purchased in town. Others, like most of Richard Endier's family, did not waste their silver on the fashionable but delicate wardrobes that could be easily and permanently stained and torn unloading baskets and bundles from their wagons.

Richard wound his way along an irregular path through the crowd of dealers. They had spread their wares on rough boards supported by old kegs, baskets of trade goods not yet opened and, at times, on the ground. Tableware, thin, painted and richly glazed; swords and war axes; cabbages, potatoes and turnips; plows and hoes were piled side by side as the traders' wares elbowed for space.

He worked his way toward the river until he reached the spot where his uncle bargained for the best price for their crop. They had chosen their place the night before. Richard and his two younger cousins had spent the late hours of the night setting out their baskets of turnips, onions, cabbages and tubers. They also sold hard little apples that never achieved a flashy perfection of size and color but, properly stored, would last through the winter and well into spring. The Endiers grew staple foods, took care to pack them carefully, and usually received a good price for their crops. Through the years the family had developed a reputation with the traders, so Richard was not surprised to see another farmer setting out his baskets where Randen Endier had reigned an hour before.

His uncle and three cousins stood off to the side, in conversation with a riverboat captain. The father and his two younger sons, Gaelin and Droene, were immediately recognizable as farmers in their sturdy, unbleached homespun shirts and trousers. They had no time for finery when baskets had to be hauled from the carts, displayed and, when sold, delivered to the riverboats.

They shared certain physical traits like wide shoulders and long, muscular legs and the strong bones and square jaws of their Endier blood, yet they were all quite different. A broken leg the winter before and a protracted illness had left Richard's uncle Randen spare in flesh. Gaelin was the most vivid member of the family with bright red hair, green eyes, a quick wit and a smaller stature. Droene, the youngest, was a hulking brute with pale coloring and a slow, though amiable mind.

Arlen, the oldest of the three brothers, stood off to the side, preening in the finery he had brought for their trip to town. He stood with his back to the rest of the family as if disclaiming any connection.

Randen Endier looked up and saw Richard approaching. He held a leather purse which he dangled by the strings as he gave Richard a wide smile.

Richard grinned back. Randen had been successful in his bargaining, and Richard would be receiving a good purse for his year's work in the fields. Richard's spirits rose as Arlen glared at the bag in his father's hand. The bag obviously held more than coppers, and Arlen had always been resentful that Richard's share was larger than his.

Randen's oldest son and heir chose to ignore the fact that the farm should have belonged to Richard all along.

The Endier freehold, a large farm in the extreme northwest corner of settled Diemed had been in the family for more generations than any of them remembered. In its time it had been inherited by Aenel Endier, Richard's father and Randen's older brother. Aenel had been severely wounded in a battle with the goblins of the Spiderfell before Richard was a year old. Knowing he was dying, Aenel had inscribed a will, leaving the property to Randen under verbal instructions to will it back to Richard at Randen's death. Randen had kept his word, to the indignation of his oldest son. Though Arlen had grown up knowing the property was Richard's by right, greed was the food of this unjustified resentment.

Richard was just skirting the wares of a glass blower when an over-exuberant bargainer swung his arm. The buyer was holding a heavy glass ewer that struck Richard on the shoulder. Caught by surprise, an off-balance Richard careened into two young men who were threading their way through the crowd. One was caught in the act of raising a wineskin to his lips, and when Richard bumped into him, the wine splashed on his velvet doublet. The other was quicker to step out of the way, but in his haste he stepped into the midden ditch. One of his soft, gleaming boots was covered with filth.

"Dolt!" the young man with the wine-soaked doublet shouted, his voice slurred with too much wine. "You ignorant country scum, you'll pay for this. . . ."

His friend, enraged over his boots, grabbed the handle of a basket that belonged to a vender of turnips and swung it at Richard's head. Richard ducked. The vegetables went flying, many into the midden ditch.

"My turnips!" cried the old woman who had been robbed of her vegetables.

"Shut up, you old hag or I'll have you up before my father," the young man snarled. He was as drunk as his friend and staggered as he pulled his short sword and advanced toward Richard.

"Run him through, Ruinel," the other shouted. "Look what he did to my doublet."

"Now see here," the enthusiastic bargainer interrupted, but he was shoved back by the young man with the wine flask.

Around the confrontation, shoppers hastily backed away. Vendors climbed over their baskets and make-shift tables to stand in the narrow path, ready to physically defend their wares.

Someone shouted, "Call the watch!"

Richard barely heard the commotion has he eyed the short sword in Ruinel's hand. The blade was a slender one, a dress sword better used for swaggering than for battle. Richard's only defense was a dirk in a sheath behind his neck, but he left it where it was. Both fashionably dressed young men were drunk. Richard had a high opinion of his strength and fighting abilities and saw no need for a weapon. He lightly jumped aside as Ruinel slashed at him.

"Stand still, you ragged fool," Ruinel ordered, his words a little slurred. "Why they even let you wretched vermin into town is . . ."

Richard had heard enough of the young dandy's insults. Ruinel was drunk, that was apparent, and his inebriation could be used against him. Richard stepped forward, inviting another slash of the sword, then stepped back when Ruinel started his swing. He let the blade whiz by and caught the city man by the arm, jerking him around, catching him off-balance. With a twist of his arm he dumped the drunk into the midden ditch. Ruinel went sprawling, splashing the filthy water on several onlookers who had not had the wit to get well out of the way.

Richard stepped back, hardly out of breath, and straight into the hands of two burly soldiers who wore the uniform of the city watch.

"That's enough," said the one who wore the insignia of a watch commander. "It will be the son of the mayor you'll be assaulting, and his father you'll be answering to."

"What's the matter, can't the mayor's son answer for his own deeds?" Richard demanded. "He had the blade, I held no weapon."

"It's true," someone from the crowd shouted.

"It should be him that does the answering," the old woman cried. "Look at me turnips!"

The second watch guard shoved her aside, ignoring her complaints as he gave a hand to Ruinel who was floundering out of the midden ditch. The watch commander ignored the remarks from Richard and the bystanders.

"I want him arrested and thrown in the dungeon!" he screamed at the soldiers.

Randen and two of his sons, Gaelin and Droene, were pushing their way through the crowd. Richard suspected that Arlen, who he could not see, had managed to once again distance himself from trouble. Richard shook his head at his kinsmen, warning them away. They could do him no good and might just end up getting in trouble themselves.

"Now see here," the heavy-set bargainer stepped up, laying a restraining hand on the arm of the watch commander. The shopper huffed and puffed, and seemed to lose his train of thought, but the soldier waited patiently.

"Do you know who I am?"

"Aye, Master Jamael, it is your moneylender's shop and your walled residence I have passed on my rounds these ten years." Respect dripped from the watch commander's voice.

"The original fault was mine," Master Jamael announced. "And too, I will vouch for this young man in that he did not intentionally start the trouble."

"Aye, Master, but he did throw the mayor's son in the ditch, and if we allow commoners to show that sort of disrespect to the gentry, where will we be?"

"Disrespect you may call it," the master replied with

a smile, "But he could have done a lot more damage with that knife in the sheath behind his neck."

Richard gazed at the man and noticed that for all his soft plumpness, he had shrewd eyes.

The watch commander pulled Richard's knife from its sheath and inspected it. Anyone with the knowledge of arms would have known the heavy twelve inch blade had a shorter reach than the dress sword, but its weight and strength would have given Richard the edge.

Ruinel's face was purple with rage. He stood dripping muck from his embroidered slash sleeves and his gold-trimmed doublet. His bright red hose sagged around his knees. He screamed at the ranking soldier.

"He'll pay for this!"

"Then let him pay," Master Jamael announced. With a quick hand and flick of his own dagger, he clipped the strings on Richard's small, nearly empty purse and threw it to the dripping Ruinel. "That probably contains his earnings for a year or more. Take it and be satisfied, else when this young man is brought before your father, I will be there to see your part in the story is properly told."

Richard's own rage became hard to control. He had paid for his boots and had not yet received his share of the profits from the crops so his purse contained only a few coppers, but having to pay the drunken Ruinel anything was unjust. He had not started the fight, and to his mind, anyone who entered an altercation should accept the consequences regardless of rank.

Ruinel opened the purse and emptied the contents into his hand. He swore at the few coppers it contained and threw the coins on the ground. He stepped forward and threw the purse in Richard's face.

"Get out of Moerel," he snarled. "Consider yourself fortunate you do not spend the next year in the dungeons!"

Behind him the old woman scrambled forward and picked up the coins, a fit payment for the turnips she had lost.

Ruinel strode away, followed at a distance by his friend with the wine flask. The watch commander eyed Master Jamael and released his hold on Richard's arm.

"It's as you say," the ranking soldier said and walked off, his subordinate following.

"Thank you, Master Jamael," Richard said, dipping his head slightly. He still bristled at losing the coppers. The loss of the coins would not hurt him, but the injustice would rankle for years. Still, he knew he owed the master a better expression of gratitude. "I hope, sir, that your defense of me does not lead to trouble for you."

"Never liked that preening cat-bird," Master Jamael said, half hiding a grin as he gazed after the departing Ruinel. "And even the mayor runs short of personal funds, so I have no fears." He remembered to whom he spoke and his face formed into stern lines. "Still, you have made a powerful enemy, so it would be better for you if you left Moerel immediately and stayed away." He turned back to the glass vender; Richard had been disposed of and he had bargaining to do. "Now then, where were we. . . . ?"

As the crowd dispersed Richard joined his uncle and two cousins. Randen's face was stiff with anxiety. Droene, the largest and youngest, gazed from Richard to his father, and over the heads of the shoppers as if still trying to decide if he should have taken part in the altercation. Gaelin, the wit of the family, gazed at Richard with twinkling green eyes.

"You don't have enough to do buying boots, you have to pick a fight with the mayor's son?" Gaelin asked.

Richard didn't reply. If Gaelin had not seen the start

of the trouble, he had learned all about it in seconds. He was a ferret when it came to information of any kind. The three young men followed Randen to the rear of the market. When they were out of hearing of the shoppers and sellers, he motioned for them to gather around.

"Boy, I'm not faulting you for what happened," he said, running a hand through his short, gray beard, a habit when displeased. "Still, you had better be on your way home." He handed Richard the purse with his share of the profits from the sale of the crops.

"I'm not leaving without my boots," Richard announced. "The shop is closed until sundown, when the boot maker returns from his dinner. I'll leave then."

And he would leave reluctantly. He saw no reason to let some drunken—what did Master Jamael call the mayor's son?—preening cat-bird drive him out of the river town. Though, if he stayed and trouble resulted, his uncle and his cousins might find themselves in the middle of it.

"That lord said to go, and he was a guildmaster," Droene said slowly. "Best we leave."

As usual, Droene's humility irritated Richard, but he never lost his temper with the hulking brute who was half earth wisdom, half simpleton, and uncritically loyal to his brother Gaelin and his cousin.

"Why? Why should I run away because a guild-master tells me to?" Richard demanded. "Is he any better than I am? Any better than you are? Look at yourself, Droene, you're probably twice as strong as he is, probably more honest and honorable—"

"We'll have no more of that," Randen snapped. "It's your highborn ideas that cause trouble, and you'll not be filling Droene and Gaelin with them."

Richard knew what his uncle meant. His father had been a man of property and Richard's pride had been inherited. His mother was a mystery to all the living Endiers. She had died giving birth to Richard, but Randen had always thought she was a daughter of wealth and power who had fallen in love with Aenel and had eloped with him. She was a delicate creature who had arrived on the family farm with rich clothing and more knowledge of directing servants than working with her hands. Richard's parents had managed to keep her true identity and family history a close secret. That secret died with them.

"You'll be a propertied man when I'm gone," Randen said. "Until that time you're naught but a farmhand, and it'll serve you best to behave like one."

Richard bit his lip and nodded. He understood his uncle was trying to teach him humility, a lesson even he knew he needed to learn. Though Randen never mistreated his nephew he wanted Richard to understand the vulnerability of the people who would one day be his responsibility.

"I'll stay just until I've picked up my boots," Richard agreed. He would not seek out Ruinel and would go out of his way to avoid more trouble in Moerel.

But there was still Aerele, he thought, for the first time savoring the idea of leaving the farm and traveling to the capital city of Diemed.

The baron of Diemed had sent out a call for all young men between the ages of twenty and twenty-five to report for militia training during the winter months. Like many other rulers, the baron found it too expensive to keep a huge standing army. He maintained a core of professional soldiers and called up a civilian militia in emergencies. Richard, Gaelin and Droene had been ordered to report to Aerele for two months of training. To keep their militia duties from interfering with the planting and harvesting, the instruction would be given between mid-Sehnir and mid-Keltier, cold months during which the fields were fallow.

They would return home to the farm to help cut and bring in firewood. When the farm had been readied for the winter they would make the sixty-five mile journey to Aerele.

In an effort to keep the three young men out of trouble, Randen walked up the street to an inn and brought back two pitchers of ale and a basket of thick rolls filled with crusty, succulent boar meat. He stayed with them until sundown, when Richard went alone to the boot maker. He was wearing his new boots when he stepped out of the shop and noticed a familiar figure.

Master Jamael was just entering a shop across the street. Above the door hung the sign of a carved and painted coin. Richard crossed the street and entered. He found no welcome in the shop.

"You thanked me, now be on your way," Jamael said crossly.

"I've heard it said that a moneylender is a farmer of coins—that he plants them and reaps a harvest," Richard said, pulling out the leather pouch his uncle had given him.

The moneylender eyed the purse and frowned. He was clearly thinking he had given Richard's money to Ruinel.

"You're not a cutpurse, are you?"

"I'm Richard Endier. You knew my father Aenel and may know my uncle. This is my share from selling our crop." He handed over the purse.

Master Jamael's eyes widened slightly when he heard the name. He laughed, his entire body shaking. "So you're not the bumpkin you appear to be." He nodded slowly, his expression one of a man looking back into the past. "Yes, Aenel Endier was a friend of mine. . . ."

The moneylender shook his head and laughed, shaking Richard's purse. "Perhaps I'll lend this to the mayor—would the interest be a fitting revenge?"

"Just don't let it out to Ruinel or I may lose it entirely," Richard replied.

Jamael nodded. "And you're as shrewd as you are quick. I'd not trust that young sod to repay a copper."

"I was thinking he might not be able to," Richard replied, the tranquility of his voice belied by his snapping eyes. "Unless I mistook his age, he will also be going to Aerele, where his father's position cannot protect him."

Master Jamael suddenly looked cold. "Take care, young man. He is still gentry, and you're not even a property owner's son. If you step above your place, you'll find out what power means." He handed Richard a neatly cut scrap of parchment that attested to the monies left in his keeping.

Richard gazed at the man, thinking he probably knew more about the feeling of power than Master Jamael. As Aenel Endier's son, he had a long heritage of power. What came from his mother and her mysterious past he did not know, but Randen had suggested she might even be of the blood. Richard would never accept the idea that the mayor's son was even his equal. He gave a nod, and bade the moneylender, whose warning fell on deaf ears, farewell.

Three

Richard swung the axe. A chip of wood flew out of the notch. The sound of cracking wood warned him the tree was ready to fall. He stepped back and watched it crash to the ground.

"About time," Arlen grumbled, waiting for the fallen tree to settle before he stepped up to it, swinging his own axe with almost leisurely strokes as he trimmed small branches off a thick limb.

Richard left him to it and walked over to the first of the four large carts, two fully loaded with firewood and another partially filled. He unhooked a dipper gourd from the side of the cart and removed the lid on the small keg of drinking water. He was just raising the gourd to his mouth when Arlen turned around.

"Stop loafing on the job and start on these limbs," Arlen shouted.

"Do it yourself," Richard shouted back, wiping his sweaty face with grimy hands. He pulled the sweatband off his forehead, snapped it against his leg to shake out the excess water and replaced it. Autumn was pouring out the last of its heat with a fury, but winter would soon smother the warmth, and the firewood had to be cut and stored.

Richard was tired, hot, and angry. The winter woodcutting was taking longer than usual because three were doing the work usually done by five. For the first year in Richard's memory, Randen Endier had not led the woodcutting party. A broken leg and illness the winter before had weakened Randen to the point that Richard had actually been able to talk his uncle into leaving the difficult chore to the younger men. Until his health had deserted him, Randen had wielded a busy axe and had seen to it that his three sons and nephew kept pace. Without his father to oversee the work, Arlen, the oldest, decided to take command, and for the past two weeks he had put most of his energy into giving orders and criticizing.

"The next time father complains, I'll tell him why the cutting is taking so long," Arlen complained, taking a couple of half-hearted swings at a thick limb.

"And so will we," called Gaelin. He and Droene were cutting up the trunk of the last tree Richard had felled. "You've not pulled your load for more than half an hour at a time since we began. Much more talk from you and he'll learn of it."

"I'll teach you to run your mouth and cause trouble," Arlen snarled and started toward his brother, but Gaelin stood flat footed, his axe resting lightly in his hands. Droene, whose slower mind was usually placid and who never initiated trouble, stepped across the trunk of the fallen tree and stood beside his smaller brother.

Throughout their childhood the three younger Endiers had suffered from Arlen's bullying. He had knocked them about whenever he chose, but since the others had reached their full height he seldom tried anything anymore. Gaelin would never reach the height and weight of the rest of the family, but Droene could easily overpower his older brother.

Arlen stopped, glowering at Droene.

"What do you think you're doing, you shambling oaf?" he demanded. In answer, Droene took a menacing step forward, and Arlen paused. "I've no time for you, we need to get this wood cut." As he turned back to the newly felled tree, the others grinned at his self-righteous tone.

Trouble averted for the moment, they went back to work for another hour and stopped when the sun was high. They climbed a small hill to take advantage of the breeze and sat beneath the shade of a stand of tall, spindly saplings. Grateful for the rest, they ate their noon meal of bread, roasted meat, cheese, and apples they had brought from the farm kitchen that morning.

Richard sat facing west, toward the River Maesil three miles away. He could just see its almost mile wide expanse in the distance, half hidden by the rising waves of heat. The huge Endier farm formed a three mile square, and they were cutting wood in the northeastern corner. To the southwest he could see the ring of trees that gave shade to the main house and the outbuildings in the distance. Between the hill and the buildings beyond, orderly squares of field and pasture lay tucked between hedgerows of thorn bushes that penned in the horses, cattle and goats, keeping them out of the tilled fields. The stock had been turned into many of the fallow fields, grazing to build a layer of fat that would keep them healthy through the winter. In the distance Richard could see one of the hirelings moving a string of cows down a farm path to new grazing.

To the north were the dark and dangerous eaves of the Spiderfell. The danger from the forest was a constant threat. Richard's own father had been killed repelling an invasion of the spider-riding goblins. A quarter mile of open territory acted as a no-man's-land between the forest and the farm. Many of the neighboring farmers and freesteaders braved the eaves of the Spiderfell to cut their winter supply of wood, but the Endiers stayed on their own land. They had owned it, passing it from father to son since the time of the emperor and had long ago recognized the need to grow their own timber. Bordering the quarter mile wide strip of no-man's-land they planted saplings, fast growing conifers that rapidly expanded in girth and height and were ready for harvesting in a few years.

"It's a waste," Gaelin muttered as he chewed on a fresh, crusty roll filled with venison, a bonus to the larder provided by Richard two days before.

"What?" Arlen, who could not stand to be left out of the conversation, glowered at his brother.

"The Spiderfell," Gaelin said. He had seen the direction of Richard's gaze. "All that land going to waste because of that monster."

"Go and tell him you want his land," scoffed his older brother.

"You don't want me to do that," Gaelin grinned. "You might have to work if I wasn't here to do my share . . . and part of yours."

Arlen scowled, but Droene, who seldom noticed the altercations in the family if they did not lead to physical violence, diffused the coming explosion. His amiable mind was always ready to follow Gaelin and Richard's ideas, even the most far-fetched.

"If we could make farms on the open land along the river, we could all have one. Then we'd all be land owners. Wouldn't you want one, Arlen?"

"Don't be more stupid than you can help," the eldest Endier snapped. "Who would be stuck on a farm, sweating behind a plow, mucking out stables when he could live in a city?"

"A city with paved streets?" Gaelin laughed. On their recent visit to Moerel, Richard had told the others about the stretch of cobblestones. While he had picked up his boots, the three brothers had toured the urban improvements and Arlen had tripped over an uneven stone. He nursed a skinned elbow, using it as an excuse not to chop the firewood until Gaelin discovered the small abrasion had healed. He still moaned over his new shirt with its torn sleeve.

"There are places more civilized than Moerel," Arlen sneered. "I've been to Aerele, and *that* is a city. They have houses—"

"Hush!" Richard raised his left hand while pointing with his right. Arlen's face darkened until his gaze followed Richard's pointing finger.

Down the hill, where the half-loaded wagons waited, shadows were moving from tree to tree. The oxen, who had grazed contentedly where they had been tethered were moving about restlessly and lowing in distress.

"Goblins, from the Spiderfell," Drone said, starting to rise.

"Easy," Richard warned. "They expect to surprise us. Let's see how they like the unexpected."

"What's your idea?" Gaelin asked.

"I'll decide what we're to do," Arlen announced, but the others ignored him. Gaelin had the quickest wit, but he was no leader and, like the slower thinking Droene, he looked to Richard.

"Let's creep down that line of bushes, stay low, and get as close as we can," Richard said, pointing out their routes. They each had a bow and arrows but no swords. Their knives and the single-blade woodcutting axes were their only other weapons.

"Listen to me!" Arlen objected." We should get

back to the fa—"

Gaelin cut him off with a sharp bark of, "Quiet!"

He moved off after Richard and Droene, who were already advancing on the goblins. Richard crept down the hill, staying close to the low bushes and in the shadows of the young trees until he was within arrow range. He paused, waiting for Gaelin and Droene to approach close enough to attack. They had chosen paths with less cover and were moving more slowly.

The goblins too were being careful as they approached their targets, the oxen. Arlen, who made it plain he was not fighting goblins, suddenly stood up in plain sight and shouted, his right arm extended, shaking his pointing finger at his cousin.

"You listen to me, Richard! I won't have you leading my brothers into trouble!"

He had not finished speaking when a goblin, correctly deciding someone lurked in the bushes where Richard hid, threw a spear that missed the human by inches. The goblin's companion drew back his arm to cast his own throw.

Gaelin pronounced an oath that, if he had been a sorcerer, would have burned Arlen to cinders. The bright-haired Endier rose from his hiding place and sent an arrow into the arm of the second goblin, spoiling his aim.

Droene, no hand with a bow, rose from his hiding place and charged down the hill, bellowing a challenge as he plowed through the undergrowth.

Richard stood and sent an arrow toward the goblin that had nearly skewered him. He missed his intended target, but the arrow pierced the leg of a new arrival who stepped out from behind a tree to see what was happening.

"Good shot!" Gaelin called back to Richard as he dashed forward after Droene. They had fought off goblins before, and it appeared that Droene thought of this fight as an interesting break from the boring job of cutting wood.

Richard spared his cousin a frown before sprinting down the slope to help the others. He was not afraid of goblins. From what he could see there were only ten of them. He and his cousins were outnumbered, but that meant little. The humanoids were common goblins, four feet tall, with little stomach for facing determined, armed resistance. By their looks they were foragers, scavengers, not a band of well-trained warriors.

Four of the goblins fled before Droene, who was still yelling his war cries. To them he must have looked like a mad giant. The others took shelter behind a row of thin saplings that Richard had helped to plant a few years before. Three of the goblins backed away from Gaelin's merry charge as he swung his axe and called to them, "C'mon and taste my woodcutting abilities— on your little wooden heads!"

Two others had already been wounded and that was enough for them. The cowardly goblins fled the belt of woods, hurrying toward the dark depths of the Spiderfell. Gaelin leaned against a tree and jeered at them as they ran away, but Richard knew that one of the humanoids had not left with its companions. He looked around and saw the last of the goblins crawling into a clump of bushes. Richard's arrow was still in its leg.

Arlen, moving slowly down the hill, had also seen the wounded goblin. He shouldered his bow—he still had a full quiver of arrows—and hefted his axe, moving toward the clump of bushes. The goblin, seeing him, gave a snarl of forced bravado, a desperate sound, full of pain.

Richard glared at his oldest cousin and slid his hand down to the tip of his bow, holding it out at arm's length to block Arlen' path. Killing any creature unable to fight back seemed to Richard an act of dishonor.

"You're brave enough with the wounded," he snapped. "Let it go, we taught it a lesson."

Richard never enjoyed a fight, but he hated cowardice, and Arlen's affected him like a rotting stink on the wind.

"It's a goblin—vermin, and you kill vermin," Arlen retorted.

"Is that what you considered us?" Richard demanded. "You deliberately gave away our position and spoiled our ambush."

"It was a bad thing to do." Droene, who almost never expressed censure of his brothers, gave his older brother a look of reproach.

"Don't blame me because you followed a fool down the hill," Arlen retorted. "Kill the goblin and let's get back to work."

"If Richard wants it, let him keep it," Gaelin's green eyes twinkled as he unstrung his bow. "He can march it around as a trophy."

Droene, likewise taking the strain off his bow, frowned at his smaller brother. His expressions were so placid not even his frowns were given much effort.

"I don't see why he would want to keep a goblin. What's it good for?"

The wounded creature, sitting between two bushes, stared at the four humans and obviously understood their speech. It had rightly guessed Richard was the one to appeal to.

"Didn't do nothing," it snarled. Petulance and pain eroded most of its defiance.

"What could you do?" Richard asked, not willing to kill the injured goblin, but unable to resist taunting it a bit. A goblin captive would be more trouble than it could ever be worth.

"Do plenty," the goblin said, taking a tighter grip on its spear. It kept the weapon handy, but had not threatened Richard. Its small eyes darted about as if looking for escape.

"Sure, you're one of the Spider's lieutenants, and he'll come for you with all his armies," Gaelin laughed.

At first the goblin seemed willing to accept the rank the human gave it. Then its gaze faltered.

"He won't come for you," Arlen sneered. "He doesn't even know you exist. You've probably never even seen him."

"I seen him," the goblin retorted and gave an involuntary shudder.

"If you want your freedom, tell us about the Spider," Richard said. He had always been avid to learn all he could about the awnshegh that lived in the forest to the north. He reached in his belt pouch and pulled out a strip of cloth. He had used it to wipe the sweat off his face and hands, it was grimy, but cleaner than the goblin.

"Use this to tie up your leg."

The goblin unsuccessfully tried to stifle its moan of pain as it pulled the arrow from its leg and wrapped the cloth tightly around the wound to staunch the bleeding. Arlen gave a snort of disgust and paced the immediate area, but the others waited patiently.

As if the binding of its leg had unleashed its tongue, the goblin looked up at Richard, its wide nose twitching as if it could sniff out the intent of the humans.

"Plenty powerful, the Spider King," it said. "Him hate stinking elves."

"He's not the only one with power," Gaelin observed and Richard wondered what he meant, but did not want to ask in front of the goblin. Gaelin liked to talk, and his remark struck Richard as a bit of bravado.

"He has no reason to hate us," Droene said. "We don't cut wood in the Spiderfell. We don't hunt there, either."

"Tell me more about Tal-Qazar," Richard prompted.

"Always looking for more learning," the goblin said. By its tone the humanoid thought the search for knowledge was a weakness. "Plenty curious is Tal-Qazar."

"What is he curious about?" Richard asked.

"What is to be asked and known," the goblin shrugged as if the question was too large for it to handle.

Arlen suddenly took two steps toward the goblin, his right arm out-thrust, his forefinger shaking, the same motion he had used when giving away the ambush.

"The Spider King is insane! You follow a crazy leader, did you know that?"

The goblin glared at the human who shouted at it and shook its head.

"Tal-Qazar not all time crazy. Plenty smart thinking he does sometimes. Plenty strong, do many things when he thinks good and not so good."

Richard and Gaelin traded speaking looks. Arlen had, in his ill temper, verified something they had heard as a rumor. Some tales said the Spider King was insane. Apparently it was at least partially true, if even a goblin would admit it. They tacitly reached an agreement. The goblin had told them all it could. To spend more time questioning it would be useless. What was the point if the awnshegh was mad? Nothing about the monster's activities would be predictable.

"Get yourself back to the forest," Richard said, then turned away, leading the others back to the carts and the woodcutting. With luck they would finish loading the wagons in another two hours.

four

That evening, when the four Endiers returned to the farm, Richard said nothing to his uncle about the trouble with the goblins or Arlen's behavior. Richard suspected one of the others had eventually complained. Maybe Randen, who was no fool, had figured out what happened, because for the next three days he accompanied the woodcutting party. He also brought along four of the hirelings to load the cut wood into the wagons.

Under his father's eye, Arlen worked along with the others and the woodshed would hold only one more day's cutting when they started on the sixth day. They had nearly filled all four carts by the time the sun reached its zenith. Fhiele, Randen's fifteen-year-old daughter, brought their midday meal up to the cutting site. She had ridden one of the plow horses and had allowed Jenna, Richard's five-year-old cousin to ride on the croup. While the woodcutters ate their noon meal, little Jenna played in the grass, laboring industriously at one of her many little projects.

Richard finished his meal and, still drinking stream-chilled ale from a gourd cup, wandered over to where little Jenna worked with a pile of grass. As she squatted on the ground, her small, sleeveless jumper covered her knees and feet and bared her deeply tanned shoulders and arms. Her light brown hair, sun-streaked by her summer in the sun, hung down her back in a thick braid. Little strands had escaped the tight plaiting and curled around her face. She wiped away the sweat with a grubby hand and continued her work as if her life depended on it.

She had pulled all the grass from one spot, baring a circle of earth a foot in diameter. Using the long blades of the plants she had uprooted, she wove the surrounding, still rooted, stalks into a loose basket. She had already curved some of the longer stems to create a sloped, loosely woven roof over the little basket structure.

Jenna was an imaginative child, always busy with some grandiose plan, and Richard always enjoyed hearing her ideas. At times his momentary interest in her gave him problems; knowing she could find a listening ear, she often followed him around the farm, prattling at him. Still, he could not resist kneeling to watch.

"Well built," he said. "What is it for?"

She looked up at him, dark eyes shining out of a dirty face, her forehead wrinkled with concentration.

"I'm making a magic house," she said as if he should have known. Her busy little hands kept weaving the strands of grass.

"Oh. Will it grow to be large and sturdy, do you think?"

In answer she gave him a look children reserve for stupid questions asked by adults. "Of course not! Magic will live in it. Magic will come to this place and we can take it out, using it for—" she twisted her mouth and shut her eyes tight, her habitual expression when trying to concentrate. "We can use it for all sorts of things, but telling what we use it for will make it go away."

"So we must keep our use of it a secret?" Richard raised his gourd cup to his mouth to hide his grin.

"That's right. If you tell, you'll drive away the magic."

"How did you learn to do this?" he asked.

"A lady—very beautiful, with silvery, feathered wings—came and told me about it while I was sleeping." Jenna looked up, her eyes unfocused as if she could see something he could not.

Richard smiled at her, thinking of Jenna's good fortune. In a world where monsters abounded—the threat of the awnsheghlien and other horrors brought nightmares to the bravest—Jenna dreamed of beautiful creatures. One had been a huge fuzzy worm that sang songs and turned wild flowers into honey. For several days after that dream she had planted flowering weeds around all the outbuildings. The first Jenna Endier, Randen's wife, died giving birth to their youngest child, who had been given her mother's name. Little Jenna was much indulged by her father and the rest of the Endier family. She had two sisters, Fhiele and nineteen-year-old Rieva, who, since her mother's death, had been mistress of the house.

The others had finished their meal and Fhiele called to Jenna to help repack the baskets. Richard, who had been kneeling beside the child, rose with her and had just handed Jenna his cup when old Durchan, the placid plow horse the girls had ridden from the house, whinnied in fear and reared, breaking free of the tree where he had been tied. He galloped down the farm track that led to the stables. The behavior of the horse frightened the child and she ran up the hill to her father.

"Whoa!" Randen shouted and stared after the frightened animal. "What happened to him?"

On the side of the low hill near the day's cutting site, the oxen, securely tethered to stakes that had been driven deep into the hard ground, lowed and stamped. Agitated, they pulled at the ropes with surprising ferocity. When the stakes came up, the oxen, still harnessed to the carts, followed the horse. Lengths of cut logs bounced from the carts as they rumbled down the hill.

After years of living so near the Spiderfell, the men knew to keep a careful eye on the mood of their animals. They grabbed their weapons and looked toward the dark forest, but the quarter mile of rolling grassland between the stand of Endier trees and the thick woods seemed devoid of any threat. Gaelin trotted down the hill to join Richard and nearly stepped on Jenna's little grass house as he looked around.

They were just turning away when Richard saw movement near a clump of bushes and stopped. Every sense said run, but for a few seconds fear froze him to the spot. The foliage was thin and he could see a shape behind it. The silhouette stood out against the brightness of the sunlit grassland beyond. He could see the cephalothorax stretching out behind a goblin-shaped body and the arch of eight spider legs.

According to one ancient tale, it was death to look any of the awnsheghlien in the eyes, so Richard averted his gaze, fixing it on the distant wood. All his concentration was on the beast by the clump of bushes. The Spider King stood staring at them, offering no threat at the moment, but Richard was sure the respite would be short lived.

During the moments while he seemed frozen with fear, his mind was working double-time. The horse and the oxen had fled, leaving the humans behind. The four young men might have a chance to escape, but Randen with his limp, and the girls, Fhiele and Jenna, would not. Richard did not trust Arlen to stay and defend his family, but Gaelin and Droene would. Still, they had little to no chance in a fight against such a creature.

The Spider King had not moved, and Richard risked a quick glance. It was not looking at the humans, but at the dome of loosely woven grass at his feet. An idea burst like a jewel in his mind. What had the goblin said? That the awnshegh was constantly hungry for knowledge and power? He told himself his idea was ridiculous, but he was in no greater danger if he tried to bluff the awnshegh than if he tried to run. The Spider King was said to be able to leap fifty feet or more, and throw a sticky web over a large area. As the closest to the monster, Richard and Gaelin would be the first to die if they fought.

Gaelin, who was staring down the ribbon of trees planted by the Endiers, stood with his back to the bushes and had not seen the Spider King.

"Gaelin, look at me," Richard said softly, then repeated, "Look only at me." He waited until his cousin's frowning gaze was turned on him. "As you love your father and your sisters don't turn around. Walk back to the others and lead them slowly down the hill toward the farm."

"But—" Gaelin almost turned before Richard interrupted him.

"You are their only hope. You are *my* only hope. Do as I say, and we may all come out of this alive. If you try to come to my defense, we'll all die."

As Gaelin stared at his cousin, Richard saw him shiver and could imagine the self-control it took for the younger man not to turn and see what was behind him. It was not a lack of courage, but a measure of his trust in Richard's judgment that gave him the strength to walk away.

As soon as he was gone, Richard knelt, pulled a piece of grass and started to work on the little woven structure. His skin crawled, but he did not raise his eyes from his work. In moments he heard the rustle of grass, the creak of ancient spider legs and the swish of tall grass against the massive cephalothorax as the awnshegh moved toward him. Two large goblins stood within the shelter of the underbrush.

When the shadow loomed over him, Richard struggled to keep his courage as he slowly raised his head. He jerked back as if he had not expected to see the Spider King. Then he realized he was looking directly into the creature's eyes and was still living. He had felt a pull on his will, but when he looked away, he found he could still breathe. His mind was capable of clear thought.

The awnshegh was larger than Richard had expected. It stood nearly seven feet tall and the cephalothorax stretched out nine feet behind it. The old tales said it had once been a goblin, but the upper part of its body, the head and arms, were all that resembled a humanoid. The face was still goblin-like, with small eyes, and a wide, flat nose, and fangs projecting from a big, cruel mouth. Pointed ears rose nearly to the top of its head which seemed small when compared to the wide shoulders and long arms. From the creature's fingers extended long claws, good for fighting, but little else.

Richard had no need to exaggerate the fear that went with his carefully rehearsed first words, but he did not get a chance to use them immediately. Tal-Qazar spoke first.

"What walks on two legs

"And tills the earth,

"Brings war and magic

"And has no worth?

"A human. But has it a name for its busy-work in the face of Tal-Qazar?"

"If you kill me before it is finished you will never

have the use of it," Richard said, his voice shaking. "Only one person can construct it. If more than one tries, it will gain no power, and if you block the sunlight while it's being built, neither of us can use it."

"And why would I want it?" The voice seemed to come from deep within some hollow cavern. The words were clear, but the sound was neither human nor goblin. Still, the awnshegh had moved to the side so the sunlight fell on Richard's work.

"I am great in power. I am Tal-Qazar, King of the Spiderfell. Do you not know that, puny human? Do you think you can impress me with your little magic?"

"Only a fool would not know the great Tal-Qazar when he sees him," Richard said, wondering if flattery would help his cause and how much. Not much, he decided, not if his plan was to succeed. "There are many powers, even in this land, but the greatest for a far distance is Tal-Qazar."

"For how far?" the awnshegh demanded.

Richard chewed on the inside of his mouth, trying to think of an answer, which was difficult. He found it hard to think around his fear and the necessity of continuing to weave the stalks of grass into the little structure. Since the power of the awnshegh came from the evil god Azrai, he suspected it might be able to tell the truth from a lie, so he knew he should be careful.

"In truth, great Spider King, I do not know, since I only hear tales of such as the Raven, the Gorgon, and the Hydra. Mayhap the repeated telling of the stories before they reached us has made their powers greater than they are." He paused and took a breath. "And then there are tales of the lady of the silver wings, and her promise of the grass house."

Tal-Qazar shifted. "What lady with the silver wings?"

"I do not know her name, the extent of her power, or her reasoning, only that she gave directions for constructions such as these. I am told she will fill them with magic power that others can use, but more I do not know."

"So it is true," Tal-Qazar glared at Richard. "The fool who took an arrow in the leg did hear you boast of power."

Richard's mind spun with the effort to remember the boast. He dimly remembered Gaelin's remark to the wounded humanoid. Later, when Richard had questioned Gaelin, his cousin grinned and said he was just spouting trash.

"It was not I that boasted," Richard replied. "The remark was made by one who is not here." He hoped Gaelin and the others had escaped. "He may have been speaking of the magic left by the silver-winged lady. I am not certain."

"She will come here and leave the magic?" the awnshegh asked. He shifted again, his eight spider legs working as if they had developed a restless consciousness of their own. He rubbed his hands together, the claws at the ends of his fingers clicked.

"If I understand the magic, and I speak true great Tal-Qazar when I say I cannot be sure of success, then I am to leave it once it is constructed and return on the morrow to find the power she has left." A sudden fallacy in his plan occurred to him, and he decided to mend the chink in his reasoning.

"It will be necessary for me to walk all the way from the farm. I wish I could have built it closer to the house, but I dared not take the chance of blood on the ground."

"What blood?"

"She will not come where blood has been spilled," Richard explained. "The only grass on the farm tall enough to build the grass receptacle is in the pastures. Occasionally your goblins raid the farm and kill stock, so I could not be sure the ground was pure enough for her."

"Pure enough for her . . . Yes, I see . . . Yes, I see . . . plenty pure," Tal-Qazar's eyes gleamed wickedly. "She will come here because the ground is pure. She will come here and leave part of her power . . . Yes, her power . . . plenty power. Lucky I did not kill the goblin with the arrow in his leg. He will be rewarded, he brought me word of the power." Saliva dripped from the corners of the Spider King's mouth. He paced back and forth. The slender, pointed tail at the end of his cephalothorax twitched, sending sticky, coiling strands from his spinneret. His eyes wandered and he rubbed his hands together and looked gleefully at the structure. The joy in his face bordered on madness.

"You will finish building the structure," he ordered Richard. "Then you will make a good meal to hold me while I wait for your lady with the wings."

"And she will never come," Richard said. "I told you she will not set foot on tainted ground."

"This is so, this is so—she will not come where blood is spilled," the awnshegh agreed as if he knew Richard spoke the truth. "You will be rewarded with your life and the ground will remain pure. Finish it! Finish it!"

Richard continued his work, carefully reinforcing the little structure. To declare himself finished too soon might rouse suspicion in the awnshegh. Tal-Qazar might be half insane, but he was not stupid, and goblins were suspicious by nature. His strong desire to run scrambled Richard's sense of time, so he stripped six blades of grass and announced they were all that would be needed to finish.

Tal-Qazar watched, pacing back and forth, but staying well behind the human so his shadow did not fall on the weaving. He muttered constantly about the power and the lady, embellishing the tale out of his own twisted imagination.

When Richard finished weaving the last of the six

blades of grass, the Spider King rushed forward and pushed the human away.

"Go, go, get away, leave this place," he commanded. "She will come . . . Her with her silver wings and her silver hair. She that wears the nasty white of snow and ice and rides on the moonlight! Yes, rides on the moonlight. She will come and I will destroy her . . . *hee, hee, hee* . . . I will destroy her and her power will be mine!"

Richard heard no more of the insane jabbering. He walked away, resisting the urge to run until he was out of sight of the awnshegh. He hurried across the fallow land and slipped through a thorn hedge. If the awnshegh changed his mind and came after him, the hedges would afford Richard little protection, but they were all he could think of. He skittered to the side as Gaelin and Droene stepped into his path.

"We were coming back for you," Gaelin said. The skin around his sparkling green eyes wrinkled with worry.

"What happened?" Droene asked.

"You'll never believe it," Richard breathlessly replied.

* * * * *

The assassin sat in the top of a high tree at the edge of the Spiderfell and watched Tal-Qazar. His eyes had the long-sight of an elf and his ears could hear better than any creature in the forest. At present, he was in the shape of a spider only two inches long.

He watched as the human rose, having completed his strange work in the grass, and walked off. Before long, the man disappeared behind a hedge of thorns. The awnshegh paced around the little mound of grass and muttered, rubbing his hands in anticipation. As the afternoon wore on, the Spider King continued his pacing and the tiny spider watched, and listened.

Just after sunset the assassin climbed down the tree. He could have used his spinnerets but he chose to walk down the bole. When he reached a suitable limb he walked out on it and by the third step, three of his eight spider legs had disappeared and he was larger. Another six steps and he had lost three more, his feet were clawed and covered with knobby skin. Another few paces and he was covered with feathers, his wings were outspread. He looked with owl eyes on the scene as he drifted out of the tree and across the quarter mile of grassy plain.

In the strip of Endier wood, he lit on the ground and walked toward the hillside where the awnshegh waited. Before he had gone ten feet, he had become a vole. He ducked into a convenient hole and worked his way to a small opening under the tree nearest the place where the Spider King waited.

"She will come. Yes, she will come . . . and I will gain her power. I will get her magic, yes her magic. I will be the greatest power on Cerilia! Me, that was Tal-Qazar, a goblin . . . a goblin. Me, that was Tal-Qazar, that was an el—*no!* No! Not an elf, a goblin, a goblin. . . ."

Thankfully, voles were silent creatures and had no sound for laughter. The assassin had never laughed so hard. The human had made a fool of the awnshegh and the assassin had been there to see it! Even better, the two goblin lieutenants who accompanied Tal-Qazar also witnessed the subtle humiliation of the awnshegh. The Spider King would either kill them, or threaten them with death if they spoke about it. The lieutenants would promise silence, then break their oaths. Goblins could never keep a secret. The news would spread through the Spiderfell like wildfire. The lieutenants would die because of it, but not even the Spider King would be able to kill every goblin who heard the tale.

Though the assassin lived for the time he could kill Tal-Qazar, he could wait a bit now. . . .

ANUIRE

five

"You'd think the weather could have smoothed out gradually," Gaelin complained. "Three days ago you could have laid out a slab of meat on the step stones and it would have cooked in five minutes." He was griping into a chill wind that carried a suspicion of rain, possibly even snow. The long autumn had been unseasonably hot, but now a sudden turn of the wind had taken them from mid-summer heat to mid-winter cold with no respite between.

The change in the weather was harder on Gaelin, Droene, and Richard, because they were on their way to the city of Aerele, the capital of Diemed. There they would take their militia training, and register for the levy. Periodically, as the Baron saw fit, young men from all over Diemed were called in to undergo a spate of rigorous training. Since no call had gone out for four years, Gaelin, twenty-three; Richard, twenty-two; and Droene, twenty, all fell within the age group ordered to report.

Richard laughed suddenly. "Arlen should have come along," he said.

Arlen, who had taken his training ten years before, had complained about the unfairness of the other three leaving at one time. At first he insisted one of the brothers stay to help with the work, even though that would mean defying the law of the land. When his father refused to listen, Arlen insisted he should travel with the others, to keep them out of trouble.

"He's probably under his bed, hiding from the Spider King," Droene said with a grin.

Richard had told the tale of the little grass house and described Tal-Qazar standing over it, rubbing his misshapen hands and muttering insanely. Most of the family had laughed with the abandon of people just released from terror. Arlen had accused Richard of angering the awnshegh and deliberately endangering the family.

"Hold there!" Randen had snapped. "Would you rather the monster had killed Richard, then come after the rest of us?" The elder Endier glared at his son. Arlen, not daring to thwart his father, kept his eyes glued to Richard, his hatred plain.

"I noticed you reached the safety of the house long before we did," Fhiele said, her dark eyes snapping. "We're alive because we did not have to depend on *your* courage."

"I came on ahead to send Colin for troops," Arlen retorted.

"That you did, and they'll be riding the western borderlands by tomorrow," Randen said. "But you'll not deny that Richard drew the awnshegh's attention to himself while we escaped. Not another word will you say in criticism."

Arlen had not said another word, but the next night Richard found the window above his bed open to the rain, much of his clothing prepared for the journey was inexplicably filthy, and Arlen had tried to "accidentally" trip him when he descended the stairs. Two days later the three younger men left on the first leg of their journey to Aerele.

Between the Endier farm and the capital city stretched sixty-five miles of Dieman countryside, but a trip to Moerel and the winding road made their journey longer. When in Moerel to sell the crops, Randen Endier had instructed a tailor to fit each one of the young men with two new sets of town clothes, and the three Endiers had returned to the river port to pick up their new wardrobe. Randen was not one to waste money, but they would be representing the family in Aerele. Knowing the young men would not be making many trips to a real city, Randen had given each a healthy purse, so while they looked like modest country men, their purses, when not tucked securely in their belts, jingled with the soft sound of gold.

"The rewards of adventuring among the cabbages," Gaelin had grinned when he had first felt the weight of his city spending money.

Randen might not have been pleased to know the three travelers rode toward Aerele in their homespun winter clothing, the new outfits stored neatly in their saddle bags. Poor farmers were less likely to be ambushed on the road, and the three young men preferred to travel in peace and do their adventuring in the capital.

They had begun their trip in high spirits, but by their second day on the road—they had spent a night in Moerel—they were shivering in their heavy sheepskin coats, and by mid afternoon the horses were tired from leaning into the stiff western wind. They could have continued another ten miles before dark, but Gaelin wanted to stop at a likely looking inn. Richard and Droene were more than willing to oblige him.

By making an early stop, they were in time to get a choice chamber that had two large beds and good stabling for their animals. They spent a portion of the afternoon rubbing down the horses and seeing them properly stabled, and they were still inside the main room of the inn, eating and drinking ale, before any more patrons arrived.

A party of five dwarves were the next to stop. Since the Endier farm was well away from any major road and the three young men seldom visited Moerel, their total experience with dwarves was limited to having seen one at a distance. They quietly watched the newcomers, peering out from under lowered lashes to prevent giving offense. The quintet of demihumans were armed with small crossbows and war axes and their well-worn armor suggested they could be formidable when they chose to be.

The dwarves paid no attention to the three Endiers, and if they noticed the young humans' curiosity they ignored it. They seemed to be in a dour mood, muttering among themselves in their own language, keeping the reason for their foul tempers to themselves. When the innkeeper served them they nodded, two put on false smiles of amiability, and complimented the human on the quality of his ale. The moment his back was turned their expressions again soured and they continued their muttering.

A party of traders with several passengers in their caravan were the next to arrive. The passengers entered first. Inadequately dressed for the sudden change of weather, they suffered from the cold. They gathered at the fireplace, buzzing with relieved chatter as they warmed themselves. Two were women, apparently sisters traveling with their elderly father. The traders and the wagon drivers followed more slowly after they had stabled their animals and before long the room buzzed with conversation.

Half an hour later, just before sunset, six trappers arrived. They had apparently traveled south to sell their furs the summer before, and were on their way north again. They were nearly broke and haggled with the innkeeper over every mug of ale as if it were his fault they were short on funds.

Richard and his cousins, sitting at a table not far from the fireplace, exchanged resigned glances. Until the arrival of the trappers, the atmosphere had been congenial. The dwarves had continued their muttering, but when greeted by the other travelers they were fair spoken. The people of the caravan were tired, but pleasant enough. The surliness of the trappers caused the two women among the caravan's passengers to shrink behind their men. The assembled company became careful in their speech as if they feared a wrong word might give offense to the six surly individuals.

The last patrons to arrive were two men, one about the age of the Endiers and the other older, grizzled, thin and wiry. The younger man was slender with a thin, sensitive face and wore a fur-lined cloak. He removed it to expose his close-fitting, pale blue hose, and a darker blue jacket trimmed with fur at the neck, bottom, and around the slashed sleeves. To protect his blue, perfectly dyed, low, soft boots, he wore a pair of under-boots, wooden soles held in place by leather straps. The older man was doubtless a servant to the young man of fashion. He wore sensible woolen homespun clothing, much like the Endiers'.

Richard's mouth curled in contempt. Some lord's son on the way to Aerele to take his training, he thought. He frowned as he mentally prepared himself for an argument with the landlord. The high-born young twerp would probably demand the best upper room, and the Endiers had already paid for the use of it.

The innkeeper hurried over to the new arrivals. An

argument among the trappers broke out and Richard heard only the last part of the conversation.

". . . and to tell you true, sir, it would be worth my life to try and oust that group."

"Then it's the tables for us," the young man said with a sigh.

Richard relaxed and took another drink from his flagon, emptying it. He waved his hand, signalling to the harassed innkeeper that he wanted a refill.

"One more and it should be off to bed with us," he said to the others. Two of the trappers had raised their slurred voices in an argument. Richard inclined his head in their direction. "They'll be looking for a fight before long."

"I thought we were supposed to learn how to fight on this trip," Gaelin grinned. Despite his spoken bravado, he eyed the trappers warily.

"We won't learn much in Aerele if we arrive with broken heads," Richard said. He doubted his warning was really needed. If a fight was unavoidable, the smallest of the Endiers entered it with feigned excitement and gaiety, as if he wanted nothing more out of life. But left to his own resources, Gaelin's nature was a peaceful, if playful one.

"We promised Uncle we'd stay out of trouble." Richard added.

"You and I promised," Gaelin retorted. "Father didn't ask Droene for his word, so if any trouble comes along, he throws the first punch. Father couldn't blame us for coming to his aid."

Droene gazed at his brother, his face blank, his eyes full of worry. "I don't much like fighting," he said. Droene had been the most resentful of the need to journey to Aerele. Not even the idea of seeing a big city for the first time enticed him to willingly leave the farm.

All three Endiers turned to look as the new arrival

walked across the floor toward the fireplace, his under-
boots clattering on the wooden floor. He had also
caught the attention of the trappers who, until then,
had not noticed him. As he drew nearer to the table
where the Endier's sat, they could see his face was
chapped and blue with cold. Richard thought he was
either tired to the point of exhaustion or had been ill.

"If it isn't Lord High, come down among his subjects," one of the trappers laughed. He was a burly
man with the wide, snubbed nose reminiscent of a
goblin. When he opened his mouth in a guffaw, he
bared long, sharp teeth. Obviously he was of mixed
blood.

"Look-ee, look-ee, what he wears on his feet,"
another trapper said. "Don't want to get his pretty
boots dirty among the common people."

Since it was clear the well-dressed traveler had
been seeking the warmth of the wide fireplace, the
trappers rose from their tables and stood with their
backs to the fire, blocking his path. The young man
paused and looked about uncertainly. Trouble was
clearly not his intention. All the tables were in use
and he seemed not to know what to do.

Since Richard had not forgotten the injustice of losing his purse to the mayor's son in Moerel, he had
been as resentful of the obviously well-born young
man as the trappers appeared to be. But where there
was injustice, there should be fairness, and the new
arrival had not tried to use his position to ride
roughshod over the other patrons.

Richard surprised himself as he reached one long
leg under the table and hooked his foot around the
rung of a three-legged stool that was out of sight
against the wall. He pulled it out and gestured with
his hand, palm up, inviting the young man to their
table. The stranger's face cleared and he took the seat
with only a momentary hesitation as he glanced back

at his servant. Droene pulled out another stool and the servant, with more reluctance, joined his master.

"Thank you," the young man said. "I'm Caern Tier, and this is Hirge Manan."

Gaelin, the most voluble of the Endiers, made their introductions. Richard's opinion of Caern Tier rose considerably; he had not introduced his servant as a vassal.

"You're of the Tier province?" Richard asked, relatively sure of the answer. The Tier family had ruled the northern province east of Moere for centuries, hence the name. Caern nodded, after a quick glance at the trappers to make sure they had not heard the question.

"And you're on your way to Aerele for the training too?" The second question came from Gaelin.

Caern nodded again, his eyes brightening as he realized they were all on the same mission. Before he could answer, the innkeeper bustled over, bringing a large platter of steaming meat, freshly cut from a spit just visible in the room at the rear of the inn. He bustled around the table, laying out five clean trenchers, smiling and winking broadly at the Endiers. His meaning was obvious. They had diffused a situation that could have brought him considerable discomfort and he was rewarding them. Their host was clearly afraid of trouble with the trappers, but he could not afford to offer less than the best to a member of the powerful Tier family.

After an apologetic glance at his master for eating in his presence, Hirge fell to with a will, and Droene, who was often accused of having hollow legs, joined him. Richard and Gaelin ate more for courtesy's sake than hunger, and Caern picked at his food. He seemed to be forcing it down.

The innkeeper returned with a pitcher and refilled the Endiers' mugs after he had poured for Caern and

Hirge. He was just turning away when the huge goblin-like trapper jumped up from his table and grabbed the pitcher, sloshing ale on the innkeeper and two of the dwarves. The trappers had been shouting for ale every five minutes, and the half-breed was clearly drunk. His face was flushed with ale and anger.

"Let some high muckety come in and you're mighty free with what you begrudge us," the ugly trapper said, shoving the portly innkeeper aside.

"Now, see here," the innkeeper reached for the pitcher and the trapper shoved him again, this time knocking him against Droene, who spilled his ale as he braced to keep himself and their host from tumbling to the floor.

Gaelin, closer to the wall, sat with his flagon halfway to his mouth, his startled gaze on his brother, whose arms entangled with those of the innkeeper and the trapper. The incident had been too quick for anger to develop in the spectators, but the trapper took offense.

"What are you looking at, you dirt digger?"

One of his companions, a dark, swarthy man with a scar down the side of his face had risen from the table and stepped to his friend's side.

"Just a dirty farmer, not worth fooling with," he said, laying a hand on his friend's arm.

Gaelin tensed, ready for a fight, but Richard raised a hand, ordering him to remain seated. He would not have minded throwing a punch at the drunken trappers, but they had made a promise. The innkeeper had half a dozen sturdy stable hands and swampers. They could manage the trappers.

Goblin-face waited a moment to see if Gaelin would react, and when he didn't, the drunken breed hooked a foot under Hirge's stool and jerked it out from under him, sending the servant sprawling. He gave a loud guffaw, cut short by Droene's fist. The youngest Endier had surged up and caught the man under his bearded chin in a move almost too quick to see. Like many large men, Droene's love of peace could be quickly overcome when he saw a smaller person harmed.

The trapper crashed back into the table where the dwarves had been, but expecting trouble, they had grabbed their flagons and moved back against the wall. The dwarves watched with mild interest as the trapper staggered into the benches, stumbling, and tripped over one. He scrambled to his feet and glared at the dwarves. He was not too drunk to realize they held their flagons in their left hands and their axes in their rights. Dwarves did not have the reputation for taking part in barehanded brawls if they had weapons at hand.

The two women screamed and hurried for the stairs that led to the second floor of the inn, followed by the other passengers and the traders. The wagon drivers gathered at the bottom of the steps, ready to defend their passengers and employers if necessary, but they made it plain they wanted no part of any brawl.

"Father will be mad at you," Gaelin grinned at Droene.

"You said I should start the fight," Droene said as he stooped to offer a hand to Hirge.

The innkeeper hurried across the room and pulled hard on a rope. Dimly, because of the thick walls of the inn, Richard could hear the ringing of a bell. Reinforcements would soon be on the way.

In the meantime, the other trappers had taken Droene's reaction to mean the fight was on. One grabbed his flagon and threw it across the room, narrowly missing one of the caravan owners. He charged toward the table where the Endiers and Caern Tier were hastily rising. Three were heading straight for

Richard who was on the side nearest them. He was bracing himself for the onslaught when Caern bent, grabbed his stool, and lightly tossed it, letting it skitter across the floor. It tripped a wiry man with a badly tanned coat of deer hide. He fell sideways, bringing down his companion on his left. Both had grabbed for a table where the wagon drivers had been sitting. The table overturned, spilling platters, cups, bread, cheese, meat, and ale onto the floor.

"Thanks," Richard said as he bent his knees and leaned sideways to avoid the charge of Scarface, the third trapper. As the drunken man careened into the table, Richard straightened and shoved, intending to slam Scarface into the wall. Gaelin, trying to get around the table, stepped into the path of the stumbling man and deflected him toward the roaring fire. Scarface careened off Gaelin and fell onto the hearth. He screamed as his hand touched one of the fire dogs, but in his inebriated state he seemed to have lost all coordination.

Richard took a swing at the man in the deerskin coat and leapt toward the fireplace. The trappers were obnoxious, but not even they deserved to be burned to death. He grabbed Scarface and hauled him off the hearth.

Droene caught two by the back of their coats and slammed them together, banging their heads. They slumped to the floor and stayed there. A red-bearded man with shoulders like an ox knocked Gaelin off his feet. He drew back his foot to kick the younger man with his heavy boot when Hirge hit him in the head with a stool.

The door of the inn opened with a force that sent it slamming back against the wall. Four sturdy stable hands rushed in, each gripping a heavy cudgel. Behind them stood two more. Only two trappers remained on their feet, and after a look at the odds, they relaxed into a watchful truculence. Scarface used a stool to pull himself to his feet and stood sucking his burned fingers.

Around the common room the participants and spectators were still until the dwarves, as if by some silent order from their leader, slid their weapons back into their sheaths and returned to their table. Two had to pick up their stools, but within two seconds they were eating their meal as if they had never been disturbed.

After a whisper or two, the female travelers continued up the stairs toward their bedchambers, but the men slowly descended the steps. The innkeeper glared at the trappers and pointed to the overturned tables, stools, and crockery.

"You started the fight, you clean up the mess," he ordered. "And you'd better be grateful that I don't throw you out into the night."

The six stable men and the Endiers watched while the trappers righted the two tables and nine stools that had been overturned. Since the inn usually catered to travelers of a less exalted rank than Caern Tier, the flagons and trenchers were wooden, and only one cup had suffered damage.

While the trappers were busy, Caern motioned to their host. Out of the corner of his eye Richard saw the lord's son reach into his purse and push something into the hand of the innkeeper, who seemed satisfied with the result.

"I'll bring more ale," the innkeeper said.

"Send it up to our chamber," Richard suggested, deciding he did not want another round with the trappers that night. He turned to Caern and found himself offering to share the room he had been ready to fight over less than an hour before.

ANUIRE

SIX

Two days later, after a cold and miserable ride, the Endiers entered Aerele. The capital city of Diemed had been built on the rocky shores of the Aerelebae, a deep water inlet that extended nearly eighteen miles in from the seacoast. It was a natural harbor frequented by ships escaping storms and squalls at sea and had become a natural seaport of increasing importance.

The more valuable it became to sea trade the more the city grew in strategic importance, making it more likely to draw jealous eyes. Realizing his capital city would be coveted by his powerful neighbors, Baron Diern Diem, the great-grandfather of the present ruler, had ordered the building of stone fortifications. The oldest towered over the stone wharves, but knowing boatloads of invaders could beach along the shoreline and attack from the north, the entire city had eventually been enclosed in walls thirty feet high and ten feet thick. In addition, elongs had been built at intervals three hundred yards apart. The elongs were walls a hundred feet long, built perpendicular to the city fortifications, that terminated in bartizans. Above their crenelated walls rose the wooden and steel frames of catapults and trebuchets.

Surrounding the city were the numerous small farms the party had been passing for hours, but only grass grew between the elongs. Grazing cattle and goats kept the grass smooth and short. No bushes or stands of trees gave an enemy cover for more than a quarter of a mile around the city walls.

The Endiers gazed on the fortifications with undisguised awe. Caern Tier, who now rode with them, had been to Aerele several times, but was hardly less impressed.

"If there's trouble while we're here, I don't want to be stuck out there," Gaelin said, indicating the bartizans at the ends of the elongs.

"If you're given a choice between serving on an elong or the wall, take the elong," Caern advised. "During the last attack, more than thirty years ago, the operators of a catapult intended to throw a bladder of boiling oil on a group of invaders who were trying to set up scaling ladders. They missed."

"They got the wall instead?" Richard asked.

"And the defenders."

"Let's just take our training and go home," Droene said. "I doubt that Arlen will make sure the hirelings do a good enough job turning under the barley stalks in the north fields. If he doesn't, we'll not get a good crop next year."

"You like farming," Caern observed.

"It's all I know," Droene admitted, but after a little thought, "Aye, you can say I like it."

"So do I," Caern said with a sigh.

Richard understood his new friend's regret. Caern

was the eighth son of Lord Fraele Tier. With seven older brothers, he could look forward to little if any inheritance. Usually busy on the farm, and generally content with his work, Richard had never given any thought to what happened to the younger sons of the wealthy land owners and lords. Richard knew he was to inherit the Endier farm, and had always expected that Arlen, Gaelin, and Droene would remain there to help him, taking a share of the profits in return. But most landlords expected their younger sons to take their training at Aerele, then make their own way in the world from then on. They were usually given enough money to start them out in life, but once they finished their military training, they were left to make a place for themselves, rather than becoming a drain on the family property.

Richard had given all this little thought until he met Caern. At first Richard wondered how Caern could manage. The young man seemed so delicate and meek, but that impression faded as Caern continued to regain his strength after his recent illness. He had been given some bad meat at an inn on his way south and had been sick for days before he was able to continue the journey. By the time they reached Aerele the grey pallor had disappeared, his eyes were clearer, and his lips firmed with renewed strength. He seemed to enjoy the company of the Endiers, but he particularly liked the placid Droene.

The party rode up to the gates of the city and stopped, waiting while the guards questioned the driver of a cart and checked his load of crated chickens. The carter gave his oxen the office to move on and the party was urging their horses forward when a clatter on the road behind them announced the arrival of other riders.

"Out of the way," the first rider called out. "Clear the road, you riffraff, and let your betters through!"

Richard's head jerked up with resentment. He turned to see six fashionably dressed young men, and among them were Ruinel and his companion from the market in Moerel. Richard's fingers itched with the desire to knock the arrogant speaker out of the saddle, but he held his temper. First he would absorb the training he had come to get. Many lords and wealthy landowner's sons received some military training at home. The same had been true for the Endiers. Theirs had been a necessity because of their nearness to the Spiderfell, but the three youngest Endiers had been trained to fight goblins, not humans.

Richard believed he would have a better chance to win his battles once he had learned a few tricks. Then too, he had promised Randen Endier he'd stay out of fights, and he had already broken his word once, even though that particular fight had been forced on them.

No doubt Caern Tier outranked the party of riders, but he moved aside with the Endiers. Richard smiled to himself, hoping he might get his wish to shove Ruinel Goerent into another midden ditch.

Inside the city the Endiers parted company with Caern and Hirge. Richard and his cousins followed the directions they had been given at the gate, found a stable that would care for their horses, and reported to their assigned barracks.

They stepped into a low room fully a hundred feet long and a quarter as wide. Abutting the long walls were narrow, three-tiered bunks, their headboards against the walls. Sturdy timbers had been shaped and roped together for the frames and ropes wove a support for the straw mattresses. A basket had been affixed to the foot of each bed. A hundred and twenty men could sleep in that one room, and by the number already gathered, Richard wondered if there would be enough space for him and his cousins.

Young men wandered about, sat on the beds talking, or around one of the five fire pits that were evenly spaced in the center of the floor. The sound of talk and laughter was deafening.

"At least we won't be lonely," Gaelin observed.

"I hope we can find places to sleep," Richard replied. He took two steps, leading the way down the crowded room before he was stopped by a shout.

"Hold it hoe-men. Where do you think you're going?"

A guard wearing the uniform of a pikeman lounged on a stool near the door. As the Endiers entered he rose and looked them over with an insolent eye.

"We thought we were going to settle in and get ready for the training," Richard snapped back.

"You'll give me your names, and *I'll* tell you where you go, what you do, when you sleep, eat, and take your training," the guard replied. "For the next two months I'll tell you when you can speak—when you can *breathe*, understand?"

"Yes, my *lord*," Richard replied with the same insolent tone. He knew he was acting the fool, but he was tired and hungry, though his temper seemed to be in fine health.

The noise level had dropped at their end of the barrack, and at Richard's last remark, thirty or more young men fell silent, watching and waiting to see what would happen.

"You will address me as First Pikeman Kiemet." The soldier eyed Richard with calm speculation and a glint of humor flashed in his eyes before he dropped them to check the lists he was holding. "Your names and province?"

They identified themselves, and he gave them directions to their bunks. "Put your gear in the baskets at the ends of the bunks," he instructed. "Follow the others to the eating hall when the gong sounds."

"Who gave their word they would stay out of trouble?" Gaelin murmured as they threaded their way through the crowds. "I think you've made an enemy—the wrong kind."

"I was a fool," Richard admitted. He fully intended to take advantage of all the training he could get. The farm's proximity to the Spiderfell was the best incentive he knew for wanting to learn all he could.

Since they were nearly the last to arrive, they had all been assigned to top bunks. Richard climbed up to his, stored his clothing and saw Gaelin, five bunks away, doing the same. Across the room, two trainees seemed to be in an argument with each other and Droene. The discussion ended with a hasty reshuffling of belongings. The occupant of the bottom bunk moved up to the top, freeing the lower level for Droene. Richard grinned. The tiered bunks seemed sturdy enough, but he wouldn't want his huge cousin sleeping above him, either.

From the height of his bed Richard looked out over the long room. The stone walls were in good repair and the roof seemed dry, though the proof of that would come with the next rain. The five fire pits kept the long building warm and smelling of wool and warm bodies, but the prevailing odor was of hay. Probably from the mattresses, he thought, but when he turned to the wall, he noticed the smell emanated from the stone. Apparently the barrack served as a hay barn when the levy was not in training.

By the next morning, Richard was in a better humor. Baron Naele Diem was proving himself wise in his treatment of the levy trainees. They had eaten well and the hay-filled pallet sacks were thick and made for good sleeping. On the way to the training ground outside the walls, Gaelin sighed.

"Here's where we pay for our dinner," he said.

Richard knew Gaelin and Droene dreaded the training. His cousins were as brave as any, but neither had the temperament for fighting.

They walked through the town in a semi-orderly formation, four abreast, with First Pikeman Kiemet leading the way. Another ten soldiers from the regular army brought up the rear. The morning was chilly, but the bite of the cold snap had lost most of its teeth. They marched down well-worn cobblestone streets and felt the wind, trapped in the narrow confines of two and three story buildings, whip around them. Kiemet led them to a grassy patch between the elongs where two carts waited. They were loaded with hoes, scythes, weeding rakes, and axes.

"We didn't come to do their farming," someone behind Richard muttered. Soft whispering and objections echoed down the lines, but Richard had noticed the implements were all made of wood. He didn't realize he was nodding his approval.

"Silence!" Kiemet shouted down the objections. He glared at Richard.

"You had enough to say last night, but you don't seem to be objecting now. Why?"

Richard stared at the big soldier, reminding himself he did not need to make an enemy of his trainer.

"Because if we were attacked in our fields, our hoes, scythes, or weeders could be the only weapons at hand," he replied. "Not all fighting is done in military rank."

Kiemet seemed surprised. He glared at the farmer for a moment longer, then ordered Richard forward. The first pikeman took a pair of wooden scythes from a cart and tossed one to Richard. Even without a metal blade, the mock tool was heavier than a real one. The curved wood that represented the blade was thick and blunt, and the long handle was two inches in diameter. The baron had no intention of letting the recruits cut each other to pieces, though they might split each other's skulls with the heavy weapons.

"Since you've worked it out so well, let's see what you can do with this."

Kiemet moved in fast, clashing his weapon against Richard's. His intent had been to catch the novice unaware and use the curve of the scythe to pull Richard's weapon out of his hands. Richard realized his intent and turned his scythe. He let Kiemet's weapon slide harmlessly down the back of his own handle until the pikeman was sure his ploy had not worked. Then, giving his scythe a quick twist, Richard caught the curve of Kiemet's weapon and jerked, pulling the pikeman forward as he stepped to the side. Off-balance, Kiemet was easy to trip. The instructor went sprawling.

Twitters of laughter came from the assembled group, and the whispers started again as a red-faced Kiemet scrambled to his feet.

"Clever," he snarled.

"Not clever," Richard replied, deciding his best course would be to help the instructor save his pride. "I'm from the northern border where we occasionally fight goblins from the Spiderfell. Our lives can depend on fighting with anything at hand." The explanation was enough, he decided. He had no intention of sacrificing his own self-respect in an apology.

Kiemet glared at him and turned away, ordering the disposition of the mock tools and setting the others to practice. Richard's next weapon was a hoe. He spent the day matching his skills with various opponents. He took his training seriously, worked out new theories, tried them, and did as much teaching as learning.

For two weeks Richard went to bed with bruises

that stiffened in the night and made the first half hour of the next day's training a misery. Still, he approved of what he was learning. War was an occasional danger, but brigands and unfriendly humanoids were constantly on the prowl, and often caught the field workers unaware.

The levy trainees were confined to the barracks area from Firlen—the first day of the week—until the evening of Mierlen, the seventh day. Taelen, the eighth, they were free to wander about Aerele. The city-bred trainees: shop assistants, household servants and hirelings complained. Most were used to the custom of working six days and having two of at least partial rest. The farm-bred trainees, who never had a day free of feeding and caring for their animals, shrugged away the extra day's work. Even when they were not engaged in training, most of their time was spent in the company of their fellow trainees.

The first day they had been free to wander in the city, Richard bought a new knife, and he spent his evenings using his whet stone to bring up the edge. They were in their second week of training when he was sitting on one of the benches by the fire, only half listening to a riddle game as he worked on his knife.

"I have one," Reilin, the baker's son who slept on the bottom tier of Richard's bunk, announced.

"They run away,
"But are never free,
"No matter the way,
"They're always with me."

"Your feet," Richard said without thinking about it.

"That was quick," Gaelin said. "I never knew you liked riddles.

"I don't know anything about them," Richard replied. They were not a usual pastime for the Endiers.

"Well, you'd better learn fast, because you have to

ask one now." Gaelin laughed. "Rules of the game."

"But I don't know any. I wasn't playing."

"You solved my riddle, now you must give us one," Reilin insisted with a grin. "Make up something."

Richard sighed and gazed about the room, seeking inspiration, but nothing offered itself as an obvious answer. Everyone in the circle was staring at him expectantly. A few of the trainees were sprawled on their beds. One earnest recruit sat cross-legged on his bunk with a scrap of hide and a piece of charcoal from the fire, laboriously making his letters. Gaelin had been helping him learn to read and write.

Richard took a deep breath and started.

"I travel without moving,

"I venture without danger,

"I see places I have never been,

"I'm moved to laughter and to anger."

He waited, but the others just stared at him, completely puzzled. He began sharpening his knife again, waiting for someone to answer. Vaguely he was aware of their shaking heads.

"You stumped everyone, so what is it?" Gaelin demanded.

"You should know, you're teaching Coedon."

"Reading!" Gaelin squawked, disgusted. "Okay, you stumped us, you'll have to do another."

"Why, I didn't do that one right?"

"You did it right, you were just too good at it," said a tall, lanky farmer's son who sat on the other side of the circle. "Do another."

Richard sought inspiration again.

"Big to little,

"Here and gone,

"Rooted, but seldom still,

"Many or one,

"They are us, tree or hill."

The silence fell again until finally a small man from the other side of the circle asked tentatively, "Shadows?"

"Correct," Richard announced, glad someone else would have to pay the forfeit of knowledge, and he was out of the game.

"Did you make them up?" Gaelin asked while the others were busy trying to solve the next riddle.

"I had to, you know we've never played that game at home."

"You're good at it," Richard's cousin replied. He turned to listen to someone else answer and then ask a riddle of his own. Richard had guessed correctly on the two that followed his, but he kept his knowledge to himself. He wanted to sharpen his knife.

After two weeks the recruits advanced to training in marching order, holding their positions over uneven terrain, charging in a phalanx, and in the use of the weapons they would be expected to carry into an organized battle: spears or battle-axes, and shields—if they were among the favored few of the levy who received weapons. Otherwise they would bring their own, even scythes and hoes, if that was all they had.

They used real spears for throwing, but for one-on-one battle practice they used weapons with leather padding. The purpose was still to learn, not hack each other to pieces.

"Shields up, swing and parry, swing and parry, swing and parry . . ." Kiemet's blaring voice carried over the constant thud of wood against wood. "Forward, back, forward, back . . ." He droned his way through day after weary day.

"I'll be great in battle if the enemy is dancing to the same step," Gaelin complained at evening meal on their fourth Mierlen. "Last night I woke up moving my feet and swinging my arm."

"Just hold on, we're halfway through," Richard said. "And tomorrow is Taelen, so you can rest."

Across the table, Reboen, a slender man with a shock of white-blonde hair, leaned forward. His eyes were big with news.

"I overheard an officer talking to Kiemet this afternoon. On Firlen we're to join with another group and fight a mock battle."

"What group?" Gaelin asked without much interest.

"I don't know. They didn't say."

"An officer?" Richard's eyes gleamed, but he wanted to confirm what he had heard.

"Captain. I saw his insignia, and he said it was his group we're to fight." Reboen tried to hide his concern, but his eyes were full of dread. "You don't suppose they're going to match us against real soldiers, do you?"

"I doubt it," Richard said, careful to keep his mouth straight. He kept his grin inside, and resolved to get a good night's sleep Taelen night. If he was right in his theory, he wanted to be ready for Firlen, the first day of the coming week.

ANUIRE

seven

"Droene! Droene Endier!"

All three Endiers turned to see who hailed Droene, and watched as Caern Tier hurried out of a nearby shop. They had not seen the son of the Lord of Tier since they'd begun their training. Caern smiled as he hurried forward to greet his former travelling companions. He seemed pathetically glad to see them.

"I wouldn't have known you if I hadn't recognized the blonde head on this walking mountain," he said, grinning up at Droene.

None of the Endiers were surprised at his reaction. They were wearing their gentleman's clothing. Droene was a formidable sight in his close fitting blue hose. The heavy muscles of his legs were exposed to advantage, and the full, slashed sleeves of his light blue coat added breadth to his already wide shoulders. Gaelin's green coat was trimmed in silver braid and he too looked like a town-bred gentleman, but

Caern stared longest at Richard.

Richard disliked the peacockish pomp of the wealthy. Unlike many, his feeling was not born of envy, but was a result of his clear and discerning eye for the ridiculous. In his gray hose and black short coat trimmed black on black, Richard thought he would melt into the background, but Caern, after staring at him, nodded.

"You look more like the son of a lord than many walking these streets today," he said.

"How goes the training?" Richard asked, turning the conversation to a subject that interested him.

"Truth to tell, I'll be glad when it's over," Caern said. "I don't think I'm much of a fighter." He shrugged. "I'm holding my own, I think. I just don't care for it much."

"We may all be glad of it if the tension with Coeranys gets any worse," Gaelin said. Of all the Endiers he was the most outgoing. Except for the few minutes a day when he worked with Coedon on his reading, Gaelin spent his off hours in the midst of a chatting, laughing group. He knew every bit of gossip in Aerele, including the fact that Baron Naele Diem's cousin, who ruled Coeranys, wanted to take advantage of this kinship to put his son on the throne of Diemed.

"Too bad you don't care for fighting, you might join the regular army," Droene said.

They were walking down the street toward the center of town. Caern had fallen in step with them and they walked for five minutes before he looked around and raised his eyebrows.

"Where are you going?"

"To see the Baron's palace," Gaelin said.

"Just using up the day," Richard added.

"If you really want to see something that ugly we should have turned left at the last corner," Caern said.

"Something that ugly?" Richard asked.

"The palace," Caern explained.

He was right. The three story stone building with its narrow windows might have been beautiful inside, but the outside was a disappointingly feature- less square. Not even the grounds were interesting. They started back toward the northern section of town and the barracks.

Most of the streets in Aerele were cobbled and dry, but an air of damp clung to the ground level of the deeply cantilevered half-timbered buildings. Since Taelen was a rest day, no carts traveled the streets so the four walked abreast until a large, heavy traveling carriage forced them to the side. They were just pass- ing a doorway when it opened and three young men came hurtling out, followed by two young ladies.

Richard immediately recognized Ruinel Goerent and his friend of the wine-soaked coat, but they did not appear to remember Richard. They did recognize Caern Tier.

Their introductions were gentlemen to gentlemen.

"I make you known to Lady Aeroena Thriess," said Shaene Alderis, the third young man, a stranger to Richard until the introduction. Shaene looked on Lady Aeroena with a wistful air; clearly he was in love with her and was hoping for her affection in return. Richard wished him well; she was a beautiful girl.

The second girl was barely more than a child, but something about her seemed familiar to Richard. Although there was no chance he might have, Richard couldn't help feeling he'd met this girl before. Perhaps she simply reminded him of one of his cousins, but still. . . .

"And this is her cousin," Shaene continued, gestur- ing at the other girl, "the young Lady Tonaere Allaen."

Richard and his companions returned her curtsey with slight bows and it seemed only seconds before Shaene was offering his apologies to Caern Tier. Ruinel Goerent had still not recognized Richard, nor had his friend, and Richard was relieved to see the party escorting Lady Aeroena rush off down the street.

"How is it a few scraps of cloth can make such a difference?" Gaelin asked pensively. The others ignored the obvious question.

"Do you know what your training program is going to be tomorrow?" Richard asked, again changing the subject.

"We're to go into mock combat with another company," Caern said. "I don't know who our opponents will be."

"Us, probably, since we heard the same," Gaelin said, glancing at Richard. "Now I know why you liked the news."

They found a small inn that catered to the gentry and sat at a table drinking ale. Caern kept frowning at the others until Gaelin asked what bothered him.

"Why are you with the hoe-men?" he asked. "I didn't recognize the name when we rode south, but I've since learned you have one of the largest farms in the Moere Province."

"Because we *are* hoe-men," Gaelin said. "We're farmers, farmers that work the land. We don't really pretend to be gentlemen of the town or the court. We prefer farming to politics."

Richard said nothing. The truth suddenly dawned on him. He felt a growing knot of shame in his stomach and his throat tightened until he could hardly swallow. Because they were sons of a major landowner, Gaelin and Droene could have joined the sons of the gentry, but as only a cousin, Richard could not. It didn't even matter that the farm was only in his uncle's hands in trust for him. Since he was not one of the traditional heirs, he was excluded from privilege. His uncle, Gaelin and Droene must have discussed the subject before the three young men came south. Neither Gaelin nor Droene had given Richard a hint. His frustration over his position, and his shame at holding his cousins back, gave him an even greater need to best Ruinel in battle.

The next morning he hurried to dress and stepped outside, glad to find a crisp, clear morning. He wanted a good, sustaining meal, but he wanted it to settle before he faced his opponent, so he was one of the first to enter the dining hall. Richard knew his biggest problem would be getting himself into position to fight Ruinel. He needed an opportunity to move up or down the line. As he ate, he formed a plan and put it into action immediately, speaking to several people who might be willing to do him a favor and trade places with him.

When they reached the practice field, Richard mused over the choice of a battle-axe or a spear and finally chose the axe. The reach was nearer to the length of the wooden practice sword he expected Ruinel Goerent to be using.

Half an hour later, the two companies were drawn up facing each other. As luck would have it, Richard faced Caern while Gaelin, four places down the line, stood in front of Ruinel. As soon as Kiemet's back was turned, the two cousins quickly traded places. Ruinel's eyes widened as he recognized his opponent from the midden and realized he had met Richard again only the day before. A lot of the arrogance was missing from Ruinel's manner.

Since the officer who commanded the training of the gentry was senior to the pikeman, he gave the opening comments.

"We learn to attack in formation," the officer said,

raising his voice nearly to a shout. "Any army that can maintain its formation during a battle has a much better chance of being victorious. I don't believe, in the history of warfare, it has ever happened." He waited for them to appreciate his joke and his own troops dutifully laughed.

"In the confusion of a major battle, knights and cavalry will find themselves facing the levy, the levy will fight knights and pikemen, and dodge the artillery. If you are called to war, all of you will benefit from facing each other. You should be familiar with the tactics used with weapons unlike your own. Each of you stands facing an opponent, you will engage at the gong."

Across a space of ten feet, Ruinel seemed confident, apparently believing his sword to be more than a match for Richard's axe. When the gong sounded Ruinel stepped forward and slashed out with his wooden sword. Richard easily deflected the blow with his shield and swung his axe. Ruinel caught the blow on his own shield, but he had been holding it out too far and Richard caught it with one side of his padded double blade. He nearly pulled the shield off Ruinel's arm. The mayor's son was forced to moved forward until he was able to turn the shield and free himself of the axe.

His error in strategy made him angry and Ruinel hacked and thrust with his sword, never able to get past Richard's shield. He ignored Richard's axe as if it did not exist, unless Richard used it to deflect the wooden blade. Richard's prowess made Ruinel so angry he lost all control and started hacking at the handle of the axe instead of his enemy. Richard stepped back, disgusted with the fiasco.

I've been anxious to prove myself against this bumbling fool? Richard thought.

"If you're loyal to Baron Naele, you should fight for

the enemy," he snarled at Ruinel. "Your bumbling stupidity would give your opponent too much courage."

Ruinel stared at him with an open mouth.

"If I had another midden ditch handy I'd throw you in it," Richard said, then sighed. "But I don't, so give me that sword!" He jerked the mock blade from Ruinel's hand and thrust the axe at him. When Richard realized he had to teach his enemy to fight in order to prove he could best him, he fleetingly thought how life could play some strange tricks.

"Now swing that axe slowly and watch how I use the blade. Remember you can't go blade to blade between axe and sword, the axe will take it every time."

Ruinel started to follow Richard's orders and then drew back. "You don't know anything about sword play."

"Neither do you," Richard retorted. "Now do as I say or I'll knock you in the head. Swing that axe and watch my shield. I can't do much with the sword to deflect your heavier weapon, but I can use it in the chinks of your defense."

Ruinel actually recognized a superior fighting mentality when he saw one, and took his instruction meekly enough. After five minutes they traded weapons again, and though Richard "hacked off" Ruinel's arm, his leg, and his head—twice—the mayor's son was still far better at his defense. They had forgotten the instruction to fall when they received a "fatal" blow, and continued their practice. Their minds entirely on learning, they also forgot their animosity.

When Ruinel stepped back and fell over a sword dropped by one of the "fatally wounded," he picked it up and handed it to Richard.

"Let's see what we can do sword to sword."

Ruinel had learned his lessons blade to blade, and

Richard found himself slightly pressed, but the weapon seemed natural in his hand. Before long he was pressing Ruinel back. He was beginning to feel even more confident with the weapon when out of the corner of his eye he noticed two figures standing off to the side, watching. Something in their stance caused him to draw back.

The captain and Kiemet were glaring at them.

"When you two finish your private war, would you like to join the rest of us for more instruction? Any time . . . we can wait." The sarcasm in the officer's voice stung like a whip.

The two companies faced off against each other for the rest of the afternoon. Richard discovered many of the other young gentlemen were adept with their weapons and understood the weaknesses of an opponent with an axe or spear. He "killed" six, and "died" three times. Richard limped to the meal hall that night and ate with a sore right elbow, but the pains were worth it. He had learned a lot that day.

The Endiers were friends as well as relatives, but had no feeling of clannishness. Gaelin was sitting with a group of rowdy jokers. Droene was at the other end of the hall, listening to a solemn discussion between two scholarly types that were destined for the priesthood of Haelyn after their training. Drone had told Richard that he seldom understood the two would-be priests, but he liked to listen to "smart talk."

When they returned to the barracks they were met by a messenger and told to report to Captain Silse. They followed without objection, but, in the light of the messenger's torch, traded speculative glances. They were led to a large building and entered a passage with steps leading to the upper floors. The building smelled of wine and damp wool and the subdued sounds of many voices behind closed doors was like the hum of bees.

In a small chamber just to the right of the entrance they found Captain Silse dictating to a scribe. He looked up as they entered and waved away the writer. The officer gave his attention to Gaelin and Droene.

"What are you doing in the hoe-men barracks?" he demanded. "You're on my list. I was ready to charge you with failure to report for training."

"When we arrived we were directed there by the guards at the gate," Gaelin said. "We had no idea we were in the wrong place."

"You should have known major landowners' sons do not train with the levy." He turned his head to give his attention to Richard. "Luckily your practice with young Goerent brought you to my attention. You have the makings of an excellent swordsman, too good to wield a hoe.

"All three of you will join my second company. They started their training yesterday. You've wasted a lot of time training with weaponry you'll never use." He waved them away without giving them a chance to object.

The messenger waited in the passage. He led them to a chamber on the fourth floor where the two beds were being moved to add a third. Other servants brought their belongings from the barracks before the beds were in place.

"It seems as if we're gentlemen after all," Gaelin said with a sigh.

"I'd rather be a hoe-man," Droene said slowly. "I feel like a hoe-man."

"You're a gentleman, so get used to it," Richard said shortly.

The next morning the Endier's began their training with the weighted wooden swords. They hacked their way through swords, pole axes, spears, pikes, and lances. They learned light artillery and tactics. Their month with the levy counted for nothing. They would spend two months in Captain Silse's group before they finished their training.

Gaelin and Droene made several new friends, and Richard often found himself in the company of Ruinel and Caern, though the son of Lord Tier spent more time with Droene. The last person Richard had expected to have as a friend was Ruinel, but sober, he was not as arrogant and unfeeling as Richard had supposed when they first met.

A month after they began their training Caern and Ruinel left for home and Richard spent most of his time alone. He was not accepted by the other trainees. Two things accounted for his exclusion: traditionally, nephews of landowners were not afforded the status of sons, and in an effort to win acceptance for his cousin, Gaelin had spread the story of Richard's confrontation with Tal-Qazar.

The scorn of disbelief totally by-passed Gaelin and Droene and landed squarely on Richard. His lips had formed the habit of a tight line by the time the training was over. His only satisfaction was the knowledge that not one of the sneering "gentlemen" had been able to stand under his weapons.

* * * * *

Richard was not the only one to suffer grief from the story of the little magic house. Back in the Web, deep in the black heart of the Spiderfell, Tal-Qazar stood on a tree limb and glared at the skeleton of a goblin, the one that had brought the news of Richard Endier's "power."

After finally realizing he had been tricked, the awnshegh had sent his spiders to spy on the Endier farm, searching for the human who had tricked him. But

Richard was no longer there. The goblin had paid the price for being a part of the trick, and now its skeleton stood apart from the others on display outside the Adytum.

"Pull it down and destroy it," Tal-Qazar shouted to his lieutenants, who were always close at hand when he was outside the Adytum. "I no longer want to look at it."

Every time he laid eyes on it he went into a frenzied rage.

Berkerig and Gosfak hurried to obey Tal-Qazar's orders. Neither of the goblin lieutenants had been able to keep quiet about the grass house, or about the awnshegh's anger when he learned he had been tricked. The sooner the skeleton of Qesgig was removed, and the Web was allowed to forget about the incident, the better it would be for the two lieutenants—and everyone else.

* * * * *

The assassin would have enjoyed the awnshegh's frustration, but he was not in the Web that day. In the shape of a bird he had flown south into the Erebannien. The tale of the awnshegh's humiliation was too good to keep to himself. He was taking a gift to his people.

They had fought so long, and grieved so much, it was time for them to have a story over which they could laugh, and, perhaps, find hope.

eight

Richard was heartily glad to leave Aerele. On a cold, blustery day in Keltier, the coldest month of the year, Richard and his two cousins rode over the last low hill and looked down on the Endier freestead. He gazed at the large farm that would one day be his—that would one day give him the right to sneer at his tormenters—and smiled.

But then why bother, he decided, most of the trainees who'd laughed at him, not believing he had faced down an awnshegh and lived, had been younger sons who could expect no inheritance. Why waste his time? Still, their scorn rankled, and would continue to rankle until he came into his own.

The Endiers urged their horses to a gallop and raced into the stable yard, shouting for the farmhands to come out and take their mounts. Colin appeared and stared at them as if he were seeing ghosts.

"What's the matter with you?" Gaelin demanded

as he jumped from the saddle. "I know we're late but we're not dead. Where's my father?"

Before the hireling could answer, a large, burly stranger stepped out of the rear door of the house. He walked with the tread of one who had spent his life on the road. His face was weather-beaten, but not old.

"Greetings, strangers. If you seek shelter, you are welcome."

Gaelin turned and eyed the man, his habitual smile lost as he stared. "And who are you to welcome us?"

The man tensed slightly, the wariness of one who is no stranger to trouble, but his eyes twinkled. "A strange greeting from one who would be a guest, but I am Liemen Lanwin, your host. This is the Lanwin holding, owned by my brother Halmied and myself. Who asks?"

"Gaelin Endier, second son of Randen Endier, the legal owner of this property."

Liemen Lanwin relaxed and the humor died out of his eyes.

"Then I have grievous news for you. Come inside out of the wind." He turned and walked back into the house and the Endiers followed with sinking hearts.

"What happened to my uncle?" Richard demanded as soon as they were in the door. He felt as if the world had somehow slid out from under him. The large fieldstone kitchen looked nearly the same. The table, the top cut and smoothed from one large tree, still dominated the room. The spit on the wide hearth was the same, but there were subtle differences.

Liemen Lanwin gestured for them to be seated and ordered a female servant to bring ale.

"Of his death I know only what I have heard. After the heat at the end of summer, a cold wind came out of the northwest and he spent days out in it, overseeing the farm hands. . . ."

"Arlen should have done that work," Gaelin

snarled, but though Liemen nodded, he went on with his narrative as if he had not been interrupted.

"Your father took a chill. I am told he had never fully regained his strength after his sickness the year before. He lived only two days after he first collapsed."

While Liemen was talking, a second man came into the room from the front of the house. He stood listening quietly. His looks, so like Liemen Lanwin, identified him as Liemen's brother, Halmied. Liemen introduced him and then continued with his tale.

"Arlen Endier, your first-born brother, desired to sell the holding, and we," he pointed to himself and his own brother, "Had tired of our wanderings, and were seeking a place to settle down."

Richard was caught up in his grief over his uncle and it took a moment for the news to register. Gaelin was quicker.

"Arlen had no right sell the farm. It was not his!"

"He was the oldest of your father's sons, so the property became his at your father's death," Halmied said. "We are not foolish enough to accept one man's word. It is inscribed in the Province House in Moerel. There too you will find the record of our purchase."

"He did not have the right." Richard spoke softly, slowly, working around his grief, yet he had to protect what was his. He explained his position in the line of the family and how, because he was too young to hold when his father died, the farm had been left to his uncle with the stipulation that it revert to him at his uncle's death.

"Tradition demands that property is inherited by the oldest son," Halmied said stubbornly. "No documents such as you describe were brought forth."

A red film of rage nearly blinded Richard. He jumped up from the table, overturning the short bench and attempted to shove his way past Halmied. When the older man refused to move from the doorway, Richard pulled his knife.

"Try to stop me and I'll kill you," he snarled.

Richard had been quick, but the flash of movement at the table was quicker. Gaelin gasped and Droene gave out with an unaccustomed oath.

"Stand away or I'll cut his throat," warned Liemen.

Richard turned to find Liemen Lanwin holding Gaelin in the grip of one strong arm. In his other hand he held the point of his knife to Gaelin's jugular vein. Richard stepped back, unable to sheathe his weapon, yet unwilling to risk Gaelin's life by threatening Halmied.

The standoff dragged through nearly a minute of silence before Halmied shrugged and stepped out of the doorway.

"Let him go," he told his brother. "We have lived in honor, we will not depart from it now. If what they say is true, we, not they, have been cheated." He gave Richard a hard and implacable glare. "Know this. If you can prove your claim, your cousin's life is forfeit. If you cannot, the holding is ours."

"I accept your terms," Richard said. "I doubt Arlen was fool enough to leave the documents, but I will see for myself."

The five men tramped up the stairs to the second floor and into the bed chamber that had been occupied by Randen Endier since the death of his brother Aenel. The massive bed and a large clothing chest remained. The small, ornately carved cask in which, for centuries, the Endiers had kept their farm accounts, was missing.

But the important papers had not been stored there. Richard walked over to the fieldstone chimney that rose from the first floor and from which a small hearth opened. He knelt, pulling out a stone at the outer corner to expose a small cavity. While Randen was alive, the niche held the documents that gave him his legal title, and guaranteed the return of the property to Richard. It had also contained a large pouch of gold, silver, and copper.

Nothing remained but dust.

"I can't believe it," Gaelin said, pushing Richard aside. He reached into the hole and felt around, his face twisted in an effort to move the stones deep in the chimney, as if he could force them to yield their contents.

"It's not there," Richard snapped. "I said he would not be fool enough to leave it."

The Lanwins tactfully withdrew, leaving the three Endiers alone. Their footsteps echoed and faded as they descended the steps and retreated back to the kitchen.

Droene stood looking down at Richard who sat on the floor. His wide, blank face held compassion, but worse, trust, trust that Richard would make everything right. The weight of that trust was as heavy as the loss.

"Will they quit their claim, do you think?" Gaelin asked.

"No," Richard replied. "They bought in good faith from the first born. Without Uncle Randen's will, they are justified in claiming the property."

"Then what will we do?" Gaelin asked. Richard looked up to see green eyes and blue staring at him, seeking an answer. He wanted to scream at them that they were not his responsibility. He would have provided for them if he had inherited the farm, but he had nothing, so what did they expect? His hurt was too deep even to allow for rage.

They heard footsteps on the stairs again and Halmied appeared in the doorway.

"We've a ham just off the spit, and baked tubers," he said. "Come while they're hot. There's some things still to say."

They followed the retired adventurer down the stairs and took their customary places at the table, not even thinking the brothers might have claimed those spots for themselves. The food was good, but Richard ate because of his body's need, he tasted nothing.

"There's still things, clothing and such, in two of the bed chambers under the eaves," Liemen said. "Be any of it yours, you're welcome to take it. We put no claim on your belongings."

"Then too, the horses you ride," Halmied added. "Doubtless, had you been here when the holding was sold, we'd consider them ours, but they weren't. We lay no claim to them."

Droene stared at them with a blank expression as if unable to take in the subtleties. Gaelin's angry expression did not alter.

"You're being fairer than we should have expected—if we had expected any of this," Richard said, thinking of their warm winter clothing, his extra boots . . . and the carefully worked hiding place in the floor under his own clothes chest.

"Are you saying we have a right to take all our personal possessions?" Richard asked.

Even Droene caught the meaning of the question. Both brothers gave away the importance of Richard's question with their quick looks. The brother adventurers exchanged meaningful glances and grinned.

"If you've hidden away your personal fortunes in another chimney, you needn't admit it," Liemen laughed. "Take what's yours. We're not robbers."

Richard gazed at the Lanwin brothers and saw the speculation and regret in the glances they exchanged. They were too canny to give up their farm, but they half-believed Richard's claim.

"I hope Arlen allowed Rieva, Fhiele, and Jenna to pack all their things," Gaelin said. "How many carts did they take?"

"He took one, but he left alone," Halmied said. "We heard in Moerel that he had indentured his sisters to tradesmen. We saw them when we first came to see the holding, but they were gone when we came back to take possession."

Gaelin rose from the table, sending his bench skittering backward. He seemed nearly blinded with rage, but not at the Lanwins. Droene sat pale and blank faced. He silently mouthed the word "indentured" as if unable to associate the word with his sisters. Richard rose too, more slowly than Gaelin, but with equal determination.

"You have been as fair as we could expect, but we will be leaving now." He choked out the words, but Liemen was on his feet, his hand on Richard's shoulder.

"Stay the night. The sun set an hour past. You'll do your women no good if you're killed by bandits or goblins in the darkness." The Lanwins were fair men. After the evening meal they assisted the three Endiers in sorting their belongings, and offered to store what they might need to leave behind until they had a place for the few bits and pieces that were too bulky to take now, having no idea where they were going.

Then the brothers made an offer that was of far more value. If the Endiers wanted to bring their sisters back to the farm, they were welcome. The older girls could oversee the house servants. The Lanwins insisted the obligation would all be on their side, since they were unused to managing the sullen and slovenly house servants.

Richard, Gaelin and Droene talked it over in the night. They discussed alternatives, but Gaelin finally made the decision. Richard gave him the right because of his closer kinship to the women of the family.

"They'd be nothing more than well-treated servants, but somehow I trust the Lanwins," Gaelin said. "At least the girls would be in a familiar place, and they would be protected."

Richard raised a loose floorboard and took out the contents of the hole beneath it. Arlen had been indirectly responsible for the hiding place. His bullying ways and willingness to steal from his brothers and cousin had driven them to carefully remove the pegs from a floorboard to hide their valuables under it.

Randen Endier had always dropped a few coins in the hands of his sons and nephew after the harvest was sold, even when they were too young to go to market with him. With no place to spend their coins they had hidden them away. As they counted the accumulated wealth, they were surprised at their total worth. Still, it would not be enough to buy back the indentures of the Endier sisters. Richard would need to visit Master Jamael to retrieve the money he had left with him.

None of the three had spent much of their money in Aerele. Looking back it seemed they sensed the greater need that would come later. The next morning they rode to Moerel. They were two days locating Rieva, who had kept Jenna with her, and was apprenticed to a tailor.

When the three Endiers pushed by the stammering clerk and into the cold workroom at the back of the shop, Jenna squealed in delight and rushed into Droene's arms. Rieva sat with four other women, their heads bent over their sewing. Her eyes were full of delight at seeing them, hope that they would rescue her, and shame at where they had found her.

"Here, I'll not have my workers interrupted," the tailor announced. His table was close to the small fire. He gave Rieva a sharp look. "She's little enough good anyway—her and her cramping hands—and a child to feed as well."

The Endiers understood. Rieva could sew a fine seam, but as a child she had broken two of her fingers. Holding a needle for longer than a few minutes caused her hand to cramp.

"If you feel you have been duped, then let us make right an unfair bargain," Richard said smoothly. After less than ten minutes of bargaining, Rieva and Jenna packed their few possessions and the Endier males left them at the inn. While Gaelin and Droene went in search of Fhiele, Richard sought out Master Jamael and collected the funds he had left with the money-lender. In the canny lord's hands it had grown slightly, and Richard suspected he would be in need of every copper. He pocketed the funds and rejoined his cousins before they found Fhiele.

She was not so easy to free. Arlen had indentured her to an innkeeper who counted on her beauty to draw customers, and in that he was right. The Endiers walked into the common room in time to see a burly, scar-faced river man pull her to him with an arm around her waist. When she struck him with an empty pitcher, he laughed and pulled it away from her.

Working together as if they had rehearsed their actions in advance, Droene knocked the river man across a table while Gaelin grabbed their sister to keep her from falling. The table broke under the river man's weight.

"I'll have no brawling in here!" the innkeeper shouted.

"You'll have no cause when you sell us my sister's indenture," Gaelin growled.

When they first entered the inn, Fhiele's face had been set in hopeless anger, but with the arrival of her brothers, tears of relief ran unheeded down her cheeks. The innkeeper refused every offer, so the Endier men commandeered a table and threatened every customer who turned an appreciative eye on Fhiele. When several of the inn's patrons decided it would be safer to do their drinking elsewhere, the innkeeper sent for the watch.

The large soldier was a fair, if slow-witted man.

"You can't keep an indentured servant from her duties," he warned the Endiers. "And you can't fault brothers for protecting their sister's honor," he informed the angry innkeeper. "Got a sister myself," he muttered under his breath so only Richard heard it.

"Best you come to terms," the watchman announced, then left with as much speed as his dignity allowed.

"I can order you out of my establishment," their unwilling host announced, and did so while the soldier of the watch was still in the building.

The Endiers were forced to leave, but they took up positions outside the entrance and warned off the approaching patrons. The night watch ignored them and they stood in the cold for three nights before the innkeeper finally agreed to the sale.

A week after they returned from Aerele, Richard and his cousins had reinstalled the three daughters of Randen Endier in the home of their births. Then, the three young men bundled their extra clothing onto old Durchan, a gift from the Lanwin brothers, and rode south, back to Moerel.

"They will be safe with the Lanwins," Droene said of his sisters, though his voice sounded doubtful.

"They're still no more than servants," Gaelin grumbled.

"Only until we can dower them," Richard replied, realizing the sisters would never find themselves in the good marriages they were brought up to expect. But the time had come to think of the future.

"The question is, what do *we* do now?"

ANUIRE

nine

Richard pulled up his collar and immediately
regretted it. The rain that had collected on the tanned
leather ran down his neck. Despite his thick woolen
chainse, he swore he could feel every freezing link of
the chain mail tunic he wore over it. It seemed half a
lifetime since he had been really dry, and a year since
he had seen the sun for more than two days at a time.

When Richard, Gaelin and Droene left the Lanwin
farm and set off to make their fortunes, they had traveled to Moerel and hired on as mercenaries to guard a
west-bound caravan. Their employer planned to journey to the foot of the Seamist Mountains and return to
Diemed within two weeks. The merchant had not
planned on the drunken brawl in Daulton, where one
of his own wagoners knifed him. He died three days
later.

At first the Endiers had tried to find another caravan traveling east and in need of hired swords. They

found none, and were ready to ride back to Diemed when they were approached by a trader in need of mercenaries.

He was headed north, to the Reconnin Mines in the northwestern corner of the province of Vanilen. He was taking in barrels of flour, spices, and cloth, and would bring back iron ore and some silver. The seventy-mile trip would take a month, allowing for a slow journey through the foothills, and frequent rests for the animals. The danger of attack by trolls, hardened brigands, and the occasional unsuccessful and embittered group of men who had spent all their resources prospecting, made guards necessary. The pay was more than twice the wage per day for traveling the tamer lands, so the Endiers took the job.

Laedon Conoed was as easygoing with his employees as he was with his animals. Both liked him, and the pay was good. When the caravan returned to Daulton, Laedon allowed the Endiers the use of two rooms over his barn, and they ate in his kitchen. In time they would have enough money put aside to provide good doweries for both Rieva and Fhiele.

During the next year the Endiers completed ten trips with Laedon, but again bad luck befell their employer at the far end of the journey. Laedon had climbed five hundred feet up the side of a mountain with one of his miner friends to look at the possible site of a new dig. He slipped on a damp stone and fell to his death. The Endiers brought back Laedon's last load and made the final deal for his family.

They eventually found another trader in the market for guards. He grumbled at their price, but they had been traveling the rutted road through the foothills that bordered the Seamist Mountains for a year, and had valuable experience. They had gained a reputation as valiant fighters and everyone knew they had been loyal to their last employer.

Ulchoen Estimied was far different from the easy-going Laedon. He had served a short stint in the army of Tuornen. Why he was not still in service was a mystery, but he boasted about being a captain, and he ran his caravan of freight wagons as though he was commanding a crack military regiment.

In town he had been fairly spoken, but on the trail he was arrogant, worked his animals too hard, and spoke to everyone on the wagon train as if they were slovenly hirelings that could be insulted into working harder. He insisted the wagons travel the roads evenly spaced, no matter that the slowing of one would make climbing the next hill harder on the beasts, or that a wagon might bog down if stopped while he reformed the line to suit his eye.

The first morning he insisted his drivers and guards form a straight line while he gave him their orders, and he faced his first confrontation with Richard. Richard didn't say a word, but the glare he gave Ulchoen was enough to send the portly little man scurrying about his business. Still, Ulchoen's resentment toward Richard seemed to grow every day. When they reached the Vendier Mines, where Ulchoen did most of his trading, Richard learned why their employer was always in need of guards for his trips.

"Watch out for trouble with him on the way back," a friendly miner advised Richard. "He has a reputation for starting arguments with his guards and firing them just before he reaches Daulton again. That way he doesn't have to pay them."

"He'll pay us," Richard remarked through closed teeth.

"You might want to know he's carrying a lot of coin," the miner said with a wink. "He did as much selling as trading on this trip."

Richard kept the miner's warning in mind as they

started south. The Vendier Mines were in the province of Taliern, only forty miles from Daulton. They were halfway back, the wagons heavily loaded with iron ingots, when Richard, riding point, gave the signal for possible trouble ahead. He could not see far. The heavily forested mountains were cloaked in their characteristic fog. The blanket of trees stretched out into the foothills, and ahead, between two small knolls, the mist had settled to the ground until the thinning forest was hidden from view.

"What's the matter?" Ulchoen called from the first wagon where he was riding with the driver that afternoon. The lead wagon came to a halt because Richard blocked the road.

"No bird song," Richard said. To him, his explanation should have been enough. The birds who lived in the Seamist Mountains did not stop their lives because of rain and fog. They continued to sing and chatter, eat and dart about, as if they lived in perpetual sunlight. Like all wild creatures, they fell silent when danger walked beneath the trees.

"What do you suggest? That we just sit here?" Ulchoen snapped.

Richard pointed to a spot a few yards ahead to indicate a break in the trees that lined the road. "A few yards beyond that break is a creek with a firm, stony bed. The wagons won't bog down. I suggest we use it to bypass that hollow." The idea had not been his. Laedon had used it several times when the hollow seemed suspect.

"Ridiculous," Ulchoen snapped, grabbed the reins from his driver, and whipped up the oxen. "I hired you and your cousins as guards. Do your duty and see us through."

As the lead wagon rumbled past, Gaelin rode up to pace Richard. His usual good humor had not been evident on this journey.

"How has this idiot managed to stay alive long enough to make more than one trip?" he asked.

"It has to be luck, and he's using his up," Richard replied. "There's an ambush ahead. I suspect they'll strike at the last two wagons. To be sure, we'll go on ahead and patrol the lowest part of the road." He gave a whistle to Droene, who was riding near the end of the train.

When Droene joined them, they pushed their horses to a trot and passed the lead wagon.

"Here, where are you going!" demanded Ulchoen, but the first wagon had already started down the slope into the hollow and Richard had no time for explanations. Ulchoen was still shouting when Richard caught a scent he had smelled before. Even in the thick mist it seemed dry, musty, and at the same time unhealthy, rotten.

"Trolls," he warned the others.

"Don't much like trolls," Droene muttered as he hefted his battle-axe. He had bought a large double-bladed axe head and had an armorer fit it with a long handle. For most men the weapon would have been unmanageable, but Droene had the strength to wield it, and wield it well.

Droene stopped at the bottom of the incline and waited for the train to pass. Gaelin held the middle of the three hundred yard level stretch, and Richard rode forward until he reached the ascending slope where the mist thinned. Then he rode back, taking up a position halfway between Gaelin and the safer area.

In the thick mist they could not see each other, but Richard heard the rhythmic jingle of the oxen as the first team passed the bottom of the hollow. Ulchoen, still riding on the lead wagon, glared at Richard as he passed, but the stocky little man seemed less sure of himself. He held a dagger in his hand, a foolish weapon if they were attacked by trolls.

Four of the eight wagons had passed Richard when he heard a shout and Droene's whistle. He turned his mount and raced back down the edge of the rutted road. Richard reached the seventh wagon to see a troll attempting to bite one of the oxen, but the panicked animal tossed it's horned head and gored the nine foot tall monster in its mottled green leg. The driver was on the ground, a gash down his arm. He was scrambling out of the way of Gaelin's horse. Gaelin was using a spear against an orog who stood on the flat canvas that covered the cargo of iron ingots. The orog hacked at the end of the spear with an axe. Gaelin had learned the lessons of Aerele, and waited for the defensive openings inevitable in the use of a swinging weapon.

Before Richard could intervene the orog stepped to the edge of the wagon, took a swing at Gaelin, who barely managed to duck as he slid his hands up the shaft of the spear. Just as the blade passed him, he gave a thrust, nearly heaving himself out of the saddle, but he had caught his adversary in the stomach, where the orog's short metal breastplate joined the chain mail apron that reached to its knees. The attacker dropped its axe and fell off the wagon, clutching the wound in its belly.

Richard reached down, grabbed the wagoner's good arm and hauled him back onto his seat.

"Get the team moving," Richard ordered.

With a wild look around, and a nod, the driver slapped the reins, urging the oxen forward. Upset by the smell of blood, and their instinctive fear of trolls, the oxen heaved the heavy cart into motion and plodded off down the road as fast as they could pull their load.

Gaelin followed Richard as they rode back down the track. Both were worried about Droene, but they did not dare force the horses to a gallop. In that area of the hollow the mist lay like a thick blanket, obscuring the ground, thinning only slightly when it reached a height of four feet. Out of the wet grayness that surrounded them they heard the cry of a human in pain, then a shout of anger—Droene!—calling down the wrath of Haelyn. The roars of trolls and the calls of orogs interrupted the human voices.

Orogs and trolls working together? The implications raised the hair on the back of Richard's neck.

They were forced to the side of the narrow road as a team of wild-eyed oxen appeared, pulling a wagon with an empty seat as the beasts attempted to escape the ambush. Then, out of the mist, stumbled the driver, holding his head and staggering after his charges.

When the two Endiers reached the scene of the fracas, they paused when they saw four orogs holding off six trolls. As the Endiers stared in surprise, a greenish-gray troll swung a heavy club and struck the hand of an orog, crushing the smaller humanoid's fingers around the shaft of its crude axe. When the orog howled and dropped its weapon, the troll reached forward. One long, claw-fingered hand ripped the helmet from the orog's head, and with the other, it tore the head from the orog's shoulders. The other trolls, still intent on the three humanoids who stood back-to-back, howled in glee.

The fight was so fast and furious that neither side had noticed the Endiers. Richard and Gaelin cautiously backed their horses until they could turn aside and circled around the fight by going through the trees.

"What's going on?" Gaelin asked as soon as they were out of sight.

"My guess would be the orogs intended to ambush us and were caught by the trolls," Richard said. "At least they're not allied," he added gratefully. If they had been, the three Endiers would have had little chance of protecting the wagons or even coming out of the fight alive. The wagon drivers could, and would fight, but they were not trained warriors. Still, any stray troll or orog not engaged in the battle between their races would find the oxen and drivers fair game.

When the noise of the fighting orogs and trolls faded behind them, they returned to the road. In moments they found the seventh and eighth wagons.

Droene was afoot, swinging his long handled axe at a pair of orogs, driving them back, away from the oxen. The two drivers, one with a spear and the other a whip, were holding off another two attackers. Draddock, a bull of a man nearly as large as Droene, had a cut on his forehead. The blood was running down into his left eye, nearly blinding him.

Richard pulled the spear he kept in a saddle sheath and urged his horse forward. He came on the orog unaware and ran it through, sending the blade through the shoulder hole of its armor and into the humanoid's body.

"Get my spear," Richard ordered Draddock as he pushed on toward the rear wagon where another orog was trying to back the oxen and turn the wagon. Unlike the trolls, they actually seemed to be after the iron, rather than simply a meal of horse, ox, and human flesh. Orogs were excellent metalworkers, and stealing metal was easier than mining and smelting it themselves.

The humanoid trying to turn the wagon was larger than the rest, more heavily armored, and to its steel helmet a set of deer antlers had been attached. Its cloak, that hung down its back, sported the foul runes usually worn by a chief.

Richard had just passed the seventh wagon when his horse lost its footing on the wet, rutted ground. The horse fell and Richard just had time to slip his feet out of the stirrups to keep from being trapped. He vaulted off the saddle, rolled on the muddy ground, and slid sideways just in time to miss a swing from the orog chief's heavy battle-axe.

He rolled to the side of the track and scrambled behind a tree as he used it and the relative solidity of the ground around the roots to pull himself to his feet. Sheltering behind a second tree he paused and managed to unsheathe his sword before he had to duck another swing of the orog's axe.

The humanoid's head rose a hand-span above Richard, who was noticeably tall among humans. The orog's legs were shorter and stockier, and the thick body gave it weight and strength few humans, not even Droene could match. Richard's blade against the battle-axe of the orog, wielded by huge hands and arms as thick as trees, was nearly useless.

The humanoid's heavy breastplate and chain mail skirt left few vulnerable opportunities, even if Richard could find an opening around that wildly swinging axe. Richard dodged and scampered back, staying within the thick growth of trees. Without room to draw back its axe and give power to its swing, the humanoid soon grew disgusted and threw the weapon to the ground. It pulled a heavy blade, a two-handed sword that must have weighed half again as much as Richard's, but still gave the human a better chance.

Richard darted in with his sword and leapt back, leading the humanoid toward a tight group of young saplings. At each stab Richard took at the orog, the creature's eyes seemed to glow brighter with rage, until it bellowed incoherently and charged at the human.

Richard waited for the orog's temper to build and then whipped his blade around the humanoid's and jumped back into the thick growth of saplings. The orog, enraged beyond clear thinking, charged after him.

The first, smaller saplings gave way to the antlers on the humanoid's helmet, bending and snapping back behind him. Others, thicker and sturdier, stopped its advance. By the time the orog realized his mistake, the trees behind it kept it from turning quickly or jumping away.

It howled in frustration and reached up with its left hand, trying to free itself. With half its attention on its helmet and its entrapment, its parry was ineffective. Richard jumped in. Holding his sword in both hands, he knocked the orog's blade aside and felled it with a thrust through the throat. Richard stumbled back toward the road, spotted the humanoid's axe, and picked it up. It was a well-made weapon, worthy of the orogs' reputation in working metal.

He found his horse, standing by the team of oxen hitched to the rear wagon, as if the beasts who served and depended upon humans sought the security of each other's company. Two orogs lay dead on the road and Gaelin was on the seventh wagon, waiting for an opening to use his spear against an orog attacker. Gergid, the driver of the eighth wagon, was still holding off the humanoid with his whip, and the two human allies were getting in each other's way.

Droene killed his last opponent before Richard could lend assistance, then hurried forward to help Gergid and Gaelin, but their adversary realized it was alone in the battle and broke off the fight, scuttling back into the wood before Richard made it to the wagon. The defenders had not finished their first sigh of relief when from the south they heard the scream of a giant mountain cat, almost immediately followed by another.

Richard recognized the raucous howl that immediately followed the scream as a troll alarm.

"Another group announces itself," Gaelin said. He'd hardly spoken when they heard snapping twigs and running feet in the woods, followed by another cat's scream and an unidentifiable, dying wail.

"Get the wagons moving," Richard said, tying the reins of his horse to the seventh wagon.

The drivers jumped for their seats. Richard walked beside Gaelin as they started along the track. Droene brought up the rear.

They had only traveled fifty feet when they came upon one of the cats, dragging a dead or dying orog out of the road. The huge animal, more than ten feet in length, dropped its burden to roar a challenge at them before it returned to its task. In less than a minute it was out of sight.

Gaelin rode on, but Richard waited, letting the seventh cart pass, but the cat did not return for the last body. He walked by his limping horse, ready to sprint forward or backward, but the eighth wagon passed on without trouble.

Two hundred feet down the fog-shrouded road, they reached the incline that led up out of the hollow. In fifteen minutes they were out of the mist and walking in the first sunlight they had seen in weeks. In a rare clearing, Ulchoen had gathered the carts and had the drivers in a military line. He glared at the last two drivers and ordered them to stop their carts on the road and form up with the others. He called to Richard, Gaelin and Droene to do the same, but Richard was worried about his horse.

While Droene and Gaelin looked on he examined the animal's legs, running a hand down the left foreleg and checking the hock. Droene also bent to check the left foreleg, the one the horse had been favoring.

"A twist, I'd not say a sprain," he said. "No swelling, but best you not ride him for a couple days."

Ulchoen came bouncing over, walking on the springs of his outrage.

"I ordered you to form up with the others," he snapped. "I've a few things to say to you. Fine guards you turned out to be, endangering my cargo, my animals, allowing my drivers to be injured. I'll have something to say to the guild when we reach Daulton, you may be sure—"

"Shut your mouth!" Richard shouted. He was still keyed up from the fight, worried about his horse and suddenly tempted to tear the head off the bumptious little trader. He settled for some home truths and spoke loud enough for the wagon drivers as well as the trader to hear him.

"You knew the ambush was there. I told you so. You knew there was a way around it. I told you that too. *You* bear the blame of the dangers, and their injuries!"

"That does it, you contracted to guard this train under my orders and if you think I'll pay for insolence . . ."

"We've guarded it, and you'll pay," Gaelin said softly. For all his merry ways, he was the one who squeezed his coins the tightest, always thinking of the dowry they needed for his sisters.

"In fact, you'll pay now," Richard said. He named the agreed-upon wage and pulled his dagger. "Pull that sack of coins out of your saddle bags, and hand us our wages. While you're at it, pay the drivers too, because next you'll be refusing to pay them, probably saying they broke their contracts by getting injured."

Ulchoen refused, insisting he had no sack of coins with him. Richard stalked over to the trader's saddle horse, pulled a heavy leather sack from the saddle bags and began handing out the wages that should have been paid at the end of the trip.

"That's robbery," Ulchoen screamed. "You'll leave

us unprotected, the drivers will refuse to drive the wagons!" He was genuinely frightened.

"We hired on to do a job, and we'll finish it," Richard said. "We'll see the drivers stay until we reach Daulton, but you'll keep your mouth shut. Insult anyone again, and you'll find yourself tied under one of your own carts."

"What do you expect me to do, bow down and treat you like the lord of the land?" Ulchoen snapped. He backed away as he gave his final shot.

"Oh, yes, he'd like that," Gaelin laughed. "Richard always has been an arrogant type."

That night Richard dreamed of being a lord, and of Tal-Qazar, the Spider King.

ANUIRE

TEN

Back in Daulton, the Endiers, ever careful of their money, stayed at a small, nondescript inn where the prices were low, the food greasy, and the beds suspect. They did not intend to remain long.

"We may have a problem hiring on with another trader," Richard said. Draddock had told him Ulchoen would complain to the trader's guild when they reached Daulton. The guild, supported by its members, would turn a deaf ear to any excuse the Endiers might choose to make.

"Does that mean we can quit working as mercenaries?" Droene asked.

Richard had been gazing out the dirty window, but the hopeful note in his cousin's voice caught his attention and he looked around quickly. Gaelin's quickly lowered lids covered a look as wistful as the tone of Droene's voice.

"You want to go home," Richard said in wonder,

amazed that he had not been aware of their feelings. The glow on their faces was too intense for their thoughts to have grown on the instant. Gaelin's purse-pinching had convinced his cousin that the red-haired Endier wanted to make all the money he could in order to dower his sisters. Still, he should have remembered that neither of his cousins were warriors at heart.

Gaelin and Droene exchanged glances and Droene shrugged. Gaelin sighed, reluctant to speak. He raised his gaze to meet Richard's, refusing to duck any reaction to an unwelcome opinion.

"We don't have a home . . . that's the trouble," he said. "But I guess we're just not adventurers."

"We're farmers," Droene added. Another telling look passed between the brothers. Their speaking eyes were repeating thoughts and conversations to which Richard had not been privy.

"You've talked about this, the two of you," he said slowly "Have you worked out exactly what you want?"

"We've enough saved to dower Rieva and Fhiele for marriages with minor tradesmen," he said. "We can't expect to do more without leaving them in servitude for years."

"At least they'll be mistresses of their own homes," Droene added as if they needed to apologize for not doing more.

"And if we can accomplish what we'd like, we'll still be doing a lot of fighting." Gaelin whipped out the ragged scrap of hide he used to keep an accounting of the money he and Droene had saved toward their sisters' dowries. He had painstakingly scraped it until it was as thin as parchment. He laid it on the table, the figures face down, and hurried to the fire for a piece of charcoal. He returned to the table and started to sketch.

"This is the Maesil River," he said as he drew a gently waving line down the left side of the paper. Halfway down the scrap he added a straight line intersecting the river and extending off to the right. Next he drew two shorter lines that set off a square at the intersection of the river and the horizontal line. Richard did not need to have the map explained. Gaelin meant it to be the northern border of settled Diemed. North of it was the Spiderfell, and the square was the Endier—now Lanwin—freestead. Then Gaelin went to work north of the line, drawing a series of irregular half circles to indicate the edge of the Spider King's forest.

"The river men say the Spiderfell doesn't actually extend all the way to the river," he said. "Well, not in every place," he scrubbed at the drawing, blurring a line and carrying the forest closer to the river in two spots. His drawing was only meant as a visual indication of what the Endiers had heard. Neither Gaelin nor the others could accurately locate the edges of the Spiderfell.

Droene leaned forward, his pale eyes bright. "But no one has ever settled on it."

"You'd be battling the goblins nearly every day, and maybe the awnshegh as well," Richard warned, wondering if the two brothers really understood what it would mean to live in constant danger. Their faces fell, and Richard realized what they took his remark to mean.

"*We'd* be battling goblins nearly every day," he amended. They grinned at the correction.

"Then you think it's possible?" Gaelin asked.

Richard knew what they wanted to hear, but he never fed hope that could only lead to disappointment, and in this case, it might mean losing their lives.

"No I don't, but if it's what you think you want, we'll take a look. I won't promise any more than that," he said as he rose from the table. Richard refused to admit, even to himself, how the idea had taken hold of his mind. He had been raised to believe he would be a major landowner, and deep inside he wanted land as much as his cousins, possibly even more. He wondered for a moment why the idea had not occurred to him. He knew the answer. His mind would have immediately blocked any suggestion that would have led his cousins into open opposition with the goblins. He would not lead them into danger, but if they decided to go, he did not fear for himself.

"And we can't even try without the permission of Baron Diem. The Spiderfell is legally part of Diemed. Even if we get his permission, and I decide we haven't a chance, I won't try it," he warned, deciding he would not allow his ambition to lead to suicide. "You can then stay, or leave with me."

"But we can at least take a look," Droene grinned and Gaelin shifted in his seat as if he were anxious to leave at that precise moment.

They waited two more days, giving Richard's horse's leg a chance to heal. Early on the third morning they left Daulton and rode southeast toward the City of Anuire. They traveled steadily until they reached the docks and bought passage on a ferry. The Maesil was more than a mile wide at that point, just before it emptied into the Arnienbae. For two days they traveled southeast until they arrived back in Aerele, the capital of Diemed.

"Now, the question is, how do we reach the baron?" Richard remarked after they had found a cheap inn and had eaten a surprisingly good meal for such a shabby establishment.

Gaelin, who was always the most outgoing of the Endiers, found the answer. He left the inn and returned an hour later with Reilin, the baker's son who had been in training with them in the hoe-men's barracks. Richard was disappointed. They had met a number of lord's sons, and Gaelin had made a number of powerful friends, but obviously Gaelin had failed to contact any of them, or they refused to come.

"When we were in training you told me a story," Gaelin reminded the baker's son when they had treated him to a mug of ale. "Something about using the baron's impatience to advantage?"

Reilin laughed. "It takes a hefty purse to get on the official list to formally present your case to the baron, and you'll still wait three months or more."

"Three months?" Droene showed an uncharacteristic impatience. "We'd be too late to get a crop in this year."

"There's another way, faster and cheaper, but more risky," Reilin said. "Petitioners who can't afford to bribe the chamberlain bunch together and stop the baron's carriage on the street."

"It's a wonder his guard doesn't run them down," Richard said. He was also considering their limited funds. They could probably bribe the chamberlain, but it would cut into what they had accumulated to dower his cousins.

"About twenty years ago the guards ran down two petitioners and started a dangerous riot. The baron's not a brave man, and he pacifies the people when he can. But he gets impatient with these demands in the street and sometimes he makes concessions he otherwise wouldn't."

"He doesn't sound like a wise man," Gaelin grinned.

"He's been accused of a lot of things, but never wisdom," Reilin grinned. Two days from now he's supposed to inspect the new wharf." The baker winked. "We're supposed to provide bread for the workers, part of a special feast they were promised if they finished the work this month. He'll be tired on his way back. If we collected a group demanding to be heard . . ."

The Endiers laid their plans and spent the next day and a half putting them into action. The number of streets wide enough for the baron's carriage was limited, so his route was easy to estimate. On the second afternoon the Endiers stood within a group of petitioners that blocked the baron's return to his palace.

When the carriage came to a halt, more than a score of people crowded up, demanding justice. Two old crones were both claiming ownership of the same hen. The baron eyed the crowd, saw that the mob was solidly behind the woman who insisted the chicken had been stolen from her, and settled the case in her favor. He flicked his hand to his chamberlain, who rode with him, and the man reluctantly recorded the decree on a stiff parchment, using a stick of charcoal. Apparently they were prepared for such interruptions when they travelled.

A tailor demanded a decree that allowed him to collect a debt, and an indentured servant pleaded his case. He had served his allotted time, but his master would not free him. The baron's fat, pouting face was showing impatience but not enough to turn arbitrary without cause.

Richard decided his time had come.

"My lord baron, we wish to settle the land between the river and the Spiderfell," he shouted, partially drowning out the arguments of two farmers disputing a plot of ground. The baron flicked him a glance and turned back to the farmers, but Richard shouted again, this time louder. The third time he interrupted, the baron glared at him.

"Then go and do it!" he shouted back at Richard. The chamberlain had been glaring at Richard, but at the baron's retort, Richard nodded to the man and saw the official shake his head as he recorded their permission to open a new area of Diemed.

The three Endiers melted back into the crowd before the baron could change his mind.

"I foresee a problem," Richard said as they rode back toward Moerel. "We won't be able to plant money crops this year. We'll be lucky to manage a kitchen garden." He decided his remark had been too positive. "That is, if we can find a place we can risk settling."

"A year of spending without earning," Gaelin said. "We'll need everything from plows to cooking pots." His merry eyes met Richard's. "If we find a place."

Since Richard had agreed to the plan and the baron had given his permission, the brothers acted as if their holding was a foregone conclusion. No matter how many times he warned them of the dangers, and of their limited chances of success, they continued to believe they would hack out a farm somewhere along the Maesil River.

Three days later they arrived at the freestead that had been their home. The first person they saw was Halmied Lanwin, who was overseeing the planting of one of the southern fields. He greeted them with a glad shout. They dismounted and walked their tired horses. He led them toward the house, talking all the way.

". . . and the rooms have been ready since last fall. We expected you then. Sort of thought you'd spend the winter with us."

"That's kind of you," Richard said, surprised to know their welcome had extended so far. They could have fared worse after the farm was sold. The Lanwins had bought the property in good faith, and they owed nothing to the Endiers.

"Kind? One does not turn out one's own family," Halmied said with a suddenly shy grin. "Best I tell you before we reach the house. We are family now. Nigh onto eight months ago it was that Rieva made me a happy man."

"You mean. . . . ?"

"It's marriage I mean, registered at Moerel and all done proper. Come fall, the heir to the Lanwin holding will carry Endier blood." His chest puffed out with pride.

Gaelin's green eyes sparkled dangerously. Even

Droene seemed angry enough to kill the ex-adventurer. Richard tried to force out the words of congratulations, but they wouldn't come. Halmied, a man who knew people, understood.

"You'll be thinking maybe that I persuaded her against her will," he said with comfortable amiability. "You'll learn for yourself soon enough."

"You married her without dowry?" Gaelin asked, still suspicious.

"What matters a dowry to a man with means enough?" Halmied asked. "And she brought something to the marriage more needful than money. She manages the house and makes a good home for us all. Now the hirelings serve an Endier again and a chest of gold could not be more valuable to the holder of this land. Remarkable how it makes a difference, even to the field workers."

They reached the farm to find Rieva and Fhiele in the cold shed overseeing the cheese making. Their rosy cheeks and laughing eyes were proof enough they were not wanting for anything. Both were relieved to find their brothers and cousin had returned safely from their travels. Neither greeted their relatives with the desperate gladness of young women who needed to be saved from a bad situation. Jenna, rounding the house and seeing saddled horses she no longer recognized, ran to Halmied and clutched his leg.

That evening, when Halmied went out to see to the feeding of the stock, Rieva confided to her brothers and cousin that she had set her sights on Halmied, though he had not been hard to catch.

"He's a fine man indeed, and I was not for his going off to Moerel again before he was safely tied," she announced with a toss of her head. And she had other news. Arlen, with his purse bulging, had crossed the Maesil and had lived in the City of Anuire for several months, aping the manners of the rich. He had surrounded himself with a group of questionable friends and had been cheated in a game of chance. When he complained, he was challenged, and died in a knife fight. One of Halmied's adventurer friends had brought the news.

"There's money left with a lender," Fhiele told her brothers. It's for you to go after, as next kindred in line," she said to Gaelin. "At least he did name you to the lender as his heir."

Arlen Endier's death was not the only one. Liemen Lanwin had ridden away a week after Richard, Gaelin and Droene had left the farm the year before. The younger Lanwin brother had been on his way to help a friend in Mhoried and had been killed by robbers on the way. Richard's grief at the loss of his property was partially eased by knowing the death of Liemen Lanwin meant the only heirs to the farm would have Endier blood. He mentally kicked himself for his callous thoughts.

When Halmied and Rieva learned of the plan to carve holdings from land considered part of the Spiderfell, they objected. In a last-ditch effort to stop what he considered insanity, Halmied even suggested the Endier men remain at the farm. They could continue their lives as they had lived them in Randen Endier's day, as relatives, with a share of the profits at market time.

A year before, they might have accepted the offer, but the spirit of adventure had moved more strongly on them than they supposed, and their plans were firm.

Five days after their arrival at the farm, the three Endiers rode north along the river. They stayed as close to the riverbank as possible, moving slowly, looking over the land to their right. They spotted two likely looking areas, one only seven miles from the northern boundary of the Lanwin holding, the other twice as far north. While Richard agreed to think about them, his mind was racing ahead to the future.

He was looking for a larger area.

Twenty-five miles up the river the forest swept back from the riverbank, leaving a strip of meadow-land fifteen miles long. Near its center it sloped back a good seven miles from the stream. In the center was a two mile long stretch of woodland that didn't seem to be connected to the Spiderfell. A few low hills dotted the otherwise level area, but the only two that were too steep for plowing were still gentle enough for grazing cattle.

Two other factors influenced Richard's decision: a gully—a stream only during the rainiest months—had caused a collapse of the riverbank, and a little dredging would turn the small inlet into a safe harbor for a boat. In addition, they could see Laedona across the river, Avanil's northernmost river town. Even the name seemed a portent, since Laedon Conoed, who had been a friend as well as employer, had been named for that town; the amiable trader had been born there.

"I like this place," Gaelin said. Droene agreed.

"Then this is it," Richard gave the final word.

The Endiers returned to the Lanwin farm, stayed one night, then rode south to buy the supplies they would need. At Moerel they bought passage on a riverboat and returned to the City of Anuire. Gaelin carried all the proof he needed to claim the remainder of Arlen's unspent funds. As the next older brother, only he had the right. They were pleasantly surprised with the total. Arlen had not been a complete fool, and had been less of a spendthrift than they expected. Far more honorable than his brother, Gaelin immediately put the funds in Richard's name. Richard drew out a substantial amount and gave instructions that would allow both of his cousins to draw from the account whatever they needed.

"You never know," he said in explanation, "Any of us could fall prey to the goblins or river pirates."

Droene, who usually left all original thought to Richard and Gaelin, frowned at the size of the fortune left them.

"There's enough for you to buy another holding, one in a settled land with fields already cleared," he said slowly. "You don't need to risk settling on the Maesil."

The thought had already occurred to Richard, but apparently not to Gaelin, who looked up with startled eyes.

"We've set our minds on the strip by the Maesil," Richard replied.

"Droene's right," Gaelin said. "It would be foolish for you to risk your life."

"Yes, Droene's right," Richard answered, "but there's only enough for one holding, not for three of any size."

"We could go up the river alone," Gaelin offered, though his eyes seemed bleak.

Richard chewed on his lip, hating to say what was needed as much as his cousins would hate to hear it. Still it had to be said, even if it was maudlin to the point of embarrassing them all.

"Through the years, you stuck by me maybe at first because you knew I'd have the farm and be in control. Then, when I lost everything, you still stayed with me even though you didn't want to be mercenaries. Now it's my turn to stick by you. You've started dreaming about holdings of your own, and I think you've a right to them—if we can manage it."

As he expected, they were embarrassed. For nearly half an hour while they walked around the city they were silent, refusing to look each other in the eye. Still, the city and their dreams worked their magic. In less than an hour they had turned their minds back to their proposed settlement and were discussing their needs.

The Seamist Mountains provided Avanil with metal to spare, and the town's craftsmen made some of Anuire's best weapons, as well as tools and household goods. The city also boasted a good boatyard. Knowing they were less limited in their funds, they bought a sturdy riverboat with a wide sail and a centerboard that could be raised at need. They began their purchases with three good axes for felling trees, wedges and mallets for dressing logs, froes for cutting shingles, and adzes to fashion crude furniture. One plow would do them the first year, when they could only plant a kitchen garden. Bowls, cups, trenchers, cooking pots, and an assortment of odds and ends began to pile up in their rooms at the inn.

They were in the public room eating a midday meal and checking off the items on their lists when the outer door opened. It brought in a gust of damp air and a stranger they ignored until Droene glanced up and stood, a wide smile lighting his bland face.

"Caern Tier!" he boomed.

They turned to greet the lord's son, who grinned and hurried over to their table, but it was a slightly different Caern Tier than the one they had known. He was even thinner than he had been and looked considerably older. His face was etched with tension lines. He wore the rough clothing of a river man. Behind him, Hirge Manan, his faithful, grizzled servant, entered like a quiet shadow.

The Endiers learned Caern and Hirge had been working on riverboats as guards and seemed no happier with the job than Gaelin and Droene were with protecting wagon trains.

When Caern heard their plans he laughed.

"Are you hiring someone to sail your boat?" he asked lightly. He grinned, but Richard saw the hope behind Caern's eyes. He remembered the young "gentleman" of their trip south, and his wistful remark to Droene about being a farmer at heart.

Caern and others like him were the reason Richard

had continued the search on the banks of the Maesil. He had been holding out for a larger area of unforested land so they could include more hopeful young men. If numbers provided safety on the road, as the old adage suggested, it would certainly be true for the settlers.

"You're welcome to join us if you want," Richard said.

He laid out their plans. "At first we'll build one structure, as sound as we can manage. With more people we can put up defensive walls around it, and who knows where we can go from there. We'll share work and watches and only build what we can protect."

"And Richard will be our leader," Gaelin spoke up. "We'll need one voice to keep us in order and he's the obvious choice."

"I've no objection to that," Caern said.

"I do," Richard glared at his cousin. "What you may see as glory, I see as responsibility."

"Still, a group has to have a leader," Caern said with a smile. "It can't be me, I can't make up my mind half the time, and your cousins always follow you, so you're the one chosen." His weak face firmed with decision. "But if we go, Hirge gets his own land."

"Master Caern," the man objected, though his face lit with gratitude. The lord's son overrode him.

"He does his share, he gets his share," Caern said, adamant on the subject. "I can pull my own weight."

"Agreed," Richard said readily, glad to see their friend from their first journey was a fair man.

"Will you be limiting the settlement to the five of us?"

"Ten would be better," Richard said after a few minutes thought. "There's land enough for ten large holdings in the beginning, though we'd still start with only one and share the profits."

"I know two others who'd jump at the chance to

join you," Caern said. "Do you remember Hergion Rodden?"

"We remember Hergion," Gaelin said with a grin. "If he's learned to use his bow, he'd be okay with me."

They all laughed at the memory of the young trainee who, at the beginning of his training with a bow and arrow, was more of a danger to his allies than his enemies. He had developed some skill but no one would ever expect him to be an expert.

Richard nodded. "And the other?"

"Gregor Vadmird," Caern said. "He's a strange one, an adventurer from the east. He's a hulking brute and a skilled fighter, but with an easy-going nature. He'd be a valuable addition."

The Endiers traded approving glances and while they finished their meal they added to their lists. They would need more equipment if they had extra hands to do the work, and more supplies. Since Caern had to locate Hergion, and Gregor Vadmird was on a boat up river and not due to return for another three days, they had plenty of time.

Hergion joined them three days later and seemed glad enough to be going back to something he knew. He had been raised on his family's farm in the province of Duene in Diemed, but as the third son, he had to make his own way. He too had hired out as a mercenary, and his weapons were the product of this experience. Along with a bow and sword he carried a strange war axe. The handle was five feet long and the blade was nearly circular, leaving only an opening for a handle shaft. Wickedly sharp points jutted out of the blade. It was as deadly a weapon as Richard had ever seen.

Hergion had been a quiet, shy young man when he was taking his training. Since that time he had developed into an almost silent personality, but, in unguarded moments, his eyes spoke articulately. Twice Richard had seen their pleased contentment. He hoped the young adventurer turning farmer would still be pleased if trouble followed the settlers.

The day before Gregor Vadmird was due to reach the City of Anuire, they loaded their supplies aboard the boat. Along with tools for farming and cutting wood, stew pots, and metal frames for roasting meat over an open fire, they had bought a metal oven to set in the side of a stone fireplace, blankets, two tents, extra leather for mending their boots, extra weapons, two hundred metal arrowheads and fifty spearheads. They could add the shafts themselves as well as doing their own fletching.

Richard was on the boat, shifting a basket of seed tubers when he saw a pair of bright eyes peering at him from behind a roll of blankets.

"Shhh! I'm hiding." The small stature and the piping voice told Richard he was staring at a halfling.

"I don't know what your danger is, but you'll be in worse trouble if you sail with us," Richard warned.

"I'll leave in a few minutes, just don't give me away."

Richard continued his work, knowing what it was to need a secure place from time to time. He was not worried about theft. All the bundles were too large for the halfling, and were of too little value for him to risk being charged with their theft. At dark Richard left the boat after giving the dockmaster an extra coin to watch over it.

The next morning the Endiers, Hirge and Hergion were already aboard the boat when Caern arrived with Gregor Vadmird. Caern had been right, Gregor was a hulking brute. The only thing Caern had not mentioned was his friend's ancestry.

Gregor Vadmird was an *orog*.

ANUIRE

εleven

While Ruinel and the Endiers stared, Hirge and Hergion could barely contain their smiles. Gregor Vadmird stood over six and a half feet tall, and with the massive build of an orog, he was close to three hundred pounds of pure muscle. His huge hands, attached to arms thicker than Richard's legs, hung well below his knees. Above his thick neck, his heavy jowls and narrow forehead were enough to give children nightmares. Caern's eyes sparkled as he introduced the newcomer.

"Richard Endier, meet Gregor Vadmird, who goes by the name of Mother."

"That is the name my friends have given me," the orog agreed. His growl was heavily overlaid with trained modulation, and his educated articulation was a shock. "I am grateful for the opportunity to join your enterprise, and I will endeavor to do my part, both with the farm work, and in the defense of the settlement."

Richard was so stunned that Droene, Hirge and Caern cast off while he was still contemplating the creature who had carried three large packs on board and stored them in the bow. Mother arrived well armed, with a sword and bow that had obviously seen some service, and six new, well-made spears Richard had seen on sale in a local shop. Attached to the orog's wide leather belt were a pair of weapons that were different from anything Richard had ever seen.

At first Richard had trouble recognizing them for what they were. Two chains that appeared to be about three feet long ended in round leather bags stretched out of shape by their contents. Richard realized as he noticed how the worn leather had been stretched to cover a precise set of points that miniature morning stars were attached to the chains. Uncovered, they would be deadly throwing weapons—bolos with teeth.

To show his willingness to do his part, Mother took the tiller and deftly steered the boat away from the dock. When Caern finished casting off and returned to stand by Richard at the rail, the leader of the expedition gazed at him with raised eyebrows.

"An educated, intelligent orog?" Richard questioned Caern.

"*Half*-orog. Only half-orog," Caern insisted.

"Physically, he takes after his father, an orog chieftain. His mental ability—temperament, training, and schooling—come from his mother, a human," Caern continued. "Unless he's forced into a fight, he's the most gentle creature you'll ever know. Of course, if he *is* forced into a fight. . . ."

Richard watched Mother's movements as the halfbreed steered the boat upstream. If Gregor Vadmird possessed any human blood, it certainly didn't show.

"He'll never be able to plow. He'll frighten the

horses," Richard grumbled, his voice pitched low so the half-breed could not hear him.

"Until we separate to set up our own farms, you won't want to waste his time plowing," Caern retorted with a grin.

"So he's a good fighter? To patrol the fields?" Richard was glad for another sure bow. They would inevitably have to face the goblins of the Spiderfell. He sighed when Caern laughed and shook his head.

"Mother is the best *cook* you'll ever find, and his maternal grandfather was a tailor. There's a reason for his name. He's the—"

"If I patrol the fields will I get land too?"

The unexpected voice came from behind bales of blankets. Richard and Caern exchanged startled looks and pulled the bundles to one side. The halfling that had hidden on the boat the night before was still there.

He stood up and looked around with bright eyes. "It's time for me to settle down in a hole in a hillside—and a good garden," he said.

"I thought you were leaving," Richard snapped, thinking they might have to interrupt their journey to return the halfling to the City of Anuire.

"I thought so too, but you took care of that," the little man said as he climbed over the parcels and straightened, stretching until he seemed in danger of pulling himself apart. "You paid the dock watchman to keep an eye on the boat, and he certainly earned his money! I couldn't get off."

He stood just an inch or two over three feet tall, slender for his race, and boasted a curly shock of dark, reddish-brown hair. His clothing was sturdy, but well worn and patched. The small sword at his side, and the bow he retrieved from under the stack of parcels showed signs of long, hard use.

"Olramen Farlain Underdown, at your service,"

the halfling said as he favored them with a courtly bow and a sprightly grin. "Most of the big people call me Stubby. I sought refuge on your boat because I was being chased by two members of the town watch and a shopkeeper . . . a trifling disagreement over some small wares from his—"

"You're a thief," Caern said with a grin.

"In the opinion of the shopkeeper," the halfling answered haughtily. "He hired me and refused to pay my wage. I only took the worth of my work."

Stubby started the tale of his woes, but he was not allowed to finish. When he announced he was a mercenary, the others laughed until he stomped over to the gunwale and stood with arms akimbo, glaring out over the water.

Richard sighed. "We begin our settlement with an orog cook and a halfling mercenary. We should have an interesting adventure."

The boat, named *Ilsiriena*—Current Seeker in the old tongue—was a slow but well-built vessel that fought the currents as she sailed upstream like a warrior meeting an old and respected foe.

They docked at Moerel where Richard, Gaelin and Droene left the boat, picked up their horses, and bought more, including a small pony for the halfling. Richard had agreed to take him along, since halflings were reputed to have excellent eyesight and hearing far surpassing that of a human. Stubby would make a good perimeter guard since the little people had an almost magical ability to blend with the ground cover or forest and remain unseen.

When they reached the site the Endiers had chosen, their first task was to anchor the boat and erect on it a large tent that would be their living quarters until they had a shelter built, or the weather turned warmer. They were just entering the month of Pasiphiel, and according to the old tales, the month of winds would blow away the winter. They had a month—possibly six weeks—in which to begin their first shelter and clear a place for their crops before planting time.

"Lucky there's no need to clear trees from the fields," Hergion Rodden said. "I'll have that undergrowth down a week from now and have it plowed well before planting time."

Since Hergion had claimed the field work as his own, the three Endiers, Caern Tier, and Hirge Manan spent their days felling trees, lopping off the branches and hauling them to the site where they planned to build their first shelter.

Stubby the halfling patrolled the area beyond the small copse of trees, making sure the woodcutters weren't surprised by goblins. Mother stayed near the building site, hunting for stones to build a large fireplace. Once he had a place to prepare meals he kept an eye on his pots while he dug the trenches for the outside walls. When the day's cutting had been completed, his strength was a boon in raising the logs.

The settlers had been excited and happy when they first reached the site of the settlement. After a week of back-breaking work they were surly, but too tired to do more than growl at each other. A week later they were morose and silent, dropping into their beds at night after their evening meal, too tired and cold to complain. Luckily, Pasiphiel had been a dry month.

The east and south walls of their first structure were made of logs placed upright, buried deeply in the ground. These would later be extended to become the walls of the fort. Next they began the north and west walls, laying the logs horizontally and leaving spaces for doors. They divided the twenty by forty foot building in half, the northern section would be the stable.

In the beginning they returned to the boat at night.

On the first day of Sarimiere, when the outer walls and the catwalk for the watch had been built, they officially moved in. They slept on the dirt floor, within the slowly rising walls, covered with a roof of stars.

At night they could see the lights from the town of Laedona across the river. The proof of civilization not far away seemed to hearten the others, though Richard knew they couldn't expect help from the people of Avanil if they found themselves in trouble. Stubby's patrol was only meant to give warning of the approach of enemies, so Richard occasionally rode a wider patrol, looking for signs of goblins.

Riding in a half circle, five miles beyond the camp, Richard was completing the northern perimeter of his patrol and was turning his horse to start south again when he saw a boat well out on the river. It rode low in the water, half swamped. Three figures were desperately trying to bail it out. In moments it was clear that the boat was rapidly sinking. As it turned, Richard could see the roots of a half-submerged tree that had apparently been washed downstream and had collided with the craft.

The boat disappeared below the surface of the river and the three travelers swam for the shore. Richard was still watching them when he saw movement to the north and the sunlight reflected the metallic point of a goblin spear as its owner crept through the bushes.

"Not fair," he murmured to his horse and dismounted, slapping it on the rump and sending it back toward the camp.

The horse made an easy target, and the few riding animals and plow horses Richard and his party had brought with them were too valuable to risk.

He slipped through the scrub brush, listening. Just ahead he heard the growl of a goblin giving orders.

He moved to the side, where he could keep an eye on the swimmers as well as the ambush. While he waited he strung his bow and nocked an arrow to the string. The swimmers had been too far away to recognize before the boat went down, and as they approached shore, all he could see were arms rising out of the water. If the trio in the river were goblins or other humanoids, he would not interfere. He had no desire to anger the awnshegh's guards unnecessarily.

The goblins preferred the deep woods and apparently they had not discovered the settlers. Half a month had passed with no interference from the Spiderfell, and given a little more time, they would have a secure building before they faced an attack.

As the swimmers neared the shore, Richard heard the goblins passing the word from bush to bush. The first of the three in the water had reached the shallows and stood to wade the few feet to the bank.

An elf.

The demihuman looked warily at the waist-high brush and slipped his bow off his shoulder. Luckily he turned his head in time to see the spear thrown in his direction and lunged to the side. A second goblin, just to the left of the first, rose to better see his target and caught the elf's arrow in the chest. Two other ambushers showed themselves. The second elf reached shore in time to send an arrow into the throat of the first, Richard caught the other one with a shaft in the back.

With that one arrow he had announced the presence of humans on the edge of the Spiderfell.

When another goblin appeared, further to his left, Richard dropped it with a shaft through the back of its neck. At that moment he didn't have time to give much thought to the long-range consequences of his actions. He had drawn the attention of a goblin who instinctively dashed toward him, then took one look at the human and scurried back into the brush. The humanoid gave a shout and appeared again, this time with three companions.

The goblins, four feet tall and only half Richard's weight were no match for a human in hand-to-hand combat, but four together could be a serious threat, especially with their spears, which gave them a longer reach than a human with a sword. Richard stepped aside to avoid the first thrusting spear and brought down one goblin with an arrow before they were on him. Two of the others moved to the sides, flanking him, while the third made darting movements with its spear.

The three humanoids confronting Richard were slightly different from the goblin raiding parties that occasionally attacked the Endier farm. These were slightly smaller, but heavier, as if they were better fed. They all wore hardened leather breastplates, held in place by leather thongs and each wore a sloppily made steel helm, still showing the blows of the hammers that shaped them. Leather thongs hung from the top of their headgear and were strung with ornaments. The one directly in front of Richard sported a string of bright bird feathers as its decoration and the breeze kept whipping the feathers in front of its face. The goblin to the left had what appeared to be a string of rabbit tails, and the third goblin's decoration was only a string of wilted leaves.

Knowing he could not allow them to get into position, Richard lunged to the left and grabbed the shaft of Rabbit Tail's spear just behind the point. The goblin gave a startled cry, but desperately held onto the weapon. Richard jerked, twisted and turned, throwing the goblin at the other end of the shaft into its feather-headed companion. They fell in a heap, and at the same time Richard took a quick step forward, expecting an attack from the third goblin, Limp Leaf.

He wasn't disappointed. As Limp Leaf charged with its spear the point caught in the back of Richard's shirt, just barely nicking the skin, but the heavy cloth had trapped the weapon as the point went in and then out of the fabric.

Limp Leaf growled and tried to free the weapon, but while the others scrambled to their feet, Richard reached around with his right hand and jerked at the shaft, swinging its owner forward to collide with the others and knock them down again. Before they were on their feet, Richard had thrust his bow aside and pulled his knife. He waded in, grabbing Limp Leaf by the helmet and pulling the little humanoid up, ready to cut its throat. But the other two were quicker to rise than Richard expected. The two goblins plowed into him, knocking him down. When he fell, his grip on Limp Leaf tumbled the unhappy goblin onto its two companions, and all four of them went down with a resounding thud.

With three goblins on top of him, Richard could hardly breathe. With a heave and a thrust of his legs, he rolled to the side just in time to prevent Feather Top from using its knife. The blade buried itself in the ground and Richard felt as if he had cracked a rib when he rolled over the hilt.

Feather Top had lost its knife, but Limp Leaf and Rabbit Tail still had theirs. They were both trying to bring their hand weapons into position, and the human who kept them pinned to the ground was reaching with his left hand, trying to prevent Rabbit Tail from finding a target while he slashed at Limp Leaf's hand with his own knife. Feather Top, who had somehow managed to end up on the bottom of the pile was growling in gasps, and Limp Leaf screamed as Richard slashed into the goblin's hand.

Suddenly Richard was grabbed by the shoulders and jerked upright. He was on his feet before he could identify the four hands that had partially lifted him. He was ready to strike when he realized the elves had finally come to his assistance.

Richard was still staggering, attempting to catch his balance, when the third elf thrust a sword through Rabbit Tail. The other two goblins scrambled for the bushes and were quickly lost to sight, leaving their spears behind.

"You have a strange way of fighting goblins," said the elf who had killed Rabbit Tail. He spoke Anuirean with the lyrical accent of the elves.

Glad to be alive, Richard couldn't keep back his grin.

"It wasn't my usual style of battle," he replied.

"You assisted us, we assisted you. The debt is paid," said the one who had caught Richard's left arm and shoulder and hefted him to his feet.

"The debt is paid," Richard agreed, knowing no elf would want to be obligated to a human.

"I think I might be of more assistance," Richard continued. "It's a long walk to the border of Ghieste, or south to the settled lands of Diemed, but we're only three miles from our settlement. We could take you across the river to Laedona."

"And how will this assist us?" The elf who had killed Rabbit Tail asked, his voice scornful.

"If you're so sure of yourself, figure it out for yourself," Richard snapped. As the elf had said, they were all free of debt.

"As we came up the river, we saw a boat," said the one on his right. He spoke in more reasonable tones. "Would you sell it to us?"

"No, but we'll take you across the river where you might buy one in Laedona." Richard replied. His temper calmed by the third elf's courtesy.

"Even if we could not make the purchase we could travel up the other bank, away from the Spiderfell," said the first. "Forgive my distrust. It is not often we find a human ready to assist us."

Richard smiled. "We're trying to carve a settlement out of the open lands between the Spiderfell and the river," he told them. "We need all the friends we can make, especially if they travel the river."

Richard led the way south toward the settlement. On the way he learned the three elves were called Mielin, Caersidien, and Garetien, and that they were from the Sielwode. They had been returning home after a journey to the Erebannien, the elven forest on the southern coast of Aerenwe. Surprised they told him that much, Richard did not press for more information.

"You are injured?" Mielin asked, turning his head to better see the blood on the back of Richard's shirt.

"The shirt fared worse than I did, but Mother will take care of it," he replied.

"Your family is with you?" Garetien asked.

"No, we are all men together—oh, you mean Mother?" He laughed. "You'll find *Mother* the biggest surprise of all!"

ANUIRE

twelve

Richard and the elves reached the rise above the settlement just at sunset. In the distance, three figures walked at the heads of three horses that pulled logs toward the half-built structure. He saw the elves grimace at the sight of the logs.

"It is the custom of the Endiers to plant where we cut," he told them, not sure they would believe him, but a little too tired to care.

In the small, dredged inlet, a second boat bobbed on a mooring line. "And it appears," Richard added, "that you will not be our only guests."

Minutes later they approached the long, roofless building that served as living quarters on one end and stable on the other. The log structure was not yet half finished—the north and west walls were still under five feet high. The three woodcutters, Droene, Gaelin and—by the limp—Hergion, who had twisted his ankle three days before, left the logs outside the structure and led the horses into the stable area in the northern end of the enclosure.

Outside the uncompleted building, Mother had built a three-sided windbreak of branches and twigs to protect his cookfire. Jutting up out of the top of the flimsy structure was a fieldstone chimney that still needed to be topped and pointed. Smoke poured from the unfinished chimney, and the aroma of a savory stew wafted on the air.

Richard led the elves into the uncompleted building. The floor was yet to be laid, and inside a few blades of grass still attempted to grow through the covering of wood chips the settlers had brought from the cutting site. The three logs that had been placed around a fire pit in the middle of the enclosed area served as seats. Along the east wall piles of branches and bundles of straw had to suffice as beds. Eleven strangers sat on the log seats listening to Caern Tier, who was explaining their plans for developing the settlement. Caern paused and gazed at the three elves.

"You didn't say anything about elves," said a small, wiry man sitting across from Caern. He glared at the newcomers and then at Richard.

"Anyone needing shelter is welcome at our fire," Richard said quietly. He forgot the complainer as he noticed the young man sitting to his left. Ruinel Goerent was hardly recognizable as the same arrogant young man Richard had thrown into the midden ditch in Moerel a year and a half before. He was thinner, tense and watchful, as if he expected surprise attacks from all sides. Though he and Richard had developed a friendship of sorts in Aerele, his gaze shrank from Richard's. Before Ruinel dropped his eyes, Richard saw his hope.

The eleven strangers bore the unmistakable signs of homeless men, men who made a habit of limiting their belongings to what they could carry in packs. By habit they kept all their possessions and weapons within reach. By each lay a tightly wrapped bundle with well-worn shoulder straps. Within close reach were bows and some spears. Each wore a sword and a knife, and had a quiver of arrows slung across his shoulder. They all wore the usual trail clothes and heavy boots of adventurers.

They were a mixed group. Anuirean clothing seemed to be the norm, but two still wore their hair in the traditional Rjurik cut. One wore a Vos helmet of fur-trimmed metal, and another had the sallow skin and practiced, precise movements that identified him as Khinasi. The other seven appeared to be Anuirean. Obviously Caern had identified Richard as the leader before his arrival. They gazed at him with steady eyes. This was a group of men who could take care of themselves.

Gaelin and Droene entered behind the elves. They nodded to all the visitors and then noticed Richard's wound.

"Mother! Richard's been cutting up his back . . . and his clothes," Gaelin called when he noticed the blood and holes in the back of his cousin's shirt.

Richard could not resist watching the elves as the huge orog half-breed appeared around the flimsy walls of his cook shed and lumbered through the half-finished doorway to examine Richard's shirt.

"There is not much blood. You were not badly injured?" Mother asked as he put one hand on the human's shoulder and examined the shirt. His orog voice was deep, but artificially gentle, and caused all the visitors to stare.

"Just a scratch," Richard answered. The elves were trying to cover their astonishment.

"It is usually best to mend after washing, but that weave will ravel. I will add some stay-stitching first," Mother said as he returned to his fire. "I will also boil a mixture to clean the wound and keep down infection."

The elves' astonishment and suspicion of Mother brought laughter from Caern and the Endiers. When the half-orog left the shelter and went to the river to throw away the tuber peelings, Caern explained their unlikely cook.

Gregor Vadmird's mother had been captured by a band of orogs and had become one of the chief's wives. Two years later she had escaped with her child and returned to her own people. Knowing her half-breed son would face hardships among humans, she had taken care to raise him to be a gentle creature, keeping him with her as much as possible. Her teaching had made him an excellent cook and his maternal grandfather had been a tailor. The half-orog expertly plying a needle that seemed lost in his massive hands was a sight most of the settlers would have doubted if they had been told of it.

"But make no mistake, there's orog blood there," Caern cautioned. "I've seen him fight. I'd never want to make him mad at me."

None of the newcomers seemed convinced. Richard could well understand their doubts. He often watched Mother—whose nickname had come from the crews of the many riverboats he'd worked for the last two years—and Richard still had doubts of his own. Mother seemed to consider the unlikely nickname a compliment and he was always vigilant in taking care of the small comforts of the others.

Conversation stopped when Mother returned, and for a couple of minutes the talk was strained. Then Caern, whose memory for names was faultless, introduced the newcomers, then brought up the reason for the arrival of the eleven human guests.

"Word of our settlement has begun to spread," he said brightly. "We've new members if we have a place for them." His gaze swept to Richard, then onto

Gaelin and Droene, and back to Richard again.

Droene and Gaelin were watching their cousin expectantly, leaving the decision to him. The atmosphere became even more strained as Richard thought about what he wanted to say. There would be both difficulties and advantages to taking in additional settlers. The fields the first settlers had plowed and planted would not yield enough food to take them through the coming winter. Still, there was time to do some additional planting. Eleven extra fighters in the settlement would add considerably to their safety, as would the extra hands to help build the fort. The responsibility of accepting the three youngest worried him. One of the Rjurik appeared to be about seventeen—eighteen at the most. Two of the Anuireans, who appeared to be twins, were smooth-faced boys, probably in their early or midteens.

"Well, I guess that silence tells us your feelings," the thin man snapped.

"Don't try to read my mind," Richard replied. "Only a fool would give an unconsidered answer. If you accept the rules of the settlement and do your share of the work, you're welcome. Understand in the beginning that the idea of the settlement and the original financing is Endier. I've been chosen to lead the settlement and I make the rules. They are . . ."

He outlined the goals of the settlement, which was to share the work and benefits of the small fields under cultivation, and the dwellings as they were built. At first, their aim was to complete one shelter, split between stable, living quarters, and storage. The building would be fourteen feet high. The section of the roof four or more feet from the vertical outer wall would also serve as a defensive catwalk along the outer wall. Later, a second floor would be added to the building. The upper floor could serve as additional sleeping quarters or storage. Before the construction of the second floor they needed to construct a small stockade, and then more dwellings within the sturdy defensive walls. The object of the settlement was to expand, to allow each man his own land, but until they were sure of reasonable safety, they would stay together.

"Everyone takes his turn at the work in the fields, the woodcutting, and the building, except for Mother and Stubby. We all work better when our bellies are filled with good food, so unless one of you can cook better than Mother, he feeds us, does our mending, and looks after our wounds."

"Suppose we taste his cooking first," the thin man, who had given his name as Noelon Asper, suggested. The grin that softened his words had not reached his eyes. The man's attitude brought up Richard's hackles, but he reserved judgment. Many worthy people had abrasive ways. Noelon appeared to be around forty years of age, and he gave the impression of vast experience.

To the right of Noelon, Tannen Oesole, an Anuirean who was a good ten years younger and had a more pleasant expression, glanced anxiously at his companion.

Richard went on with his explanation.

"It's now the sixth of Sarimiere, and in ten days we can begin planting. We'll put all our efforts into preparing enough ground to feed the rest of us."

"And possibly a few more," Gaelin said with a grin. "We may get more people."

Richard nodded. "After we have our first crops in we'll concentrate on the fort and more buildings."

Richard looked around the group, giving each new arrival a long, questioning look. The first to receive his attention were the two Rjurik. They were both tall and muscular with light skins and dark blonde hair. Anders, the younger and still in his teens, looked to

Borg, the older, allowing him to answer for both of them. Borg nodded with the speed of doubt.

"When the *jarl* has been chosen and the rules set, it is up to us to agree to his leadership and his laws—if we choose to stay."

"But you have reservations," Richard prompted. They could use reinforcements, but not those who disagreed with their plans.

"We are Rjurik," Borg said, stating the obvious. "It is not our way to destroy the forest . . ." He paused. "We do not judge. It is obvious the settlement cannot succeed without the shelter and the defenses you plan to build. Yet we are followers of Erik and would find it hard to set an axe to a living tree."

"If you object to cutting timber, there's plenty of work in the fields, plenty of hunting, and a constant need for a watch," Richard replied. "You can also help plant new trees."

He explained that in the years to come they would need more timber and firewood. To cut trees in the Spiderfell guaranteed war with the awnshegh, so in the Endier tradition they would replant where they cut. Borg nodded again, the second time without hesitation.

Pyotr, the Vos, sighed when Richard looked at him. The afternoon light glinted off his shaved head when he removed his helmet. His long, slender mustache brushed his cheeks as he rose, strode over to the corner of the room and grasped the handle of a hoe that had been leaning against the wall. With the hoe in one hand he threw back his arms and raised his head to look up at the sky. His bellowing voice was loud enough to shake the walls.

"Look on me Kriesha, Haelyn, and all the gods who see these lands! A new page of history is written as a Vos warrior tills the soil!" He caught the hoe handle in both hands and brought it down with a mighty blow. Wood chips, used to cover the dirt floor, went flying along with a clump of soil.

"That's very good," Richard said as he held out his hand for the hoe, "But we plan on farming *outside*."

Richard understood the northern warrior's need for ceremony. The Vos considered any occupation but hunting and fighting beneath their dignity. Pyotr's pride had to be assuaged. Richard also hoped he would forego the Vos desire to wipe out insults with blood, even those that were unintentional.

Two who sat together—Mourde Eslipa and Oervel Muranch—muttered to each other and seemed to be in an amiable argument. When Richard's questioning gaze fell on them, they paused. They were an unlikely looking pair; Mourde huge and awkward, Oervel small and slender as an elf. Mourde nodded his agreement. Oervel nodded also, but posed a question.

"How long will it be before it will be safe to start our own farms and take wives?"

"I don't know," Richard said. "I for one would not want to bring a woman here for some time. Do you think she'll wait?"

Oervel's face had fallen, but he turned philosophical. "Perhaps, if she cares as much as she says," he said with a sigh. "At least it's an opportunity for land of my own, and without it I don't have a chance of being accepted by her father."

Drawn back from the others, but silently watching, were the two youngsters. They traded speaking looks as Richard said he would not bring women into the settlement. At their age they probably had yet to be interested in girls and would only consider them a nuisance. Richard at first thought they were identical twins, their features were so similar, but when they removed their helmets one had dark hair, the other was a redhead. Their slenderness was the soft kind. Life and hard work would develop their muscles, but they were still too young to have a great deal of strength.

"I don't think you'll be much good behind a plow or felling a tree, but we have plenty of less strenuous work," he told them.

"You won't find us lacking," replied Parniel Doreant, the one with dark hair. He had spoken with a voice artificially low and full of bravado. Richard sighed. Their voices had not changed. Their youth would be an added responsibility.

The evening meal had been delayed while Mother added more food to the pots. While they waited, the new arrivals chatted with the first settlers, some of them giving their histories, most of which sounded false. Richard was not surprised. Oervel, the young man with the ladylove waiting somewhere on his back trail was like Ruinel and Caern, a younger son of a wealthy family, out to make his own way. Most of the others seemed to feel the need to shroud their history behind half-told stories, but that was usually the way of mercenaries and adventurers. Their pasts did not matter.

Three of the Anuireans were from the eastern regions of the old Anuirean Empire that was being invaded and usurped by the Khinasi. They eyed Hassan Aghahn, the Khinasi, with dislike. Their suspicion did not extend to Mother, who had been raised in Khourane and whose mother had been Khinasi. His half-breed status seemed to exclude him from any political animosity, though they distrusted his orog blood.

An hour and a half later, Gaelin grinned at Noelon Asper.

"You can eat your words about Mother's cooking now that you've twice scraped your bowl clean."

"He doesn't have any room," Tannen, who had eaten as much, replied.

Ruinel Goerent looked up from his dish, which had taken his entire attention until it was empty.

"It's been a long time since I've tasted anything as good."

Even the three elf visitors nodded. Elves ate no flesh, so they had refused the meat, but they had made a good meal of the vegetables.

Mother, who had been gathering the empty dishes in a basket, grinned, not a pretty sight, since he exposed his sharp teeth and his stretched lips added width to his wide jaws. Their meal had been a venison stew with tubers and long roots, but it had been flavored with several different herbs. Most of their meals were stews, venison, rabbit, and sometimes fish from the river, but Mother varied them in taste with different seasonings so expertly that no one became bored with the repetition.

After the meal was finished, Richard warned the newcomers of the dangers they faced.

"Not all the danger comes from the east," he told them. "We are close enough to the river to fall easy prey to river pirates as well as the Spider King's goblins. The awnshegh's patrols usually keep to the forest. They don't appear to do much traveling across open land, so until now they may not have known we were here, but before dawn the awnshegh will learn the elves came ashore and were aided by a human. We could be facing an attack by his entire army. If he forces us into a fight before we've finished the walls of the fort and have some defensive plan, we'll have to abandon the settlement—take to the boats and leave. It will be our only recourse."

"I'm not leaving," Droene, who usually sat quietly listening, spoke up. "I'm holding what we have."

"And I'll stay with the Endier mountain, providing I'm fed," announced a voice from the doorway. Stubby entered and marched over to Mother, arms akimbo. The halfling's chin was out-thrust, his stance a challenge. The scene was reminiscent of a rabbit ready to attack a wolf.

"I hope you kept something back for me, else I'll have to trim your ears to size."

"I'd not dare let anyone eat *your* food," Mother said with mock humility as he dished up the rest of the stew into a bowl. The dish was so large the halfling needed both hands just to carry it back to the fire where the others were gathered.

The halfling had developed a habit of bullying the huge half-orog. Richard had worried about it for the first week. Then he realized Mother thought it a joke to be bullied by a creature he could have killed with one swing of his arm. He left them to their games and kept his mind on more important issues.

The next morning Caern and Hergion left in the boat with the three elves. The two settlers returned before nightfall from their journey across the river. They had left the elves in Laedona, where the demi-humans had been able to buy passage on a boat sailing up the Maesil. Caern brought back four more axes and two more plows.

While they were gone, Richard rode perimeter patrol, watching for goblin patrols and spider-riders. The humanoid that had escaped the fight the day before must have alerted its people. Richard was crossing a low hill a mile beyond where the woodcutters were working when he saw a shadow beneath the trees of the Spiderfell. When it emerged into the sunlight, Richard immediately recognized the grotesque shape.

Tal-Qazar, the Spider, now knew of their presence.

Thirteen

Richard wondered if the awnshegh used magic to hide his approach. The Spider's ability to make huge jumps endangered the woodcutters, as far away as they were. Again, Richard was the only thing that stood between his friends and death. By the time he had seen Tal-Qazar, Richard was too close to escape if the Spider King really wanted him. Richard jumped from his horse and for the second time in two days, slapped it on the rump and sent it trotting back to the stable, out of danger.

"Hail, great Tal-Qazar!" he called out as if greeting a welcome visitor. He stood waiting as the awnshegh paused and turned his head from side to side, as if expecting a trap.

As Tal-Qazar edged closer, he narrowed his eyes. "What is it?

"A human with it's ruses,

"And grass houses—no magic uses.

"I think I should eat it."

Venom dripped from his fangs at the last line.

Richard had anticipated the awnshegh's anger, and was prepared for it. "I don't know what *you* have to complain of," he retorted, as if unjustly accused. "You were alone while you waited for the magic that didn't come. *You* weren't made to look like a fool in front of six friends."

Tal-Qazar paused. The venom stopped flowing, though it still dripped down his chin when he grinned.

"Six companions laughed at you?"

"They'll probably never let me live it down," Richard groused. "I think that winged lady—who did you say she was? The Ice Queen? I think she played a trick on both of us."

"Kriesha . . . they call her the Ice Lady," Tal-Qazar said. The venom was dripping again. The few mortals who had spoken with an awnshegh and lived had told tales of how the immortals of the blood of darkness hated Belinik and Kriesha. The two had absorbed enough of the dead god Azrai's power to become gods themselves, so were envied by the Gorgon, the Raven, the Spider, and all the rest of the awnsheghlien. Nothing created an appetite for power like power.

"She would use trickery, yes she would," Tal-Qazar's eyes blazed red with rage. "She would like nothing better than to make a fool of me."

"And me, don't forget," Richard said, forcing anxiety into his voice. "Do you think I am in further danger from her? Or do you think she only made a fool of me because she knew I lived near the Spiderfell and could be used against you?" A common enemy might divert the awnshegh's anger from him.

"This could be . . . this could be," the awnshegh nodded as he considered the implications. He turned his head, staring toward the direction of the small copse, nearly a mile distant.

"I saw movement," he muttered.

"A crow landing, I think," Richard said. "I saw one in the sky a moment ago." Fearing what the awnshegh might have seen, he used the excuse of stepping onto a boulder for a better look. The move took him in a more northerly direction. As he suspected, Tal-Qazar turned to face him, and that put the Spider King's back toward the copse where the settlers were hiding.

Behind the awnshegh and still a good distance away, he saw Oervel and Gaelin's heads and the glint from their axes. Momentary anger welled up in him. He was risking his life to give them a chance to return to the settlement. The risk to himself was all for nothing if they persisted in approaching to protect him from the Spider King.

"Well, you can be sure of one thing," Richard said, attempting to resume the conversation and keep the awnshegh's attention. "She won't use me again to make sport of you," Richard assured the Spider. "The next time I will be on my guard, but could she subvert any of your goblins?"

"They would not serve her," Tal-Qazar sneered. "They are loyal to me." The Spider King's glare told Richard that he'd lost ground with his last suggestion. He had damaged the sympathy he had built, and needed to regain it, still he could not be too obvious about it. The rumors said the Spider was insane, but no one had ever called him stupid.

"But remember, I didn't know I was being used," Richard said. "She might hide her true identity from them, or even make them think that by serving her, they'd be aiding you."

"It is so," the awnshegh admitted. "I will question my lieutenants." He started away as if to take on the task immediately. The ancient joints of his spider legs creaked. Suddenly he turned back.

"Some human aided three elves," he said, venom dripping again. "Was it you?"

"*Me?*" Richard sounded astonished. "Aid elves—who consider humans their enemy?" Not knowing if the awnshegh could detect a lie, he had skirted a direct answer.

"You did not see them?"

"I did see them," Richard decided to let truth serve him. "I sent them away. I have no time for elves, and I am no fool. To harbor your enemies would not be wise. We will keep them out."

Tal-Qazar suddenly seemed struck by their location. He turned his head to look all around him and then back at Richard.

"Why are you here? Why are you in the Spiderfell? I do not allow humans in my land."

"But I'm not in the Spiderfell," Richard objected. "I knew you, with your great forest, would not care for this little copse of woods nearby, which is not a part of your vast domain. And you know we Endiers plant trees as we cut. We will never invade your forest, befriend the elves, nor be used by Kriesha again. She will not bring her trickery to these borders while we are here."

"It is good, you keep a watch and do not let her pass," Tal-Qazar said, his mind turned again to the evil god. "I must hurry and speak to my lieutenants. They must alert my people to be on guard against Kriesha."

The awnshegh's joints creaked as he scurried across the open land to the eaves of the Spiderfell and was soon out of sight.

Richard's knees felt weak with relief as he hurried west where Gaelin, Droene, and several of the newcomers had stayed out of sight in the underbrush, but were carefully working their way to Richard's aid. As he approached them, Gaelin stood up and grinned at his cousin.

"Meet an old friend?"

"A momentary ally," Richard said. "And be warned, we are to keep an eye out for Kriesha and not let her pass." He raised his eyebrows to underscore the surprising turn of events. "We will guard this border of the Spiderfell for the great Tal-Qazar."

The woodcutters, who followed him back to the half-built structure, tripped over branches and clods of dirt as they traded confused and questioning looks.

* * * * *

The humans were not the only ones who were confused over the meeting between Tal-Qazar and Richard Endier. Berkerig and Gosfak had crept forward, hiding in the undergrowth, and had heard the strange conversation.

Berkerig's first reaction was one of relief. The goblins who patrolled the western borders of the Spiderfell usually stayed within the eaves of the wood. They never really thought of the miles of treeless plain along the river as part of the Spiderfell. Since this open land was never patrolled the goblins had not even known about the humans.

Once Tal-Qazar learned about Richard and his people, they expected to lose their heads. Luckily the Spider King had been too interested in Richard to punish them. But why had he allowed the humans to remain? Berkerig thought Richard had tricked the awnshegh again, but he dared not mention his suspicion, not even to Gosfak.

ANUIRE

fourteen

Richard swung the axe one last time, heard the crack of breaking wood as the tree swayed off balance, and stood back as it started to fall. He pulled a soiled scrap of cloth from the pouch at his waist and wiped away the sweat that dripped from his eyebrows and into his eyes. Talienir, the month of spring flowers, had brought warm air and as the first week passed most of the settlers had laid aside their heavy clothing.

At the edge of the copse, the saddle horses, wearing harnesses for pulling the logs, rolled their eyes and sidled to the lengths of their tethers as the tree swayed. Durchan, the old plow horse who had traveled with the Endiers to the Seamist Mountains and back, was too old to do any heavy work, but he had been brought along and would pull back one of the tree limbs. Age gave the old horse a clearer insight and he watched the falling tree impassively, which was fortunate since he was not tethered. The light work was more of a concession to the old horse's need to be useful than any actual necessity on the part of the settlers.

A hundred feet away, the two young boys, Parniel and Eldried, were cutting and sorting branches from a tree felled the day before. The longest and straightest branches were being saved for making furniture. The rest would be cut into manageable lengths for firewood. The youths had shown surprisingly good judgment in their choices. They made a game of tossing the wood in piles, but though they seemed to spend the day quietly joking and laughing, they accomplished as much as any other worker.

Nearer to Richard, Ruinel Goerent had paused, glanced at the falling tree, decided he was in no danger and returned to hacking the branches from another that lay on the ground. Richard watched the fourth son of the mayor of Moerel, thinking he had never seen so much change in anyone. He was still mildly surprised that the fashionable fop he had hated less than two years before had become one of his closest friends.

Richard still had no idea who or what had knocked the arrogance and pomposity out of Ruinel, but something had changed him. When he was with the others in the settlement he sat back from the fire, tense and nervous, as if he expected to be attacked at any second. When he was working, felling trees, or helping with the planting, he seemed happier and more assured. He could drop a tree exactly where he wanted it, and when he lopped branches and limbs off the hardwoods, he worked with clean, sure strokes.

"That's the last of them today," Richard said, looking up at the lowering sun. "By the time we get them back to the stockade, the sun will be down."

Ruinel nodded as he finished clearing away the branches and strolled over to help Richard with the last of his work. The mayor's son glanced toward the dark eaves of the Spiderfell, a habit of his, but he never spoke of the danger that could be lurking there in the shadows.

"Refusing to admit he's there won't keep Tal-Qazar away," Richard said with a grin. "He'll come in his own time."

"You believe he'll come?" Ruinel asked.

"I don't doubt it for a minute. He's still chewing over what I said the last time we met. Sooner or later he'll decide we don't belong here."

"What's holding him back?"

"Age, I think. Remember, he's lived more than a thousand years. I suspect his sense of time is different from ours. Believing he'll live for another thousand years, he wouldn't see the passing days as we do." Richard paused and leaned on his axe handle as he stared east, toward the Spiderfell.

"I couldn't guess what he's thinking," Richard continued, "His mind is nearly gone. One minute he's as sly and as evil as Azrai himself. The next he's almost childlike. But don't be fooled by that. In his saner moments he's smart for a goblin, even a chief, and as evil as anything on Aebrynis."

When they finished cutting away the branches, they used chains to attach the last two logs to the horses' harnesses. Richard tied a rope to Durchan's rigging to let him drag a good sized limb, then he gave each of the animals a light slap on the rump to send them on their way toward the stockade, two miles away. The horses had no objection to returning to their stable, so the two men let the animals go on ahead while they called to Eldried and Parniel.

The young brothers had been the prime reason for Richard's concern over accepting the settlers. Their slenderness and smooth cheeks testified to their youth. Their accents were Taeghan, and like the rest of the newcomers they kept their histories to themselves. In fact, they kept *themselves* to themselves, withdrawing from the fireside to sit in the shadows in the evenings. They always volunteered to work as a pair on any task that needed two pairs of hands.

As they joined the two men on the return to the stockade, Richard hid his grin. Both walked, leading with their shoulders, an obvious facade of macho bravado they had yet to earn. He admitted to his growing fondness for the boys. They were a merry pair, though they kept their jokes to themselves and were remarkably well behaved.

The leader of the settlers turned his attention toward the fields. The plowed rows were crooked as if both the horse and the man holding the plow had been drunk, but they had not taken time to remove the large rocks from the fields. That was a task that could wait. It was enough that the light green plants were growing; potatoes, maze, carrots, cabbages, onions, and herbs.

Beyond the fields was the fort. He was still amazed at the speed of the construction. The advantages of their eleven new members had far outweighed any problems.

When Caern and Hergion had sailed across the river to Laedona, they had brought back four plows, six more axes, and more importantly, valuable information given them by their elven visitors. Seeking to lessen the unavoidable evil of the human need to cut timber, Caersidien had told Caern of a forest of conifers a short distance up the Tuor River. The evergreens grew faster than the hardwoods of the small copse and the decimation could be more quickly healed if the settlers replanted.

The tall, straight-boled trees grew right up to the banks of the river, and were easy to cut, rope together and float downstream as rafts. The first cut fell within a few feet of the river, and the rafts could be beached in the creek bed only a few yards from the fort. The time they saved dragging the logs from the copse more than two miles away was a boon to the new colonists. More than half the settlers had traveled up the Tuor, and within days the rafts were floating down to the new settlement. In three weeks they had enough timber to complete the walls of the fort and finish the second building.

Hassan, the Khinasi, was responsible for the speed of construction. He had surprised them with the design for a dragger that pulled the logs up from the river. More important to the construction of the defensive outer wall was his mobile hoisting tower that raised the logs and lowered them into position for the stockade. The Anuireans forgave him his former occupation of designing siege engines when he significantly reduced their labor. Woodcutting in the copse of hardwood trees had been reduced to some limbs and smaller logs for furniture and door frames. A general thinning of the small woodland would allow for better growth of the more prized trees.

In the month since the last group of settlers had joined the little group, three walls of the stockade had been put up and daubed with clay on the outside. The roof and walls of the first completed building were also being daubed with adobe to prevent attackers from igniting the wood with fire arrows. The walls of a second building were already waist high. Neither structure had a floor. Luxuries could wait until the settlers had protected themselves from the weather, and other enemies.

Richard entered the reinforced opening in the stockade walls where a sturdy door would soon be hung. He laughed as he saw Gaelin and Caern on the roof of the one completed building. Their clothing and faces were mottled gray and their hands were covered with the adobe they were spreading on the roof. At the side of the building, Mother, at his cook-fire, was giving his stew pots an occasional stir before turning back to a little pit that had been dug in the ground next to his makeshift hearth. When not busy with his cooking he mixed the adobe.

"I hope you remember which one is dinner," Richard shouted to the half-breed.

"Don't worry, we've only found five long roots in the mud," Gaelin called down from the roof.

Noelon Asper, his boots still caked with earth after spending the day in the fields, had entered the stockade behind Richard and the other woodcutters. He was the only one who found no humor in Gaelin's joke. Noelon was a refugee from the eastern reaches of what had once been the Anuirean Empire. Land that was being systematically conquered by the Khinasi.

"That mud you're spreading on the roof won't last through the winter," he announced, his tone contemptuous.

"I don't expect it to," Richard said, though he hoped it might, and was even then wondering how they could preserve it. If it lasted through the summer, the fall, and part of the winter, it would be enough. They could add more in the spring when the sun would bake it into semi-permanence again.

"You'll learn as you get older," Noelon sneered as he walked away.

On the roof, Gaelin and Caern exchanged glances with each other and with Ruinel. They carefully avoided looking at Richard, whose main irritation with the new settlers came from Noelon. He was the thin, wiry man who had objected to the elves, and who gave Hassan, Stubby and Mother a wide birth. He laid claim to forty years and could have been older. Whenever possible, he used his age and greater experience to criticize Richard's leadership.

At first the young man had taken the criticism seriously, though he had not mentioned his concern to anyone but Gaelin. Richard had been raised to believe he would own one of the largest freeholds in Diemed; he had been raised to leadership, he wanted it and was not about to turn it over to anyone else. Still, he was not a tyrant, he was willing to learn from anyone who had greater knowledge and listened carefully to the suggestions and ideas of the others.

To Richard, Noelon seemed intent on undermining the settler's confidence in their leader, but the thin, wiry man from the east was not contributing any useful ideas of his own. Richard put the irritation out of his mind and climbed the ladder to the roof to get a closer look at the work.

He soon realized his was not the only patience being worn thin by Noelon's attitude. Anders Johram, the younger Rjurik, had reached his breaking point.

"Complaints mean nothing if you have no answer for the problem," Anders shouted after the older man.

"Right!" Mourde Eslipa, who had been growing increasingly voluble about his dislike of Noelon, sided with Anders. "He complains, but he never strains himself."

Tannen Oesole, a quiet young man, and the only one who seemed to willingly bear Noelon's company, turned on them with angry eyes and balled fists.

"Get about your business and leave him alone!"

Mourde was usually tolerant of minor irritations, but he looked tired, was probably hungry, and not ready to accept criticism from anyone.

"And what will you do if I don't?"

Tannen launched himself at Mourde and struck at him with his fist. Mourde ducked Tannen's blow and struck him in the face. Tannen's nose gushed blood all over both himself and his adversary. They grappled and rolled on the ground, toward the wall below where Richard stood on the roof.

The fight had started too quickly for Richard to realize more than words would be exchanged. He looked around for a way to stop the battle before one or the other was injured. His solution was near at hand. He picked up a bucket of mud and poured it over the scrambling men. He had been lucky, catching them on a roll, and the mud poured down on both their faces.

They broke apart, gasping and wiping the goo from their eyes.

"Another swing and I'll throw both of you in the river," Richard said quietly, his soft voice laying a smothering blanket over their anger. "You'd better go down and wash off, and when you come back, if you still have the energy to fight, you can set half a dozen logs in the wall after you eat."

They rose and started for the river without a word, still wiping the mud from their faces. When Tannen almost stumbled into a pile of logs in his path, Mourde grabbed the other man's arm and steered him around the obstruction.

"And you can bring us another bucket of mud," Gaelin, smiling, said to Richard.

The fight stopped and the anger diffused, Richard carried up another full bucket before he also went to the river to wash away the sweat of the day's work. Maybe, when the second building was completed and the settlers felt more secure, the irritations and flare-ups would be less frequent. If Noelon continued his criticisms, there would be a confrontation. Richard wanted to avoid trouble if at all possible. They would face enough with the Spider King if he decided to attack, and no one believed the temporary peace would last.

Mourde had been wrong. Noelon did his share of the

work, and Richard admitted to himself that he had another reason for not wanting to oust Noelon from the settlement. Tannen Oesole was a sound man and one of the hardest workers in the group, but he was totally loyal to Noelon. Why, Richard did not know. Once when Noelon, in a particularly surly mood, insulted Tannen, Richard had questioned the younger man.

"I owe him a debt," was the only answer Richard received.

They occasionally had a bout of fisticuffs between tired men, but the first major trouble erupted that night—not long before sunrise—and from an unexpected direction.

Pyotr Bestre, the silent, morose Vos, was standing guard, patrolling the narrow catwalk that had been built five feet below the top of the stockade wall. The night was cloudy but warm. The spring sun had dried the ground after the showers that had fallen a week before. Eldried and Parniel, the two young Taeghans, Stubby, Mother, and the three Endiers were sleeping inside the walls of the roofless, half constructed building to relieve the crowding in the completed structure.

Stubby Underdown's quick ears caught Pyotr's short, sharp cry. The halfling shouted, waking the others, but not before the dark shadows had scaled the six-foot walls of the building.

Richard jumped to his feet, his sword in his hand, and barely managed to duck the swinging axe of a shadowy form, indistinct in the darkness. Still slightly foggy with sleep, he lashed out and caught his attacker on the arm with the tip of his sword. He heard an oath, human in voice, Anuirean in origin, and Mhorien in dialect.

River pirates!

Other shadows moved and Richard saw them scrambling over the log wall, dropping down into its shadow while selecting their targets.

Stubby had continued to shout though he too had disappeared into the shadows. One attacker gave a yelp of pain, hopping away from the wall, holding his leg.

The curse was lost beneath Mother's roar as the half-orog surged to his feet, swinging his spiked bolos. The moon, peeking out from behind a cloud fell on Mother, lighting his eyes which glowed red with the bloodlust of his humanoid ancestors.

Droene and Gaelin, Parniel and Eldried, were all on their feet, stumbling over their bedrolls as they moved into defensive positions. Richard tripped on his own bedding as he rushed forward to take advantage of the opening provided by his almost accidental wounding of his adversary. He stumbled, regained his balance and struck out, missing the Mhorien, but causing the pirate to back up, his feet slipping on the wood chips that had been spread on the ground. He stumbled sideways and into the path of the roaring half-orog's weapons. The chain that held the whirling, spiked bolos together wrapped around the pirate's neck and the lethal weapon split his skull and tore off half his face.

"Thank you, Mother," Richard muttered as he stepped back over the bedding and hurried to lend his assistance to Eldried, who was holding off two invaders as he backed away from their attack. Richard regretted not taking the time to learn if the two youths who had joined the settlement were trained with their weapons, but Eldried kept his head as he fended off the two invaders. It was soon clear that he was not strong enough to hold them for long.

Eldried was being forced into a corner and Richard side-stepped Droene, who was driving back a large brute nearly as big as himself. Eldried cried out in pain and fell backward, but the youth had not done with his opponents. He arched his body and kicked out as he fell. One of his attackers, who had been stepping in to finish him, doubled over in pain. As the wounded pirate straightened, Richard caught him in the back with his blade, and shoved the falling body against its companion. Both fell, and Eldried lashed out at the second with another kick, catching the man on the side of the head, snapping his neck.

Eldried scrambled back into the shadows of the wall and it was clear that the youth had given up the fight. Richard decided the boy had not been too badly wounded. If he was, he would not have delivered his kicks so forcefully. He left the young man in the dubious protection of the shadows and turned back to the battle.

Mother was roaring and swinging his second morning star-bolo in a half circle. Three invaders were backing away from him. Droene was chasing two more out of the unfinished entrance, and Gaelin was going to Parniel's assistance as the second youth struggled to fend off the blade of a tall, thin human.

Stubby raced away from the inner wall, chased by a long-legged, shadowy figure when three more loomed up in front of him. Richard threw himself against the halfling's pursuer, knocking him into the other three, with Stubby caught between them. All six went down in a heap. From the depths of the pile of struggling arms and legs, Richard heard the halfling give out with an oath, a triumphant gurgle, and a human voice cried out in pain.

His sword useless, Richard was reaching for his knife while he twisted to avoid the reaching arms of the man under him. Then another set of hands grabbed him and jerked him off the pile. He found himself forced to his feet by Hassan and Mourde. The area inside the half-finished structure was crowded with the rest of the settlers who had been sleeping in the finished building.

The man immediately beneath Richard rolled to the side and grabbed the halfling as a shield, holding off

Ruinel, Noelon, and Hergion while his companions scrambled to their feet and over the wall. He slung Stubby toward the defenders while he scrambled after them, giving a shrill whistle—probably a signal to retreat. The attackers broke off their individual fights, vaulted the wall, and raced away toward the river. One, the closest to Mother, who had found a discarded axe, didn't get completely over the wall. His head made it, the rest of him fell inside.

"Wait, Mother, it's me!" Gaelin shouted as he backed away from the half-orog who was advancing on him with the axe. His bloodlust up, the half-orog was still looking for someone to fight—and kill.

Richard looked around, making sure no other intruders lurked in the shadows before he vaulted the wall and raced after the survivors. He was followed by most of the settlers. They were just in time to see a boat being shoved out into the current, most of its would-be occupants clinging to the side as they forced it into deep water.

"River pirates," Caern Tier was a bit tardy in identifying them. The Maesil was home to several bands of raiders who attacked and robbed boats or small, isolated holdings near the shores of the wide river. The large number of small streams that fed the two mighty rivers provided plenty of hiding places. Since the banks of the Tuor and the Maesil were political borders, no individual ruler spent money to patrol the rivers. The trader's guild offered a token bounty, but few mercenaries wanted the job of hunting down the pirates. Most who set out to bring the pirates to justice, ended up joining them. Apparently, the money was better.

"They saw our boats and didn't guess how many they'd find," Richard said. "They won't be back."

The settlers returned to the stockade. Borg Ericton, the older Rjurik, had stayed behind and had helped Pyotr down from the wall. Pyotr had been struck with a rock, probably thrown from a sling. Hirge Manan, who had been one of the first to answer the alarm, had received a small slash on the leg, mistakenly delivered by Stubby.

"What do you expect, fighting in the dark," the half-ling demanded of Richard as if Richard had chosen the fight and the time. "All you big folk look alike to me."

The halfling applied a bandage to Hirge's leg, but kept complaining, as if he, not Hirge had received the injury. Stubby was interrupted by yet another complaint.

"I can manage!" Eldried, at the other end of the enclosure, insisted, his voice high with irritation.

"Leave him alone, I can do it for him," Parniel tried to push Mother away. The three seemed to be in a struggle, which ceased with the sound of tearing cloth. Richard frowned and the three seemed frozen in place.

"What's wrong there?" He started toward the trio when Parniel suddenly moved, sheltering Eldried from Richard's view. Almost as quickly, Parniel was joined by Mother, whose small, orog eyes were stretched wide. Together they blocked all sight of Eldried.

"You have other things to do, I will bandage the . . . boy," Mother said, his determination so fierce Richard stopped, less intimidated than astounded. And there was something odd about the way he had said the word *boy*.

As if that oddness had jerked away a curtain, Richard suddenly understood. Everything strange about the pair of youths fell into place. Their desire to spend part of their time apart from the others, their smooth faces, and that highly pitched voice that had not been irritation, but panic.

Eldried and Parniel weren't too young for their beards, they would never have any.

Two of the Endier settlers were women.

ANUIRE

fifteen

Tal-Qazar paced the Adytum. Random thoughts jumped about in his head like startled grasshoppers. Before he could catch one idea and settle down to think about it it was gone, and some new thought had taken its place.

He had awakened from a short nap knowing he needed to think, to make a decision, but about what? Why did his brain become ungovernable, sprouting thoughts like arachnid limbs that just as suddenly disappeared?

"I am Tal-Qazar," he muttered under his breath, beginning the litany that sometimes anchored his thoughts. "I am Tal-Qazar . . . I am Tal-Qazar . . . I was an elf who—*not at elf! Not an elf. . . .*" That tale had passed through the human and elven lands to make sport of him, to cause the rest of the world to laugh at him.

"I am Tal-Qazar . . . I am Tal-Qazar . . . I was the

human Tal-Qazar, a trader in spices until I met the wizard—*not a human!* Not a human. . . ." That was another tale told by his enemies to discredit him, to cause those who hated him to laugh.

He had chewed on the terrible tales until they had become a part of his mind, and he needed to purge them from his thoughts. He was a goblin—a goblin, a goblin, a goblin: He was *not* human.

But he needed to think about humans. He needed to make a decision about the human, Richard Endier, who claimed to have been tricked by Kriesha, who had tricked him, and then offered to guard the western borders of the Spiderfell.

Why would the mighty Tal-Qazar need humans to guard the borders of *his* Spiderfell? He did not need them. The human, Endier, had said the open land by the river was not a part of the forest and so not a part of his domain. A lie!

He did not want the humans to live by the river. He did not need them . . . or did he?

He considered this Endier. Spiders, goblins, humans and dwarves—they all feared him. Orogs, trolls, and gnolls quaked in his presence. The Endier had shown him respect, but had not seemed to fear the Spider King. At first Tal-Qazar had thought that the Endier was a powerful magician. Later he thought him a friend and an honest human.

An honest human? A human friend?

No!

He had been tricked. How had he been tricked? Was the Ice Lady, Kriesha, behind the ruse?

Now he knew the truth. The Endier was not protecting the Spiderfell from Kriesha, he was aiding her in taking part of Tal-Qazar's land for herself!

The Spider charged to the entrance of the Adytum and roared for his lieutenants. They hurried to the foot of the ladder, their small eyes stretched with fear.

"Marshal my spider-riders! We march on the humans at the river!"

He watched while Berkerig and Gosfak hurried down the spider silk ladder, shouting orders, then turned back to pick up the two curving, serrated swords he carried into battle. With one in each clawed hand he was descending his ladder when a goblin spider-rider came into sight. Instead of forming with one of the companies, the little goblin raced around the bustling troops and came to a stop at the foot of the stair. The remnants of woven grass cloaks, camouflage that was often worn by the patrols that guarded the eaves of the forest, clung to the goblin and its arachnid mount.

The mounted rider was a messenger, and by the tattered remnants of the disintegrating camouflage and the obvious fatigue of the spider mount, Tal-Qazar could tell this particular messenger had made a long, hard, fast journey.

"What news do you bring me?" Tal-Qazar demanded.

"Trouble on the northern border, great king," the messenger panted. "A troupe of goblins, not of our land, have been raiding the farms in southern Ghieste and hiding in the forest. The humans of Ghieste have hired mercenaries and they are invading our borders."

"We march north!" Tal-Qazar shouted to his lieutenants and bounded through the forming companies, scattering them as he went.

At the moment, the Endier and his humans were a lesser problem. As the human had said, he was not actually *in* the Spiderfell, and was less an insult and less a challenge.

Tal-Qazar would deal with Richard Endier later.

ANUIRE

sixteen

Richard sat on the bench, stretched his legs under the table, and looked around. He could not prevent the smile of satisfaction that slowly crept across his face, and Ruinel noticed it.

"Pleased with yourself?" the smaller man asked slyly. In the six weeks since the eleven new settlers had joined the group the mayor's son had lost a little of his tense wariness. Richard still did not know what had caused Ruinel's fear of his companions. Four days before, the taut, wary expression had returned when an additional seven men arrived and asked to join the settlement.

Richard had taken the time to consider the advantages and possibilities. The crops were growing well and they would have enough food to last through the winter. A few extra hands to bring in the crops would be welcome. All seven seemed pleasant enough when they arrived and they were mercenaries, all skilled with their weapons. Richard had agreed to accept them.

"Pleased with everything," Richard replied. His view was restricted by four walls of upright logs, buried in the ground and rising twenty feet to sharp points. A framework of timbers inside the stockade added support to the walls and the catwalks. Every six feet a single vertical log had been shortened to give the defenders an arrow slot while preventing exposure.

The stockade had been provided with two entrances, the one facing east had a narrow door, just wide enough for a small cart. To the west and the river, was a set of double doors, giving on a track that led to the water's edge. Both could be braced with a series of stout sliding bars. The roof for the second structure was more than half finished and the first logs had been laid the day before for an addition to the first building—a cook shed that would include a new hearth for Mother.

The day was Mierlen, the seventh day of the week. Mierlen and Taelen, the eighth day, were customarily rest days on Cerilia, and when the stockade had been completed two days before, Richard had declared the settlers would thereafter take rest days from the heavy chores of woodcutting and working the fields. Since the settlement provided little comfort, most of the members were filling their time with the less strenuous tasks of shaping primitive furniture.

Twenty-two of the twenty-six members of the settlement were scattered around the open area. Two, Anders Johram and Borg Ericton stood watch on the walls, keeping an eye on the stock that grazed just outside the stockade. The two young women had taken fresh clothing and had gone to the river to bathe.

Richard considered the two women, smiling to

himself as he remembered the shock of the rest of the men when they discovered they had been duped. Several, who in idle times had boasted of their knowledge and experience with women were noticeably silent for the first few days after the word spread. The day after the battle, Richard had taken the two young women aside and talked to them.

"We would not have lied about it," Entiene said, "but when we arrived you told Oervel you did not want women here. We planned to tell you later, after we had proved ourselves."

"Then the mistake was quite possibly mine," Richard said. "I still don't want women—" How was he to explain? "I want no one here who cannot do his—or her—share of the work . . . and fight to defend the settlement. You've proved you can do both."

They really were twins, he discovered, though not identical. Paeghen, whom they had known as Parniel, was older by an hour, but it was Entiene, whom they had called Eldried, that spoke for the pair.

"Even these are not our true names," Entiene admitted, "But to have our real ones spread about could bring trouble to the settlement. We will all be best served if you will allow us to keep our secrets."

Richard had remained silent after that remark, giving it due consideration. None of the other settlers admitted to hiding their past, but he had always believed Hassan, Borg and Anders, Mourde—and even Mother—had told some tall tales to cover their pasts. Only the women actually admitted to having a secret to hide. In that they were more honest than the men.

"The reason we took to the road and ended up here is less sinister than you might be thinking," Paeghen said, trying to read the thoughtful expression on Richard's face. "Marriage would separate us, and we are not yet ready to sever the bond of twin-ship."

Entiene nodded. "The bond is closer than with sisters—or brothers—separated by time."

"I've never known any twins, so I will accept your explanation," he replied, thinking they were truly close if they were tighter in sympathy than he, Gaelin and Droene. "But what do you expect from the settlement? Do you want your own land?" The girls had done their share of the physical work, but when the time came to divide up the cleared land, each settler would be working alone, and he wondered if the women would be able to handle it.

Entiene's eyes flashed. "Haven't we worked and fought for it just like the others?"

"You continue as you have and you'll get your share," Richard said, thinking perhaps with land as a dowry, they might chose their own husbands.

The men had been shocked and several had muttered at the ruse, but the chief problem had been growing accustomed to the new names. The women continued their work and joined in the occasional joke, but spent most of their time together. For the first few days a few of the male settlers eyed the women and let it be known they were not adverse to being more than just friends, but their advances were ignored. Within a week life settled back onto its normal course.

Richard had stopped worrying about the women and that day he was just enjoying the group's accomplishments. Droene, Hergion, Hirge and Stubby were digging a well. The rest were working with belt knives, froes, adzes and spoke-shapers, working on pieces of furniture or splitting and smoothing boards for flooring.

Richard had been trying out the first table and one of the long benches while he used his knife to scrape at what he hoped would be a leg for another table. A woodworker he was not.

As he looked up from his work, Richard's pleasure

dimmed as he saw four of the new arrivals in deep, and what looked like dissatisfied conversation with Noelon Asper. The eastern Anuirean refugee's viper tongue was at work again. Richard considered going over to join the group; he might discover they had a legitimate complaint, or he might prevent Noelon from spreading discontent. Before he could make up his mind to go, the gathering disbursed. Noelon disappeared around the end of the first building and the others milled around, looking for something to do.

Brosen, a huge ex-mercenary, was nearly as large as Droene. He fingered a ragged black beard as he wandered over and inspected the mobile log lifter that Hassan had designed. Gaelin, who took all the new people under his wing and integrated them into the group, was showing Raenwe, one of the newcomers, the carefully protected pile of hardwood limbs that had been sorted out and cured.

"That pile," Gaelin pointed to one farther down the stockade wall, "Is to be used for tables and benches for the settlement. From this one you can take what you want to make a bed frame, chest, or whatever. What you make is yours to take with you when you build your own place on your own land."

"And everyone helps to make the tables and chairs?" Raenwe asked. He was a Mhorien, a fifth son with no prospects, who seemed anxious to fit in.

"Everyone that can," Gaelin replied with a grin at Richard. "We don't like to see wood in the hands of our leader. He's as clumsy as an orog."

Richard looked up from his work and gave Gaelin a mock scowl before trading grins with Mother. The huge, half-orog sat at the end of the table, placidly mending a shirt for Borg. His huge, claw-nailed fingers looked ridiculous as he deftly worked with the needle, but his only successful work with wood was in feeding the cookfire.

No one had noticed Brosen, who had strolled over to a pile of shortened lengths of wood lying by a log seat. He picked one—a partially carved length of hardwood—and pulled out his knife, preparing to go to work on it when Richard realized what he was doing. But Entiene had just entered the river gate. She had seen him first, and hurried across the stockade.

"Thanks, but we don't need any help with that," she said hurriedly. She had spoken pleasantly as she held out her hand for the bed post she had been carving.

"What do you want, woman?" Brosen glared at her. He had made the gender designation into an insult. "Can't you find something to do without bothering a man at his work?"

"At *my* work," she corrected him. "My sister and I are working on those pieces."

Brosen gave a derisive snort and continued his carving. Entiene stepped over to the small pile and hefted a longer length of hardwood. When she spoke, the menace in her quiet voice was more than a match for her words.

"Put it down or I'll split your skull."

Richard's table leg clattered to the tabletop as he rose, but he paused. Paeghen had started to her sister's aid, but Entiene had shaken her head, signaling she could handle her own problems. Richard paused. He wanted to go to the girl's defense, but if he did he knew he would be weakening the women in the eyes of the other settlers. For the first time since they had begun the settlement, Richard wished someone else was responsible for making the decisions.

Entiene stood poised and ready, taut as a wild animal. Fresh from bathing, with her short, curly hair combed back close to her head, she reminded Richard of a sleek cat with its ears laid back.

Ruinel and Mother rose and waited. All work had stopped as the rest of the settlers watched, most taking their cue from Richard. Droene, Hergion and Stubby had left the well and were walking toward the cookfire. Their path would take them within ten feet of the altercation.

Brosen noticed the silence and looked around. His gaze raked the three who were not quite approaching, then Richard, Ruinel, and the half-orog, and he hesitated. Suddenly he jammed the carved end of the short length of wood into the ground, deep enough to bury it in the underlying dampness. He walked away, leaving Entiene to jump forward and grab it out of the dirt.

To anyone not a member of the settlement, the disagreement over a stick of wood would have seemed out of proportion, but those carefully measured and shortened limbs represented weeks of work, laying them out each morning to take advantage of the sun to dry the wood, taking them in at night to keep the dew from soaking them, and careful measuring and shaping by firelight after a hard day's labor. The roofs would be finished before the cold rains of winter set in, but without floors in the buildings, the settlers would be sleeping on the ground unless they had constructed their own beds. They would be sitting on the ground to eat unless they made their own benches.

When Brosen walked away from the women, the others went back to work, but for Richard, the big, black-bearded man had taken part of the joy out of their first rest day since early spring.

And the trouble wasn't over.

Droene, Hergion and Stubby continued on their path to the table by the cookfire and each took a drink of water from the bucket at the end of the table. The two humans walked back toward the pit that was the beginnings of what they hoped would be a well. Stubby stayed behind long enough to find a gourd cup and fill it with water for Hirge, who was still down in the pit digging. He was taking it back, passing the door just as Noelon stepped out.

The eastern Anuirean had been looking out over the area and had not seen the short little halfling in his path. Stubby had been looking down at the cup he was carrying and they collided. The halfling was knocked off his feet and the human fell over him. Richard had glanced up just in time to see what happened, and knew it was an accident. If the human had been anyone but Noelon, he would have laughed.

But as Richard expected, Noelon, always looking for trouble, made an issue of it.

"Why don't you look where you're going, you sawed-off runt!"

Stubby scrambled to his feet, his face red with anger. He scrubbed at his wet vest with his left hand while he rubbed his rump with the other. Noelon had stepped on him as he struggled to keep from falling.

"Watch it, bitter-mouth, or I'll put a blade through you," the halfling warned. He bent to pick up the gourd cup and didn't see Noelon raise his foot. The human planted it firmly against the halfling's backside and pushed, sending Stubby sprawling.

"That's enough!" Richard shouted, on his feet again. Vaguely it occurred to him that he was never to finish that table leg.

"Are you sure a rest day is a good idea?" Ruinel murmured, but Richard ignored him. He was already on his way across the stockade ground.

Stubby rolled over and came up with a knife in his left hand while he grabbed for his sword with his right. Luckily, since they were staying inside the stockade, he was not wearing the longer weapon. The little halfling mercenary considered himself the match for any of the big folk and was ready to prove it.

Noelon pulled his own blade, long enough to skewer the halfling with plenty of point to spare, but Pyotr put an end to the fight. He reached the two in three long, quick strides and hooked one hand into Stubby's belt while he caught the halfling's collar with the other. Lifting the demihuman three feet off the ground, he backed up and marched off.

Stubby waved his hands and kicked until he looked as if he were treading on air.

"Put me down, you big oaf!" the halfling growled. "You can't protect him forever, you know."

Brosen, Noelon, and one of the newcomers laughed. The rest kept straight faces out of respect for Stubby's courage. Richard's lack of humor came from anger.

"If I need to repeat the rules . . . we don't fight among ourselves!" Richard shouted so everyone could hear him.

"I'm getting tired of *your* rules, *your* stockade, *your* settlement," Noelon snarled. "I don't see any reason why we have to put up with halflings underfoot, Khinasi, and. . . ." he slewed his gaze to take in Mother, but he stopped before mentioning the huge half-orog.

"Noelon. . . ." Tannen warned, his face full of worry.

"And women!" Brosen finished for him. "Women that don't know their place."

"Their place?" Gaelin jumped to his feet, the adze he had been using was still in his hands. "You weren't here when they helped fight off the pirates. Their blades are at least as good as yours."

"And this is Richard Endier's settlement," Caern Tier, who had been fitting his own bed together, spoke up. "He bought the tools that made the settlement possible. He owns the boat, he paid for the first supplies, he—"

"Enough of that, too," Richard said. "But it *was* Endier money. We started this settlement, along with Caern, Hirge, Hergion, Stubby, and Mother. No one asked either of you to come here. You were told the rules in the beginning. You can accept them, or get out."

"And leave the work I've done?" Noelon snarled. "I put in my work and I'm not going. I say we need a new leader!"

"Are you nominating yourself?" Richard taunted him.

"Sure he is," Stubby spoke up. "He has so much experience, or so he tells us. He knows how to run things, run his mouth, and be run off his land."

Several of the listeners laughed aloud. Most, particularly Gaelin and Caern had resented Noelon's constant criticisms and his insinuation that Richard was not old enough to be the settlement's leader.

Richard glanced around at the spectators, reading resignation, dread, and even anticipation in some eyes. Most were willing, some even anxious for the trouble to be brought to a head and settled once and for all. He could not blame them; the work was hard enough without the added irritation of Noelon's complaints and some members hating each other because of their race or realm of origin.

But they did not fully appreciate his problem. He had accepted these people into the settlement. To drive them out without just cause was not the act of a responsible leader. The loss of any member weakened the settlement. Still, members who worked from the inside to weaken the fabric of their solidarity could actually be considered enemies. The settlers needed peace within the fort. At that moment he would have been glad of Noelon's added years and experience, if it would give him a surer grasp of the situation.

"I say Noelon would make a better leader," Brosen shouted. Four of the six who had arrived with him started shouting Noelon's name and walked over to stand behind the thin east-Anuirean refugee.

On the other side of the stockade yard, Droene and Hergion knelt and reached into the pit, lending a hand to Hirge, who climbed out. They crossed the cleared area together, bringing their emotional as well as their physical support to Richard. He appreciated their silent vote of confidence, but the battle of wills was his to fight.

"You've already been told this is an Endier settlement," he said, his voice ringing across the enclosure. "Accept our laws or leave."

"And if we don't chose to do either?" Noelon retorted with a sly grin. "I challenge you to defend your leadership."

"You're going to fight Richard?" Gaelin demanded, not bothering to hide his laugh. The easterner was half a head shorter than Richard, and in the one battle they had fought since their arrival, he had not appeared to be overly adept with his weapons.

"I'll fight on Noelon's behalf," Brosen said, stepping forward. The big black-bearded man topped Richard by half a head and outweighed him by more than fifty pounds.

"Then you'll fight me," Droene spoke up.

"No." Richard waved his large cousin back. "If I'm the leader they want to depose, I'm the one he fights." With a sigh Richard stepped out, away from his supporters. He regretted the need, but the decision had been made and he was ready.

Neither Brosen nor Richard was wearing a sword, but they both had heavy knives in their sheaths. Richard pulled his blade and wondered if he had made a mistake. Brosen's weapon was a good three inches longer than the knife Richard carried. Added to the big man's longer reach, Richard would be at a distinct disadvantage.

The others stood back, watching silently as the two fighters circled, each watching the footwork of the other. Brosen moved in a crouch, as if he were used to fighting men smaller than himself. Richard kept a portion of his mind on his own body, forcing his muscles to relax, saving his tension until it was needed.

The larger man wore an arrogant grin as he moved, stepping sideways, always turned toward Richard. By the muttering coming from the spectators, Brosen's attempt at intimidation was working—on them.

"You should have insisted," Gaelin hissed at Droene.

The circle of settlers watched in silence, but Stubby, with the impatience of his race, hopped up and down on one foot and shouted at Brosen.

"What's the matter, rag-beard? Realize you've a foe you can't scare?"

"Shut up, you little wart!" Brosen snarled and charged Richard. The halfling's insinuation that he was over-matched had infuriated the larger man. Richard feinted to the left, drawing Brosen off his intended course and jumped to the right. As Brosen passed, Richard leapt into the air, gave a flying kick, and struck the larger man in the backside with the flat of his foot.

Brosen careened through the circle of watchers who scrambled out of the way, and fell across the first of the tables.

Stubby gave a crow of delight, and Mother snorted an orogish laugh. Since the half-orog was only a few feet from the table, when Brosen found his feet again he turned toward Mother with a snarl.

"Your fight is with me!" Richard shouted. He had remained in the center of the circle, poised and ready but conserving his strength while Brosen's foolish act took a toll on the larger man's confidence.

When Brosen returned to the circle, the wariness in his eyes warned Richard that any further tricks would be useless. They circled and closed, each leading with his knife in his right hand. The bearded man was wary, but anxious for the fight. He swiped at Richard with his knife and Richard bent nearly double as he pulled in his midriff to avoid the slashing blow. He straightened and returned the jab, drawing first blood.

The cut on Brosen's upper arm was shallow and less dangerous to him than to Richard, whose knife caught in the shoulder of the other man's ragged vest. Unable to jump away, he found himself grabbed and thrown to the ground, Brosen on top of him.

Richard gasped as Brosen's falling weight forced the air from his lungs. His left hand had fallen on a short length of tree limb, a leftover scrap from someone's furniture making. He clutched it without realizing what he was doing. Dizzy from lack of air, he knew he had to act before he passed out. He struck at Brosen with the stick of wood, aiming for his back, but connecting with the sensitive bone in his elbow.

Arching his back and twisting, Richard rolled, tumbling the larger man to his right, pinning his own right arm and his knife under him. As Brosen rolled off him, Richard struck again with the short, heavy length of wood, catching the big man in the throat, just under his beard. Brosen gurgled and reached for his throat with his left hand. His right hung useless, his knife lost when Richard had struck the nerve in his elbow.

Richard scrabbled to his knees, brought his blade down Brosen's naked chest, leaving a thin, bloody line, and stopped the knife just below the rib cage.

"Yield or I'll kill you now," he snarled.

Brosen could barely breathe, and the blow had knocked the fight out of him. He sat unmoving. Slowly, he nodded.

Richard stood and sheathed his blade. He stepped back and turned, looking around the circle.

"Let this be an end to it," he called out. "I say this

once more and once more only. This is an Endier settlement. I set the rules, and you can abide by them or leave. Noelon, you and Brosen pack your belongings and get out."

"Who get's out?" Noelon demanded. "Maybe there's more that wants you gone than me."

"None that I'd be knowing about," Hirge Manan spoke up.

"Hirge is right," Caern shouted.

"His is not the only voice—I stand with Noelon!" one of the newcomers shouted. Richard could not remember his name.

Mother gave a growl that showed there was still an orog nature beneath the normally gentle exterior. He pulled a burning brand from the fire and lumbered over to stand by Richard, the burning stick raised high as if it were a banner.

Taking their cue from the half-orog, all the settlers moved at once, physically taking their stands with Richard or Noelon. When the movement stopped, four of the newcomers—not including Brosen, who was still sitting on the ground, panting—stood with Noelon. Tannen was one of them. He glanced apologetically at Richard and then stared at his feet. Seventeen had ranged themselves with Richard. On the walls, the two Rjurik—Borg and Anders—still stood guard duty, but thought it was fitting they announce their intention.

"We stay with Richard Endier," Borg called down.

"It is fitting to remain with the chosen *tsarevos,* Pyotr called back to them. He was standing by Mother, holding his huge blade in his hand.

Ten minutes later the six dissenters packed their belongings and left the stockade. Anders walked around the catwalk to watch the river side of the small fortress. At a nod from Richard, Stubby climbed to the catwalk to take the place of the younger Rjurik.

Anders watched for a few minutes, climbed down one of the ladders and trotted over to Richard.

"They're going upstream," he said with a frown. "They're staying close to the riverbank."

"They're going to set up their own settlement," Caern said, his eyes hot with outrage.

Pyotr rounded on Richard. "Why did you not kill this Brosen?" he demanded.

"Why should I kill him?" Richard asked, staring across the enclosure while he considered the fight, its outcome, and what it might mean to all of them. "Brosen will have problems enough."

"And bring us trouble as well," Entiene added, clearly thinking like the Vos. "If they choose a place near here and start cutting wood in the Spiderfell, they'll bring the awnshegh down on us as well as themselves."

seventeen

"They've finished their shelters and started their own stockade," Stubby said, his face suddenly serious. "They're cutting in the Spiderfell. Another eight have joined them, so they're doing a lot of cutting."

"Which means they will not last long," said Mother, with the pragmatism of his orog blood. "Because of them, we will be attacked as well."

Sitting at another table, Richard listened but said nothing. Stubby and Mother had adequately summed up the situation.

The halfling, with his native ability to slip through the brush and woods unseen, had made the ten mile journey up the river to spy on Noelon and Brosen's settlement several times. No one in the first settlement wished the others harm, but the dissidents' decision to cut their timber from the Spiderfell was sure to attract the attention of the Spider King and his armies.

Strangely, Richard resented this additional danger less than the others. He had accepted the responsibility of leadership, established laws, and dutifully shared the work, but he had never really believed in its ultimate success. His cousins, Gaelin and Droene, had followed his path for more than a year, and now he was following theirs.

Likewise, he had no real faith in Tal-Qazar's hasty decision to allow the humans to guard the eastern shore of the river. The mad awnshegh would soon realize that the humans could never protect the Spiderfell against an invasion by the evil god, Kriesha. Or the Spider might even realize that that threat never really existed in the first place. Richard was surprised at the months of peace they had enjoyed. Peace and opportunity to build their defenses, he amended. Six ballistae had been added to the walls along with three small catapults with two more under construction.

Droene, Stubby, Hergion and Hirge failed with their first well, but the settlers had completed three more buildings. A smokehouse and two low earth-covered storage sheds to store their crops and fodder for the horses had finally been constructed. The fields were still yielding some late-ripening vegetables, but most of the harvesting had been done and the food safely stored, along with enough wood for the winter. A blue tendril of aromatic smoke constantly rose from the chimney of the smokehouse, which was crammed with wild boar, venison, and fish.

Mother now had a proper kitchen where he muttered, growled, and rumbled over his oven, spit, and cooking pots. Entiene and Paeghen complained about gaining weight. Richard firmly believed that the half-orog's food was largely responsible for the amount of work the settlers had accomplished.

Half the settlers made a second journey up the river

to the pine forest and sent down more huge rafts of logs. The timber was stacked by the river bank to be brought into the stockade when the harvesting was completed. Before the winter was over they should be able to expand the outer walls and add at least two new buildings.

Hassan Aghahn, with his curling beard and finicky manners, had proved to be one of the most valuable assets in the company. When the walls of the stockade were up and the defensive weapons built, he had gone in search of clay. Mother's cookfires and ovens, the small fires in the living quarters, and even the smoldering embers in the smokehouse were lined with baking hand-shaped clay tiles. These would replace the dried mud on the roofs of the buildings and protect them from rain . . . and flaming arrows.

The settlement actually had a chance of succeeding, though not much more than a chance. They still numbered only twenty against Tal-Qazar's army of thousands.

The door of the main building opened and slammed back against the wall, sending a gust of cold air across the open area. Pyotr entered, followed by Hassan.

"You are a fool!" the Vos announced, throwing the remark back over his shoulder.

After the fight with Brosen, no one else had challenged Richard's leadership, but arguments between the settlers were common. Richard had had to physically stop several fights.

"No more a fool than the man who refuses to arm his allies," Hassan snapped back. He was a delicate little man with large, dark eyes and a habit of curling his long hair and beard around his fingers until it hung in love locks, not the usual look of a rugged adventurer. The Khinasi strolled across the room and took a seat at the table where Richard sat, drinking a cup of herb tea. He announced the subject of the argument without preamble.

"I've finished the last of the catapults and I've hardwood left over. I want to use it to make more heavy artillery and send the extra pieces up the river." He did not need to say he wanted to send them to the second stockade.

"The oil jars?" Richard asked. Hassan had developed another weapon that would add immeasurably to their defense. Twenty thin-walled jars, holding the rendered fat from their food, were sitting in the smokehouse, ready to be hurled onto their enemies in case of attack.

"They're easy to make," Hassan replied. "Anyone can do it." He glared over his shoulder at Pyotr. "And it isn't as if Noelon and Brosen could haul the ballistae and catapults down here to attack us."

"A well-armed ally would split the target for Tal-Qazar," Richard replied. "Another three days of harvesting and we'll be finished with the crops."

Caern Tier sitting across the table, looked around the room. "I don't know where we'll put the rest. The store houses are full and there's no room on the upper floors because of the stable fodder. We'll have to stuff it under the beds."

"Or send some of it up to the other settlement," Richard replied. "Noelon and Tannen did their share in the fields. We owe them some of it."

"They will see you as weak," Pyotr said, glaring at Richard, but it was Borg, the Rjurik, that answered the Vos.

"Is it strong and honorable to keep from a man what he has earned? I care nothing for Noelon and Tannen, but they were good workers. Even the three newcomers that went with them did their share during the few days they were here."

Everyone in the room tensed as Pyotr's face reddened. The Vos were quick to take insult and wash it away with blood. Pyotr glared at the Rjurik for a moment, then sighed and raised his eyes to the ceiling and shouted.

"Kriesha, bear witness! I am accepting the constraints of another's sense of honor!" He stomped across the room and slammed the door as he left.

Gaelin strolled over to stand behind Caern. Richard's cousin, his skin brightened by the chill of early autumn, was vivid with his red hair and bright green eyes. He grinned down at the five people sitting at the table.

"Perhaps it's time to start laying out farms," he grinned.

Richard understood his meaning. By the end of winter, the confinement of so many conflicting personalities could turn the stockade into a battleground. He was tempted, but rejected the idea.

"We have to settle with Tal-Qazar first," he said.

"And how do you do that?" Stubby demanded.

"When I know, I'll tell you."

Richard returned to his tea, but he could not relax. The awnshegh was on his mind. He felt as if their senses were somehow connected, and he knew the monster of the Spiderfell was turning his attention toward the two stockades by the river. He told himself he was being foolish, but the feeling would not go away.

The last three days of harvesting passed, all the food was in, but the settlers who had looked forward to a sense of relaxation in the work were disappointed. Richard sent several men to help Hassan complete the ballistae and catapults for the other settlement, and most of the rest were set to making oil pots. Droene, Pyotr and Hergion returned to the river to retie twenty logs into two rafts. Richard wanted to be sure no one was left behind if the awnshegh attacked and they had to escape. He worked the settlers relentlessly while his skin prickled with a sense of danger and the hair on the back of his neck seemed to stand at permanent attention.

Gaelin, Caern and Hergion, the most amiable of the settlers and the major peacemakers, took the food and weapons up the river in the boat. Richard hardly ate and paced the floor nearly the entire time they were gone, but they returned in good spirits.

"Noelon would have refused everything and would have shot us for trespassers if he could, but he apparently didn't hold his authority for long," Caern said, laughing. "His loyal followers turned on him fast enough when they discovered he had no idea how to hold a group together."

"Tannen is leader, and he was grateful enough," Gaelin added and gave Hassan a wink. "You were right, they're allies. I'm not sure most of them don't regret leaving here, but they're well-entrenched now."

"And Noelon is gritting his teeth because Tannen is using our rules in the new settlement," Hergion grinned. He seldom spoke, but his news was too ironic to allow his usual silence. "They'll be cutting the rest of their timber from the pine forest too."

"It's mainly because the conifers are easier to cut," Caern said.

"It's easier to drag them the few feet to the Tuor and float them down the river than to drag them more than two miles from the Spiderfell," Hergion added. "Still, it may help keep Tal-Qazar at bay."

"It won't," Richard said softly, speaking from an inner conviction that proved prophetic four days later.

* * * * *

The sun was only halfway up the sky, but the fickle autumn weather had turned as hot as midsummer.

The humidity was stifling. The settlers were tired and every breath they took drew in air so damp they felt as if they were breathing water. Richard called a halt to the work and declared a rest day, though it was only Dielen, the third day of the week. Off to the west, just on the horizon, a thin dark line of clouds indicated an approaching storm. Everyone hoped it would bring relief from the oppressive autumn heat.

Half the settlers were on the walls of the stockade, hoping for a breeze. Richard and Gaelin, who was good with figures, were working with a scrap of deer hide, trying to work out how much extra firewood they would need if they built an extra oven for baking roof tiles. Ruinel and Droene had the watch and were keeping an eye on Pyotr and Oervel, who were out in the field with the horses. The animals were taking advantage of the last of the green grass.

Droene gave a startled cry and pointed, but none of the others were in time to see what had alerted him. Then they saw the smoke rising from the dry range grass half a mile north east of the stockade.

"It's Stubby!" Ruinel—who was at the northeast corner and could see better—called out.

"Why would he be burning—" Entiene started a question, but Richard cut her off.

"To alert us to danger and slow up the goblins chasing him," Richard said and raised his voice in a shout. "To the walls! Anders! Mourde! Help Pyotr and Hirge get the horses in!"

The newest evening occupation of the settlers had been stool-making and they had brought their new seats up on the catwalk. Richard kicked his to get it out of the way. It went spinning off across the roof of the south building.

Hirge and the Vos heard the commotion and Hirge grabbed a stick and struck the nearest animals on the rump, sending them back toward the walls. Pyotr jumped on the back of Richard's horse and galloped across the fields. He barely slowed to grab the halfling before he turned and raced back again. By the time he had reached Stubby, the halfling had sent up four more fire arrows and the flames were spreading.

"He might cook us too," Ruinel shouted, but Richard wasn't worried. They had prepared the stockade against fire and he doubted the moist air would let the blazes get out of hand.

Entiene had taken up a station by one of the catapults. "Stones or oil jugs?" she asked as she swiveled the war engine to target on a narrow passage between two of the spreading fires.

"Stones for now, we don't want to bring out the oil until the last minute," Richard said. The hotter the oil, the faster it would burn.

Out in the fields, Hirge had grabbed the halter of the last free horse and stood watching Pyotr gallop toward the little fort. When Pyotr passed him, Hirge jumped on the back of old Durchan and galloped after the Vos. The free horses had sensed danger and smelled fire, and the first three were jostling each other to be the first into the small eastern door.

Richard divided his attention between the horses and what looked like a shadow moving over the low hill in the distance.

"Spider-riders!" shouted Caern, who had the sharpest vision.

"Hundreds," Richard said and looked around, checking the defenses on the northern and southern walls. He had developed an escape plan, and ran over it in his mind. It depended on not allowing the stockade to be surrounded. The rafts and the boat each could be freed of their moorings with a single stroke of an axe. He checked to be sure the three axes were waiting by the double doors that led to the river path.

"Pass the word, don't shout," he said to Entiene,

the closest defender to his right. He had no idea how sharp Tal-Qazar's hearing might be. "Your prime target is the awnshegh. If we can wound or kill him, the goblins might lose heart."

"Can an awnshegh be killed?" she asked, her face pale.

"Of course, but don't get the idea it'll be easy."

"It is said that burning the fields makes next year's food grow well." Mother, who had climbed the steps and stood near Richard, held his spears loosely as he watched the approaching army. He had left his spiked bolos at the foot of the ladder. They would only be used if the invaders broke into the stockade. Richard had decided the settlers would be well away before he would allow his few people to face that horde. The half-orog seemed undisturbed by the approaching numbers. He took Richard's speculative gaze to be one of censure and shrugged.

"I banked the fires and took the meat off the spit. Midday meal will be late, but it will not burn."

If there was anyone left to eat it. Richard firmly put the thought out of his mind and watched the oncoming horde. A breeze, coming from the north, was spreading the fires. He decided Stubby's little blazes were the work of genius. The halfling had started them within the range of the catapults and the ballistae, creating barriers so attackers would be forced into the narrow necks of safe ground, and the artillery would have easy targets.

When the first spider-riders started through the gap, Richard gave Entiene the order, and she let go with a load of small boulders. Three goblins fell from their mounts, and one of the five foot long spiders was struck on the head. It reared up on its back legs, tried to turn, and stepped into the blazing grass. The hair on the legs of the spider caught fire immediately, and it attempted to flee the pain. It charged back in the direction it had come, spreading fire through the ranks and causing the spider mounts to panic.

Entiene crowed with triumph, but Richard saved his energy to haul at the crank to reset the catapult. The eastern wall of the fort was also the eastern walls of the two large buildings. The wide roofs, with only enough slope to allow the water to run off, doubled as space to store the ballista shafts, rocks and oil jars for the catapults.

Since they were not permanent storage areas, Mother scrambled down the ladder and with Borg and Droene's help, tossed up the large arrows and stones for the heavy artillery. Droene brought out several oil jugs from the smokehouse. When the big half-orog was back on the catwalk he frowned up at the sky.

"It darkens," he said. "First I thought it was only the smoke from the fires."

Richard spared the time to glance around and understood what bothered the half-orog. The darkness came from the west, the bank of storm clouds they had seen that morning was beginning to move, not an unusual occurrence with the abrupt weather changes of autumn. A sudden rain would put out the fires in the fields and allow Tal-Qazar's riders to advance en masse.

Ruinel and Caern gave a victory shout. They had fired one of Hassan's four-shaft ballistae and three of the missiles had found targets as another troop of spider-riders bunched to charge through a gap between the fires. Two spider mounts were down and a goblin rider had been lifted from its seat when one of the large shafts went completely through its chest.

"If we can keep the fires burning, we'll hold them off," Stubby shouted. He had climbed up to sit on one of the shortened logs that provided an arrow slit.

He was right. If they could keep the fires lit, his

strategy would work—this time. It might even work a few more times during the winter, but what about the summer, when they would be burning the food they planted?

One thing at a time, Richard warned himself. He had enough to think about. Through the smoke and fire he saw Tal-Qazar. The awnshegh gave a sudden, seemingly impossible leap and cleared the flames, landing twenty feet beyond them.

The defenders on the walls gasped at the sight of the abomination—half goblin, half spider. Stubby scrambled down from his perch and crouched on the catwalk. The others just stared, so awed by the fiend that they had forgotten their weapons.

ANUIRE

eighteen

Richard's heart sank when he saw the terror in the eyes of his people. He shoved Entiene out of the way, almost knocking her off the catwalk as he hauled the catapult around, aiming it at Tal-Qazar. The load of rocks sailed over the head of the awnshegh, but when the Spider King saw them coming, he flinched and scuttled to the side. This was enough to show the defenders on the walls of the fort that the Spider considered himself vulnerable.

The settlers came to life, shedding their panic almost as quickly as they had acquired it. Even before the first load of rocks hit the ground behind the awnshegh, Ruinel and Caern were cranking their ballista around to aim at the abomination. At the southeastern corner, Gaelin and Droene were on target with four shafts from their ballista.

Out on the field, Tal-Qazar leapt sideways to escape the incoming missiles, a maneuver that placed him directly into the path of the rocks slung by the catapult. Richard raised his head to see Pyotr and Paeghen nodding to each other as the monster roared and raised his left foreleg.

Tal-Qazar had been struck, but not injured. Still, he drew back as if suddenly aware that he was not invulnerable to a large weapon. He looked around at the few gaps in the flames that allowed his army access to the wood and adobe palisade. A sudden wind had sprung up and the small spaces between the fires were beginning to narrow. The fire was blowing to the east, driving the goblin spider-riders back toward the Spiderfell.

Tal-Qazar glared toward the small fort, then turned his head to look at the fire, then back toward the humans behind the wall. He opened his mouth to roar, and the sound seemed to shake the walls of the stockade. The noise continued after the awnshegh closed his mouth and Richard realized they were hearing thunder as well as the awnshegh's challenge.

So much for their defensive fire, he thought, as a bolt of lightning crackled down from the dark clouds, immediately followed by another roll of thunder. Something struck Richard on the shoulder.

Suddenly Pyotr stood up in full sight of the awnshegh and the goblins as he stretched his arms to the sky, his hands empty and open. "Kriesha! The Ice Lady comes to our aid!" he roared. By accident or a sense of dramatics not evident in the Vos warrior, a loud roll of thunder preceded his shout and one immediately followed it as if nature itself had bracketed his words with emphasis. It seemed as if Kriesha herself had given his voice volume.

Before Richard could decide what hit him he was struck again and again. He held out his hand and stared as a ball of hail, as big around as his thumb, stuck his palm and left it stinging with the force of the strike and the sudden shock of cold.

The melting hail doused the fires in seconds, but the spider-riders were having trouble with their mounts. The icy missiles from the sky were terrifying the spiders. They were charging into each other. Closer to the fort, the awnshegh was roaring at the sky, leaping about as the hail struck him.

"Behold, Kriesha!" Pyotr shouted again. "Strike down your enemy!"

Out on the field, Tal-Qazar roared and raised his tail. From his spinneret came a long, thick strand that sailed directly toward the Vos.

"Grab him!" Richard shouted, but his order came too late.

The thick, sticky cable arced over the wall. Entiene had seen it coming and had thrown herself against the Vos, knocking him off the catwalk and onto the roof of the first building. They had only fallen a foot, and the long strand came down across the Vos's legs, wrapping around them as if it had a life—and mind—of its own.

Richard jumped down and hacked through the thick strand with his sword. He used the tip of his blade to flip the severed end toward a thick, vertical beam that supported the catwalk. The strand wrapped itself around the heavy log. Entiene used her blade to free Pyotr's legs and at Richard's gesture, he jumped back to the catwalk and raised his arms again.

"See, Kriesha, I stand against the awnshegh, he has no power to pull me off the wall!"

Tal-Qazar roared in answer and jerked at the strand, but the end wrapped around the beam held; the support was set deep in the ground. As the hideous monster pulled and jerked, Pyotr laughed.

Above the fort the storm released a barrage of large hailstones and the humans hunched their shoulders

and grabbed their shields to protect themselves from
the bruising blows. Tal-Qazar glared at the spider
strand and roared at the Vos. When the large balls of
hail fell harder the awnshegh skittered sideways as if
he could avoid the blows of the falling ice. He glared
up at the sky, turning and searching, as if looking for
an enemy.

Out on the field, beyond the steaming black streaks
where the fire had burned, the spider-riders were
retreating in a disorderly mob, borne away by their
panicked mounts. Tal-Qazar turned his back on the
fort and bounded after them. In minutes the attackers
were lost behind a silvery curtain of hail.

"We'll keep five guards on the wall, the rest get to
shelter," Richard shouted and decided to be part of
the first watch himself.

Entiene and Paeghen left immediately with
Mother, but the rest took time to reload the catapults
and ballistae before retreating to the warmth and
shelter of the buildings. The females returned in minutes, bringing five stiff, half-cured hides so the guards
could protect themselves from the hail. Richard stood
guard with Stubby, who had climbed up to seat himself again on the shortened log of an arrow slit.

"Do you think Kriesha really helped us?" the halfling asked Richard as they peered through the sheets
of rain and hail. The halfling never mocked the
human gods, but as far as Richard knew, the demihuman offered no god his allegiance.

"I hope not," Richard said quietly. "I don't like the
idea of being obligated to a god that holds part of the
evil power of Azrai."

"But the hail," Stubby objected. "Ice. They call her
the Ice Lady. Pyotr cried out to her and it came so
suddenly—"

"It wasn't sudden," Richard replied "The storm has
been building in the west all morning. It wasn't even

unusual. In this part of Cerilia we often have hail in autumn."

The halfling was not satisfied. His round face was a chubby circle of worry.

"Then why would it panic the awnshegh? After a thousand years he should have been used to it. And I thought he could control the spiders from the Spiderfell. They panicked."

"I don't pretend to know his mind, but part of his trouble had to do with my conversations with him, and Pyotr added the final touch to Tal-Qazar's doubt," Richard explained. He told the halfling about his two meetings with the awnshegh and how the awnshegh's hatred and fear of the Ice Lady had formed a greater part of their conversations. Despite his worry, the halfling laughed at the story of the woven grass hut.

"He's partly insane, even the goblins know it," Richard continued. "He was the one who decided the lady who put magic in the little grass house was Kriesha, and later I planted the idea that she had been using me to trick him. Then Pyotr capped all his fears by calling out to her, so like you, he attributed the hail to Kriesha as well as the strand wrapped around the beam."

"And in his panic, he lost control of his army," Stubby nodded. "That should set him back a bit and make him doubtful."

"For now," Richard agreed, "But not for long. Good fortune and blind luck was on our side this time. We can't count on them to win all our battles."

Like most of the autumn hailstorms that struck the Southern Coast, this one only lasted a short time. An hour later the sun was shining and the only evidence of the saving ice was heaped in piles in the shadowy corners of the stockade.

From the height of the catwalk they could see for

three miles. A deer had left the shadows of the small woods to graze in the sunlight. They saw no other signs of life. Stubby slipped out to patrol the area. North, south, and east of the cleared fields, the low brush was tall enough to hide the little halfling. He returned just before dark without having seen a single goblin.

For two days the stockade was quiet, but on the third, they were inundated with new settlers. The strangers arrived on four large rafts made of cut logs roped together. The primitive watercraft were piled high with plows and pots, axes and adzes, bedrolls and furniture. The strangers came hats in hands, telling a tale of battles between adventurers and landowners in Mhoried, and their need for new homes.

"It's not pushing in on you that we want," said Antiet, the grizzled farmer who appeared to be the leader. We've our own food, and can build our own place, but we asked at the fort above, and they said we should ask you, as it'll be your decision."

"You'll have a cold time of it, and you may be facing an army of goblins," Richard warned.

"Aye, but once we get the horses across the river we can use the timber from most of the rafts, and if we build not too far away, we could, mayhap, aid each other," Antiet said hopefully. "We've left our women behind with our kinsmen, and we've a need to make a place for them."

"We could lend them the crane," Hassan said. "It comes apart easily enough—or I could go with them and build another one."

"We could spare a few of the conifers we cut," Droene said, with Pyotr and Borg nodding. As the largest settlers, they had swung the most effective axes.

"It looks as if you've just been given permission to

stay," Richard grinned, though he did not feel light-hearted. He didn't care for the idea of bringing women and children where goblin armies might attack at any time. Three miles south of the stockade, the Spiderfell retreated back from the banks of the river for five miles and a creek had washed a depression in the bluff, leaving a small cove sheltered from the main current of the river. The cove was inadequate for five rafts, but it could be made larger if need be.

They invited the newcomers to stay the night and when most everyone was asleep, Richard, Gaelin, and Droene gathered in Mother's kitchen.

"You didn't speak up," Richard said to Gaelin. He might be the acknowledged leader, but Richard still considered the settlement an Endier project, and he trusted the opinions of his cousins. Droene was a bit slow-witted, but he had better instincts than most. Gaelin was as quick as Droene was slow. Richard had always believed Gaelin was the sharpest member of the family.

"There are twenty of them here in the fort and six across the river with the animals," Gaelin said. There are twenty of us and thirteen in the northern stockade. That's fifty-nine altogether, with the possibility of women and children arriving in the spring." Gaelin made his tally with the tone of a person who has more to say but needed to be prompted.

"So?" Richard prompted.

"I think it's time to ask the baron for a military patrol."

They had discussed the possibility after the second stockade had been started, but Richard had shied away from the idea. He liked the thought of having the protection of the Diemed military, but Droene and Gaelin had insisted he should be the one to go to Aerele and speak for the settlers. He had not wanted to leave the settlement, fearing Tal-Qazar would attack in his absence.

"And now is the time to do it," Gaelin pressed. "The farmers can stay here and walk back and forth to their site. We have enough people to protect the stockade, and after the hailstorm, the awnshegh will stew for a while."

Richard knew his cousin was right and the next day he packed a leather sack with his dress clothes and Hergion took him across the river to Laedona. From there he caught a packet boat sailing down the river to Moerel and bought a horse for his ride across country. He joined a party of travelers that were being escorted to the capital by a company of mounted soldiers, and five days after leaving the stockade, he was back in Aerele.

The morning after he arrived, he dressed in his finest clothing, the black velvet with the tiny rows of black leather trim, and paid a visit to Shaene Alderis.

Luck was with him. Shaene Alderis remembered him. Shaene, a younger son, had done well for himself. He had married his second cousin, the elder daughter of his uncle, a wealthy merchant. His soft, rich life was already telling on him. He had put on weight, and though it was not yet noon, he had downed enough wine to be weaving slightly, but even in his cups he was genial company.

"Nothing easier," Shaene replied after reading his friend Ruinel's introduction, explaining that Richard needed to reach the ear of the Baron.

"I'm a companion of Stenel Diem, the baron's son. I can get you into the court, but I can't help you with your mission." He grinned with the deprecating charm that had won him his wealthy wife. "I've no power, you see. I'm just good company."

Richard did not envy Shaene at all. He was, however, amazed at the speed with which Ruinel's friend was able to honor his request. That evening he found himself dining in the castle. The baron, a short, stout man with a pouting mouth, sat in the center of the head table. It was raised a foot above the two other long tables that stretched down the dining hall. To Richard, accustomed to the barn-like buildings erected in the settlement, the chamber and the table seemed small for the ruler of a nation as large as Diemed. There were places for five at the head table, and no more than ten could be seated at each of the sides.

Across from him, separated by the width of the two tables and three feet of open space that allowed the servants to serve the diners, Shaene was drinking heavily and telling a tale that made his listeners laugh. One, an older man, his face red with too much wine over a long period of time, turned a bleary eye toward Richard.

"Where did you get the idea for the magic house?" he shouted across the room, interrupting several other conversations.

"What magic house?" demanded the baron. He had been speaking to a tall, thin man on his left and appeared to resent the interruption.

The stocky man tried to repeat the story of Richard's first meeting with the Spider King and managed to garble the tale. Shaene constantly interrupted him, making corrections, and by the time they completed the story it bore little relation to reality, but Richard let it go.

"And what I want to know, is where he learned to make a magic house," the drunk pursued.

"I can only tell you that if you give me your word you won't tell Tal-Qazar," Richard said with a laugh.

"I promise, on my honor," the stocky man said, holding one finger up to his mouth. His bond caused the rest of the diners to laugh. For the first time Richard told the true story of little Jenna and her active imagination.

"It was a child's toy?" The thin man sitting by the baron roared with laughter. When the room was reasonably quiet again, the baron smiled at Richard.

"If I were you, young man, I would not risk meeting that monster again."

Richard smiled gratefully at Shaene Alderis, who had not only brought him to the attention of the baron, but had succeeded in giving him the opening he needed to present his case.

"But I have met him again, sire—twice." He leaned forward in an abbreviated bow to the ruler of Diemed. "Acting according to the permission you gave me back in Faniele, I have the honor and privilege of working to expand the settled borders of your land, my lord."

The baron seemed startled. He turned an inquiring gaze on his chamberlain.

"Did I agree to this?"

The chamberlain reluctantly nodded. A lord on the other side of the baron, deep into his cups, demanded to hear the rest of the story.

The diners forgot their food as Richard told them of the two stockades and the third that was even then being built. Several chuckled over the tale of his second meeting with Tal-Qazar, but to them it did not hold the humor of the first tale, which they had thought to be only a joke.

No one laughed as he described the attack on the first stockade and the hailstorm that had confused and frightened the Spider King.

"All the Spiderfell is a part of your dominion, sire, but no one has yet dared to settle it. The most valuable area is the land by the river, and that we intend to hold for you, but we need a company of soldiers to make the land more secure."

Not even a single expelled breath broke the silence in the dining hall. Baron Naele Diem fingered the stem of his wine goblet while his eyes searched the faces of his advisors. When he seemed unwilling to speak, the tall, thin man on his left—Richard had not caught his name—leaned forward. His thin face, beaked nose, and black eyes reminded Richard of a hawk.

"We all admire the courage that allowed you to undertake such a venture, but do you think your daring justifies asking the baron to bear the expense of troops to protect you?"

"My lord, two months ago I would have said no," Richard replied. Since the unnamed advisor had the temerity to speak in the place of the baron, he could be no less than a lord. "Today, my answer is this: Diemed will not be spending, but investing, an investment that I believe will add significantly to the treasury before much time passes."

The thin man smiled, and Richard shivered at the evil he felt behind the expression.

"Do you really believe these fields, that you admit you cannot protect, will yield crops of such value that your taxes will support the soldiers?"

"Not at all," Richard replied smoothly. He deliberately omitted the honorific, the only hint of the anger flaring inside him. "I believe we can offer something of far greater value."

Desperate to give the baron a solid reason for sending soldiers to help hold back the Spider King's armies, Richard described a plan that had been forming in his mind. Below the fork in the rivers, where the Maesil turned east and the Tuor River ran north, the banks were high. In many places the bluffs rose more than twenty feet above the surface of the water. All three forts were located on streams that flowed into the water, chosen because the settlers needed inlets for their boats. It had been only by accident, when the first settlers sank pilings to build the rudiments of a pier, that they discovered the current of the river, diverted by those six logs, was washing back, digging away the bank and creating a sheltered cove.

Richard had been toying with the idea of sinking more pilings, and if the current of the Maesil assisted in gouging an even larger cove, the stockade could provide a much needed break for the river traders beating their way upstream. Docking fees, a good inn for wealthy travelers, and shops to sell stores needed by the river men could bring in more wealth than simple farming.

He had told no one but Gaelin of his idea and then in only the broadest terms. His mind galloped through ideas that had not even occurred to him as he outlined his plan for the baron and his advisors.

"And Diemed's power over its stretch of the river would be more than doubled," he added, knowing every ruler whose lands abutted the Maesil was jealous of the baron's claim on it.

"But I don't know if my guild would approve of that," said the tall, thin man.

Too late, Richard realized he had made a grave error. Shaene had not told him a member of the Trader's Guild would be present at the dinner.

For centuries the Trader's Guild had found it to be in their best interests to keep many rulers at loggerheads so none gained too great a power over the trade routes. Diemed already had more than its share of major land routes as well as seaports, and Richard was proposing to further the baron's power by doubling his control along one side of the Maesil.

Richard might have made himself an enemy.

ANUIRE

nineteen

"I wish I had warned you," Shaene said for the seventh time. "I had no inkling you had such long-range plans. Master Seone Hamnet is a power in the court."

"You're not to blame," Richard repeated for the seventh time as he secured his bedroll and good clothing to the back of his saddle. Late on the day after the dinner, the baron had sent him a message. The three settlements would get their military support "at such time as Diemed had troops to spare."

The "at such time" warned Richard that the baron was treading a cautious political path. There would be no military protection for the settlers because it could anger the trader's guild. Patrols would be sent only if and when the settlers were strong enough to be a concern in the capital, and by that time the soldiers would no longer be needed.

The morning after receiving the message, Richard took his leave of the capital city of Diemed. He spurred his horse through the gate of the city just after dawn, determined to return, not only a landowner, but the lord of a new province of Diemed.

Autumn had left the last flares of heat behind it, and unlike his first trip on the road between Aerele and Moerel, the weather made for fair, enjoyable riding. Richard rode along a well-kept road between neat farms and the occasional small village. He looked around him with a proprietary air, imagining he was seeing the unforested land by the banks of the Maesil. He was seeing what he wanted for his settlers, and his mind roamed through courses of action and possibilities as he explored the possibility of turning his dreams into reality.

He was so busy with his thoughts that he had ridden through most of the first morning before he realized he was being followed. His pace had been set by his mood. Twice, his ambition burning in him, he had urged his horse to a gallop. Then reason had taken over and he slowed to spare his mount. Behind him, another rider was keeping pace. As the road topped a gentle rise and curved, Richard looked back, and saw that he was still being followed. And behind the first, a second rider was doing the same.

Road bandits? He doubted it. He wore his worn and tattered clothing, and his horse, while chosen for strength and stamina, was an ugly brute that looked to be worthless. No stranger would think him worth robbing. Anyone who had learned of him in Aerele would know he carried little of value except his court clothing. His pursuers were after him for a different reason. Would Baron Diem think he was a danger and send assassins after him? He dismissed the idea, but his mind centered on the master of the Trader's Guild. The baron might not have believed in the coves by the river, but the master of the guild might not want to risk their construction.

The men following him were in for a surprise, Richard decided as he continued on his way. Two miles ahead he found what he sought. The road ran through a small wood and turned just after it crossed a shallow stream. When he knew he was out of sight of his pursuers, he turned into the wood and tethered his horse. He pulled his sword and walked quietly back to the road.

On the way, he stepped over a fallen limb, stopped and looked at it. He sheathed his sword and picked it up. After snapping off most of the branches he stood waiting behind a massive tree as the splashing from the stream alerted him to his first pursuer's approach. He let the mounted man pass and stepped out into the road, swinging the thick limb. The rider fell from the saddle and struck the ground with a thump and the clatter of armor.

"Not so easy to catch, am I?" Richard scoffed as the man rolled over to face his ambusher.

Richard stared. A rude, homespun cloak covered the man's armor and a tunic with the markings of a knight- priest, a paladin of Haelyn, god of war and honor.

"That was a scurvy trick," the paladin snapped.

"Your pardon, priestly knight. I thought you were an assassin. He would not deserve honorable treatment."

"Honor is not what you owe your enemy, but what you owe yourself," the paladin growled as he stood and rubbed his left shoulder.

"You were following me," Richard said, already tired of the lecture.

"To offer your settlement my services, and the blessings of Haelyn. But someone is on my trail—or yours," the paladin added. "You may face your assassin yet. I suggest we get off the trail."

Richard didn't argue. He gripped his sturdy

weapon and stepped back into the shadows behind the large tree while the paladin led his mount into the wood on the other side of the road. When the second rider crossed the stream and rounded the turn in the road, they both stepped out into plain sight.

Neither Richard or the paladin offered a challenge though the warrior-priest of Haelyn gave a snort of disgust. Beneath the heavy, hooded traveling cloak of the mounted woman, they could see the white and gold robes of a priestess of Sarimie.

She gazed at the paladin and smiled, softening a strong, angular face. "I take it, Werberan, we are on the same mission?"

"You may accept it, Daire. I should have known the servants of Sarimie would move rapidly to seek a foothold in any newly settled land." Werberan's voice was less friendly than hers.

"No less so than the servants of Haelyn," she retorted. "You were ahead of me."

"And of more use to the settlers, since I can help to fight their enemies," Werberan said.

"It is to be expected that the warriors of Haelyn think all victories are won with a sword."

"If I understand correctly, the decision is mine," Richard spoke up, stopping the verbal battle.

"Yours is the decision," Daire said, softening her voice and smiling at Richard, though her eyes still snapped with anger. Werberan nodded and kept his gaze on Richard.

Richard sighed. The last thing he needed was a priest of Haelyn or a priestess of Sarimie. Either or both would immediately start demanding temples while the settlers were still holding on by their fingernails.

Many countries in Cerilia were ruled by the high priests or priestesses working behind the thrones, and some had even taken the crowns themselves. Still, did he dare anger the gods they served? The trader's guild might already be after him. Just how many powerful enemies could he handle?

If he had to have the representative of one god, better they have one of each, he decided. Neither would allow the other the upper hand. While they jockeyed between themselves for supremacy, Richard might still be able to run his own settlement. Then there was the problem of Kriesha. He doubted the evil of the Ice Lady had acted to benefit the settlers, but the Vos called on her and Pyotr could have drawn her attention to the settlement. If Richard could prevent it, Kriesha would not rule the new colonies.

"A question," Richard asked, ashamed he did not already know the answer. While no Endier mocked the gods, the family had always relied on their own strength. "How do Haelyn and Sarimie feel about each other? We have enough war without the gods battling above our land."

Werberan and Daire exchanged startled, wary glances. Priests never explained themselves, but these two had quickly discovered that Richard Endier was not one who would bow and accept without question.

"Haelyn and Sarimie do not fight each other," Werberan answered. His arrogance tucked beneath his need to win acceptance in the settlement. "There is a pact among the gods. They will never again war on the plane of this world. Not even they want another Mount Deismaar."

"Lawful gods respect the rights of their peers," Daire said. She was also less haughty. "If we, the servants of the gods, argue among ourselves, accept it as our dedication to those we serve. A mortal failing, no more, that should not be blamed on the deities."

"Why were you following me?" Richard asked. "Why not openly approach me in Aerele?"

"I didn't know where to find you," Werberan said and Daire nodded as if she had faced the same difficulty. "I was too late to meet you at the city gate, and once on the road, I realized one of us was being followed. I stayed between you and your pursuer. If I was the target, to endanger you would not augur well for my purpose."

"I too knew you were being followed and I stayed well back, keeping the possible adversary between us," Daire smiled at the irony.

"I'm glad I was so well protected," Richard replied, chagrined that they thought he was in need of help, yet still grateful for their willingness. "Before I formally accept you into the settlement, there are several things you must accept. You will be the first dedicated to the service of Haelyn and Sarimie, but before you is a Khinasi, who reveres Avani, two Rjurik who look to Erik and a Vos who calls on Kriesha." Both Werberan and Daire frowned at the mention of the Ice Lady. "They have earned their place in our settlement and since I accepted them with their beliefs, they may not be persecuted for them. Also, at the moment we are still fighting for our lives. We have shelter, but not enough yet for comfort. We have no time to build temples."

"Perhaps, at least, an altar?" Daire asked.

"If you build it yourself, or find believers to help you when they've finished their daily chores," Richard said, determined to make the safety and comfort of the settlers his first priority.

Daire and Werberan grudgingly accepted Richard's terms and they rode on. Just before sunset they arrived at the same inn Richard had used on his previous journeys, where he had fought the trappers on his first trip south. They were accepted by the innkeeper, but with less welcome fervor than Richard had experienced on his earlier visits. Paladins and priestesses were accustomed to and demanded the best, but never expected to pay for their food and lodging.

The next morning they were up before dawn and on the road as the sun rose. Richard set a good pace, as fast as the horses could travel without exhausting them. Most of the land in Diemed had been tamed. Farms adjoined farms and for most of their journey they rode between well tended fields, lying fallow after the harvests, and they were seldom out of sight of sturdy farm buildings. Here and there were small woodland areas that could hide wandering bands of raiding humanoids or road bandits. Richard never forgot his mount should be fresh enough to outrun a potential enemy if he encountered a group too large to fight.

Halfway through the morning he slowed his horse as they approached a dense woodland in their path. The small forest stretched, with few breaks, from the Spiderfell to the sea. He was not anticipating any trouble because the Diemed military made it a regular part of their patrol, but he was always wary when his vision was limited.

"You plan ahead," Werberan observed.

"Dangers can be halved or avoided entirely if you prepare for trouble," Richard remarked as they entered the shadow of the forest that lined both sides of the road.

But they encountered no trouble. They stayed their second night in Moerel. Since they would travel over-land to the settlements, Richard bought another horse, a strong brute who was trained to the plow, and loaded it with extra supplies, mostly blankets and furs.

The third night they spent at the Lanwin freehold. Despite the fact that he was opening a new land, Richard still felt the pull of the homestead that should have been his. His loss was lessened when Rieva showed off her infant son. The soft features of the baby had a strong resemblance to Randen Endier.

"Not a lot of me in him," Halmied said as he tickled the chubby infant under the chin. "Looks like his hair will be light like mine, though."

As if answering his father, the baby gave a gurgle and a slight frown as he kicked his fat feet.

"I'd say he's determined to be himself," Daire suggested with a smile.

The next morning they continued their journey, additionally loaded with bags of apples and new clothing the Endier sisters had sewed for their brothers and Richard. They began their journey in the darkness. Knowing the farm roads, Richard led the way through the fields and they left the property behind just at dawn.

The first seven miles north of the Lanwin freehold was the most dangerous. In that area the trees of the Spiderfell crowded close to the riverbank, so they were in Tal-Qazar's domain. Believing the banks of the river might be patrolled by goblins, Richard stayed well inside the forest, trying to remain at least a mile from the river. The forest was too thick to gallop, but he set a fast pace and halfway through the morning they rode out into the open without encountering an enemy.

"The goblins don't much care for the open fields," he explained to his two companions as he slowed the pace to rest the horses. "Some say they have trouble seeing in the sunlight, but I think they feel vulnerable to attack on open ground."

Throughout the day Richard set a reasonable pace, breaking every two hours to walk and lead the horses to rest them. The sun was low over the river when they reached the third—the most southerly and the newest—stockade. As they approached, they could see one of Hassan's cranes rearing up over the half-finished walls. Richard rode up to the gate and pushed, the large doors were unbolted and his calls brought no answering hails. Looking around he was amazed at the amount of work that had been accomplished, but he saw no evidence of occupation, so they rode on, following a well-packed trail of hooves and human feet.

A mile north of the new stockade they heard shouts and rode to the top of a low hill to see a score of settlers crouched down behind several clumps of bushes while twice as many spider-riders were milling about beneath the eaves of a group of trees, too few to be called a wood. Five horses were disappearing over the rise to the north. The builders had sent the animals on ahead to shelter and safety.

"I hoped to be back before the trouble started again," Richard said, then realized the arrogance of his remark. If Tal-Qazar attacked with enough force to destroy the stockades, his one bow and one sword would make little difference. Still, as leader, he felt it was his responsibility to meet any danger at the side of his people.

"This is where you could use my assistance," Daire said. She dismounted, removed her traveling cloak as well as the white and gold robes of her office. Beneath it she wore a long tunic of light chain mail. Her hands were busy in a pouch, then she suddenly disappeared.

"I too have a ring of invisibility," Werberan sneered. "To a paladin of Haelyn, hiding from the sight of the enemy is not an honorable move." The priestly knight dismounted, removed his own traveling cloak and the thinner garment, covered in the runes that proclaimed his office. He took the latter and spread it over his horse's neck and back, letting it drape so the magic runes protected the horse's flanks.

He drew an amulet from beneath his tunic and climbed back in the saddle. Richard watched, unbelieving. The paladin and his horse glowed and seemed to grow until they were twice their original size. Then, singing a paean to Haelyn, Werberan charged down the hill, his sword in his hand.

"Sorry, old boy, but after that, we won't make much of a show," he said to his horse. He turned Daire's mount and the pack horse to head toward the beaten trail and gave each a slap on the rump. The animals galloped away, staying on the track as if they knew the path led to safety.

Richard too charged toward the wood, guiding his mount with his knees and yelling at the top of his voice as he pulled his bow and set an arrow to the string. He waited until he was just within range before he let his first arrow fly. It passed through the first ranks of the spider-riders, but behind them, one of the huge arachnids reared up with a high-pitched cry. Richard's arrow had pierced its jaw.

Behind the wounded spider a goblin screamed in pain and fell from its mount. He had not hit the ground before a second and a third were struck by some unseen force. Richard saw Daire become visible and duck behind a bush. Then Werberan was among the spider-riders, slashing with his sword. A goblin screeched; its arm flew up—hacked off—and was sent flying by Werberan.

A triumphant shout rose from the settlers and Richard just had time to see them rise from their hiding places. They rushed forward with bows, swords, and axes. Richard's next two arrows found targets, the first in the eye of a goblin rider, and the second in its companion's chest. When he was too close to use his bow again he pushed it over his left shoulder and pulled his sword.

The ugly, raw-boned horse he rode proved its courage as Richard charged into the ranks of the spider-riders. The horse screamed a challenge at the huge spiders and swerved, answering the commands Richard gave with the pressure of his knees.

Richard slashed at the first spider-rider whose own blade deflected the blow. The raw-boned horse shied, angling away from a spear thrust at them by another rider, and Richard deflected the point with his sword. He grabbed the weapon just behind the point and jerked, pulling the goblin from its spider mount. He swung the spear butt first, knocking two goblins from their seats, and brought the heavy wooden shaft down on the head of the first huge spider. He heard the crack of bone and the arachnid collapsed. Behind the first ranks of the goblin riders came the screams of dying goblins and the gibbering of huge wounded spiders.

The farmers had taken heart at the sight of the huge paladin, and arrived at the scene of the battle in a rush. Their axes hacked away at the goblin blades. Despite their numbers, and the leadership of the awnshegh, the goblins of the Spiderfell were bravest when they far outnumbered their foes. Between the success of Haelyn's paladin, Richard, and the invisible fighter behind them, they had lost nearly half their numbers. Several shouted to the others and braved the invisible danger as they fled.

One, a large goblin with a rank insignia on its boiled leather helmet, rode a spider that topped the others by more than a handspan. The humanoid pressed its mount forward, toward Richard. The goblin gave a command that caused the spider to rise on it's four hind legs. Richard gripped his mount with his knees as the horse shied, but it had not moved away in time. The spider bit the horse on the neck before Richard brought the butt of the spear down on the arachnid's head hard enough to crack the skull.

In trying to protect the horse, he had left himself open to the goblin's sword, and felt the sting of a dirty blade as it cut into his right arm. The blood spurted, but mercifully he felt no pain. Beneath him the horse wobbled and fell. Richard dropped the spear and his sword as he used his left hand to balance himself when he jumped off his collapsing mount.

The horse fell on Richard's sword, so he bent to pick up the spear and straightened just in time to miss the second thrust of the large goblin's sword. Richard whirled and, again holding the spear butt forward, jumped at the goblin. Luck guided him. The blunt end struck the goblin in the mouth, breaking off one of its tusk-like bottom teeth, and the spear butt rammed down its throat. The humanoid leader fell, grasping the shaft of the spear with both hands as it gave a bloody, dying gurgle.

Richard only heard part of it. A black mist descended over his vision and he felt himself start to fall. He was unconscious before he hit the ground.

ANUIRE

TWENTY

Richard dreamed he was flying, bound to some great bird that carried him across the sky. He regained consciousness to discover that he was tied to Werberan's horse. He felt weak and sick and his right arm hurt when he tried to move it.

"Keep still," ordered Daire, who walked beside the animal. "Your wound is not completely healed."

Richard's head swam and his thoughts were too fuzzy to argue. Instead he concentrated on working out what had brought him to his present condition. When he remembered the fight with the spider-riders, he looked around. The sun had set and in the near darkness he could see a group of settlers walking along behind. He gave up trying to count them. What would the number tell him, since he was unsure how many had been ambushed by the goblins? They walked with a jaunty step and their voices were triumphant. None seemed to be mourning friends.

Ahead, Borg led the way; he was leading the ugly, raw-boned horse Richard had bought in Moerel. Maybe his mind was confused. He thought the horse had been bitten by one of the huge spiders. Surely the venom would have killed it.

Daire saw the direction of his gaze.

"The druid drew out most of the poison. The horse will not die." Even in the dimness he could see her displeasure. "You said there were no other priests at the settlement."

"Borg?"

The two Rjurik mourned the timber cut for the settlement and used no axes themselves, but he had no idea one or both were druids. Though their magic was different from priests, they served the god Erik and would have powers of their own.

Richard was still considering what he had learned when they reached the stockade and entered through the wide river gate. He wanted to look around, to see and attempt to judge the progress made while he was away, but Daire verbally bullied him into lying still. Mother hauled him from the horse, carried him into the second building and put him on his bed. He was too weak from the loss of blood to fight them.

When he awoke the next day he could see the shortened shadows within the palisade. When he shifted and sat up slowly, he discovered the weakness and dizziness of the night before had left him. He rose slowly, careful of his arm as he dressed and put on his boots.

Outside he found several of the settlers shaping wood into furniture, but the stockade seemed nearly empty. Entiene and Mourde were standing guard on the walls. Gaelin sat on a stool by a fire pit, using a red hot iron to burn a hole in a short length of wood that would become another bed frame. He grinned as Richard approached.

"Welcome back to the world of the living. The second healing spell did the trick, I see."

"The second spell? I don't remember either one, or what happened to end the battle."

"I'll tell you all I know," Gaelin said. "Several of our people were with the farmers, helping them with the new stockade. They saw the spider-riders and were setting up a defensive position when you and your priests arrived." Gaelin described what he had heard of the battle, much of which Richard remembered. "Your arm was slashed and you passed out from loss of blood, but by that time the goblins had had enough of your giant warrior and invisible fighter."

"Was anyone killed?" Richard asked.

"No, several were wounded, that's why they only partially healed you last night. They were using up their spells. Did you know Borg's a *druid?* Apparently he can't heal people, only animals, so he drew most of the spider poison out of the horse last night and the rest today. Why didn't you tell us about him?"

"I didn't know," Richard said slowly. "I should have guessed, the way Anders hangs on his every word. I guess the boy is his pupil."

"We didn't even know that Paeghen and Entiene were *females* . . . at first," Gaelin said, staring out over the yard of the stockade. "I wonder if the others are hiding secrets too."

"At least Mother didn't hide his ability to cook," Richard said as he turned away. "I'm starving."

Gaelin left his work and walked with Richard to the cookfires. In fair weather, Mother still preferred to work outside. He had built himself a second fieldstone hearth that was partially for cooking. More than half was taken up by an oven that baked the clay roof tiles.

"Since we've finished the walls and gates for the fort, we retied all the timber and rafted it down to the new location and sent Hassan's crane with them," Gaelin said. "Antiet has promised to help us cut more timber for our other buildings when they're set up."

"They've worked hard," Richard said. "I was surprised at what they've accomplished."

"If the goblins don't attack again, they'll finish the gates and the roof today," Gaelin said. "They hope to move in tomorrow. They're calling their fort 'Farmstead.' What do you think of 'Rivervale' for us?"

Richard approved of the names and the work accomplished on the third fort, particularly since through the open east gate he could see that the residue of the crops had been turned under, leaving the fields ready for the spring planting. He had been away just over two weeks. Two very busy weeks for the settlers.

Cutting more timber would give the settlers something to do in the winter months. Without occupation they would be restless. Boredom could cause more trouble than the awnshegh.

Werberan and Daire immediately began their campaigns, trying to draw the settlers into their religions. Both seemed to consider personal popularity a strong draw. The priestess of Sarimie endeared herself to the settlers of Rivervale and Farmstead by pinpointing spots where wells should be dug. She gave the credit to her god, but Richard wondered if she had used some sort of magic. He was too happy with the result for the doubt to bother him. They were reaching the point where their largest vulnerability in time of battle would be water.

The ex-mercenaries and ex-adventurers of Rivervale needed little from Werberan, but the farmers were taking instruction in the handling of weapons and hanging on his every word.

At the insistence of Daire and Werberan, Richard rested for two days, but by the third he was so restless he would have been willing to ride Tal-Qazar's back. The meat in the smokehouse was fully cured and the cool weather would allow them to move part of it into the storage buildings that were half structure, half pit. Richard decided to go hunting. If they could refill the smokehouse and help supply meat for the new fort, the farmers there would be less likely to endanger themselves by hunting near the Spiderfell.

Werberan, whose talents did not include wood-working or farming was also restless, so they rode out together. Richard was glad for a chance to talk with the paladin away from the others.

"When I told you we had no priests, I had no idea Borg was a druid," Richard told him. "I didn't deliberately lie, and Borg didn't lie to me, since I'd never asked him. He has earned his place in the settlement."

Werberan gazed at Richard for an uncomfortable moment and then shrugged. "Haelyn has no quarrel with Erik, but Sarimie is a jealous god."

"Borg stays," Richard said stubbornly. "Another subject bothers me more—not a subject, ignorance, even of how much I can ask." He knew he was not expressing himself well, but he pursued anyway. "When we planned our defense of the first stockade, we tried to make use of everyone's abilities. I will question Borg again, but I need to know what you and Daire can offer if we are attacked by Tal-Qazar."

"Daire will have to speak for herself, but understand, neither of us have the powers of Lord Duraine or Lord Masimil."

Lord Duraine, a high priest of Haelyn, had recently emerged as the paladin-ruler of Ghieste, the land north of the Spiderfell. And all Cerilia was hearing rumors of Lord Masimil, priest of Sera, as Sarimie was known in Brechtur. Most of the controlling threads of commerce in that land ran through his servants' hands, and he was reputed to be using his power to forge his own crown.

"Neither of us have been in the service of our gods long enough to . . . well, I would say you've seen most of what we can offer."

Richard sighed. He had hoped they had more magic than he had seen, and Werberan saw his disappointment.

"Look on the positive side," he said. "If we don't offer much more than an ordinary fighter's defense, we are not strong enough to be a threat to your position."

"At least not yet," Richard said thoughtfully, then wondered if it had been a good idea, expressing the thought aloud.

Werberan laughed softly as he slowed his horse, allowing it to choose its own path through one of the rock screes that occasionally reared its head above the river plain.

"I intend to grow, Richard Endier, but from what I have seen of you, you'll at least keep pace. Haelyn's favors in return for strength and honor are not limited to those publicly dedicated to his service. I suspect he noticed you long before I entered your life. Perhaps that is why I was drawn here."

Richard started to wonder if Werberan's praise was meant as a palliative to his suspicions, but at that moment a wild boar broke from the brush directly in their path. They had ridden out with spears as well as bows, hoping for just such an encounter. The subject of their discussion was forgotten as they slid from their horses.

"He's a big one," Richard said as he anchored the butt of his weapon in the ground.

"We'll need two, and then be hard pressed to hold him," Werberan replied. His eyes danced with the challenge and Richard could feel his own blood pounding in anticipation. The monster boar that squealed its challenge and snorted in preparation for its attack was not only needed food for the settlers, but an opponent to test both men's mettle.

Their weapons soundly anchored and waiting, they mimicked the boar's squeal, returning the challenge. The monster pig had been turning its head, as if having trouble locating its adversary, but then its small, red eyes focused on Richard and it charged, head down, its long, curving tusks nearly touching the ground. Its hooves, that seemed impossibly tiny for its weight, sent stones flying from its path.

"Heart strike's mine," Werberan announced as the boar drew closer. Richard agreed, since the paladin was on his right and in the best position. Richard would try for the heavy muscle in the boar's right shoulder.

The boar charged straight at them, completely ignoring the spears pointed in its direction. Then, within inches of the sharp metal points, it swerved as if to go around them. Werberan missed his aim at the heart and his spear entered the tough hide of the left foreleg. Richard's weapon caught the beast in the chest, but missed the heart.

Not even the two spears stopped the boar. With an ear piercing squeal it charged on, driving the points deeper into its body as it tried to reach its enemies. The shock of impact jerked Werberan's spear butt from its anchor and he was thrown sideways as the boar twisted. The paladin kept a tight grip on his weapon and his feet slid. Small rocks clattered beneath his feet as he was pushed back. Richard's spear cracked the length of the shaft and he felt the break pinch his hands as he desperately tried to hold it together.

Both men held their grip until the boar faltered and then they shoved together. The boar was unsteady and their combined force tumbled it on its right side. It fell, sharp hooves flashing as it kicked. Richard was thrown to his knees, but he kept his grip on his spear, twisting and shoving. He felt an obstruction that suddenly gave way and knew he had found the heart.

With another grunt and a kick that struck Werberan and knocked him off his feet, the boar died. The body still twitched, but the life had gone out of it. Richard rose from his knees, his legs trembling. He eyed the boar and stepped over to offer Werberan a hand.

"Did he get you with a hoof?" The hooves of a boar could be as deadly as a sword.

"No, thank Haelyn, but I'm well bruised," the paladin said as he struggled to his feet. He looked down at the boar and nodded. "It was a good death. He kept his courage and honored the battle."

"I think I'd rather have less courage and less battle from my meals," Richard said, surveying the scuffed ground. The beast had charged at them and then had tried to turn aside at the last moment. But boars never turned aside unless something more important than their enemy redirected their attention. Possibly a den in the rocks behind them?

Richard turned and his blood nearly froze as he saw what had caught the boar's attention. Backed into a dark, shadowy depression, a huge spider crouched, ready to spring.

Since his first spear was firmly lodged in the carcass of their prey and the other was a good fifteen feet away, Richard grabbed at his sword, but his hand was blocked by Werberan, who caught his arm and pulled him back.

"Wait, this is no true spider," the paladin ordered. He raised his hand and muttered strange words. At first Richard thought it was an incantation, but it ended with a sight rise in tone, a question? A question in the language of magic, words that seemed to fog in the ears of any but a magic user.

Richard stared as the monster seemed to lose definition, blurred, and changed shape. The body of the spider, a good five feet in length and three feet high, even when crouching, shortened in length and grew in height. It blurred even more until it was like a roil of thick black smoke before it took on shape and sharp edges again.

In front of them stood an elf. He held no weapons and Richard thought it fortunate, because his face was full of hatred. When he spoke, his voice was musical—as if bells chimed in the background of his speech—but his words were Anuirean.

" 'Ware humans. I will not be as easy to kill as that dumb creature."

"We have no fight with elves unless you want one, but spiders are our enemies." Richard had gripped the quillon of his sword again, but he made a show of removing his hand.

"Then why do you trap me?"

"The accident of finding our prey here," Werberan answered as he stepped aside. With a sweep of his arm he indicated the path was free.

The elf took one tentative step forward, but Richard also moved, not far enough to block the demihuman's path, just enough to show he was not through with the conversation. The elf paused, his face closed and wary.

"You are free to go, but know you are close to the Spiderfell and in danger from the goblins." He doubted an elf with the magic to turn himself into spider form was unaware of his location. Still, he needed to make his position clear. The warning had been the best he could think of as an opening gambit. "If you are ever in need of shelter, we have a small fort three miles west of here at the river's edge. We harbor no hatred for elves and you can depend upon our aid. You would not be the first of your people to find a safe night's sleep with us."

"I take no shelter from humans," the elf snarled and pulled his blade. "Stand away, or I will kill you."

"We are not enemies," Richard said, stepping back. The elf stepped past him and around an outcrop on the rocky tor.

Werberan watched the stranger leave. When he turned, his eyes sparkled and a little smile curved his lips.

"You know more of him than I do?" Richard asked, intrigued by the paladin's humor.

"If I am right he has his secrets and we should let him keep them." When he turned his attention back to Richard, his smile disappeared and his gaze was speculative. "You asked questions of Daire and me, Richard Endier, but I am beginning to realize how little you told us."

"What am I supposed to have told you?" Richard demanded. "As far as I know, there's nothing about our settlement you would not expect, save Borg being a druid, and that you knew before I did."

"You had not told me you were an elf-friend."

"I don't know that I am," Richard said slowly. "I do know the elves hate Tal-Qazar even more than humans. That makes us allies of a sort. I don't want to throw the knowledge of my aid to elves in Tal-Qazar's face, but any aid I give the demihumans could come back to us when we most need it."

"As I said, you are a planner," Werberan said. "Even the wisest of leaders does not always know when he plants the seeds that will reap a crop of fortune. Making friends is the surest way to power, as well as luck."

"I don't know that I've done much planting," Richard said as they began to butcher the carcass. The elf had not behaved like a friend.

ANUIRE

twenty-one

Tal-Qazar crouched on the floor of the Adytum. All around him tiny spiders were at work mending the floor and walls. Most of the rents he had torn in his rage had already been closed by the tiny workers. He chafed at the need to be still, but if he did not allow them time for the repairs he could fall through one of the gaps.

"I am Tal-Qazar, goblin king," he repeated softly, trying to bring his mind back into focus again. He had warned himself repeatedly that his rages prevented him from thinking clearly. He needed clear thought.

He needed clear thought to drive away the humans by the river. Yes, very clear thought, he repeated to himself. He needed to think about Richard Endier.

Even before he received his powers at Mount Deismaar he had never been a friend of humans and had seen very few more than once. Since he had become an awnshegh he had never seen any human more than once, and very few had escaped his wrath. So why had he allowed Richard Endier to trick him, deceive him and then drive him away from a battle he should have won?

In his frustration he tore another hole in the floor and moved away as the small spiders rushed to repair it.

Tal-Qazar knew what he had been thinking at the time. At his first meeting with Richard he had been deceived by the human's words and his own desire to trap Kriesha. He should have killed the human at their second meeting, but again the human had held him off by convincing him that Kriesha was using them against each other.

He, the great Tal-Qazar, had been a fool!

By the time he returned to the Adytum he had realized that the hailstorms were frequent at that time of year, but he had chosen not to return and renew the attack. He knew he could destroy Richard Endier, who was only a mortal, and a human at that. Tal-Qazar's power was greater than any mortal and most awnshegh.

But would Richard Endier find a way to make a fool of him again? He shivered as he thought about it, about his own forces, who might laugh at him. Never to his face—they would never let him see what they were thinking. Still, to laugh at someone was to lose the awe and the fear that held his empire together.

No, he would not attack the stockades again until he had a plan the human could not thwart.

What was he thinking of? One puny human could not continue to trick Tal-Qazar, Spider King, awnshegh carrying the blood power of Azrai, elf . . . human . . . *Goblin!* A goblin! A *goblin!*

Tal-Qazar, Spider King, awnshegh, could out-think and destroy any human! Richard Endier was full of tricks and ploys, but he could never be a match for

Tal-Qazar, the Spider King. He could do it. He must never distrust himself again.

He would still need to work out his plans. . . .

"In the meantime, my patrols can harry the settlers," he said aloud. "Hopefully lessen the numbers of both. The sacrifice of a few goblin lives will insure proper outrage in the rest." His armies were growing too large anyway. They were denuding the forest of food and might soon start raiding into Ghieste and Diemed, bringing the armies of those two lands to give him trouble. If the settlers killed off a few he would have less trouble and perhaps his goblins would get a few of them. At least they would all be occupied until he was ready to take on Richard Endier again.

He sat thinking about the human, convincing himself he was the wiser.

"I am Tal-Qazar, and no human can trick me," he muttered. "I am Tal-Qazar, through me runs the blood of Azrai . . ." The litany to build up his faith in himself continued for hours.

* * * * *

Ever watchful and always alert, Berkerig and Gosfak exchanged guarded glances. They had heard the muttering of the Spider King. He was afraid of Richard Endier. Tal-Qazar was striving to build his confidence, to be sure the human did not trick him again.

Was that a sign that his mind was clearing? Or that he was slipping deeper into his madness? Berkerig wondered if he could escape the Spiderfell and join another band in the northern mountains. . . .

ANUIRE

twenty-two

"So, if it's entirely up to us to hold what we've settled, we're a land apart," Tannen said.

Richard gazed across the table at the small, slender man who had taken over the leadership of the northern fort. Tannen had left the first stockade with Noelon and Brosen, following Noelon because of a debt he owed his fellow countryman. Within a week after the fight and the desertion, the rest had discovered Noelon's true talents were in criticism, not leadership.

With their lives at stake, the other four had changed their loyalty from Noelon to Tannen, and the second leader of the new group had made the journey to consult with Richard.

Tannen gave Richard a rueful smile. "I didn't understand how hard it was to be a good leader until I was stuck with the position." His expression turned serious. "We made a mistake, you know. We realize it now."

Richard's face closed. He felt it stiffen. He did not

want the settlers of the northern fort to return to Rivervale. Noelon and Brosen had caused too much trouble, and were no longer welcome. As he looked into the clear calm of Tannen's eyes he knew the leader of the northern settlement would not oust them. In addition, they had taken in more people, so they now numbered more than thirty. Tannen seemed to have read Richard's expression. He raised a hand as if to physically hold back Richard's objections.

"I didn't mean we want to return. We've invested too much labor in our own settlement, and it will pay off next autumn when we bring in our first crops. The weapons and food you sent will help us get through the winter. I didn't come begging. I came to learn just what you've told me, that we can't count on Diemed for protection. If we're all on our own, then we should do what we can to assist each other. If we're a land apart, we'll need a leader for it, and I've no objection to it being you." He grinned. "In a gesture of recognition for what you taught us, we've even named our settlement Endier."

"What do you suggest we do for each other?" Richard asked. His heart had swelled when he heard the northern settlement had been named for him, but he deliberately submerged his pride in practicality.

Tannen laughed. "Now that I've made the grand gesture, I don't know. We're too far away to assist each other if the Spider King attacks. But if we're able to deal with him, we'll soon be facing the problem of the baron and other nations. We need to keep in touch and stand united."

"We're still a part of Diemed," Richard cautioned. He had never planned on leading an insurrection.

"If we can hold what we settled, we'll at least be a province," Tannen replied. "Think about it."

For a week after the leader of Endier left, Richard had trouble thinking of anything else. A few days later, Borg had been called to Farmstead to attend a sick horse. The druid had told the farmers about Tannen's suggestions.

Antiet, the leader of Farmstead, returned with the Rjurik druid. He was a short, stocky man, twice Richard's age with short, grizzled hair and a thick graying beard. The weathered skin of his face was crinkled into folds and his black eyes sparkled as he greeted Richard. Before he even tasted the cup of red-root tea Mother put in front of him he was praising Tannen's idea.

If they could hold their land they would become at least a province of Diemed, and would fare better if they were united. Acknowledging their chosen lord of the province would show solidarity to the rest of Cerilia, particularly the baron and Diemed's closest neighbors.

In the week that followed Antiet's visit, Richard's self-acknowledged ambition had swelled with pride, only to be punctured with doubt. What did he know about governing a province? Still, if he were given the leadership, he would lead.

He had expected some objections, but all the settlers were enthusiastic. Mother, with orog pragmatism, and a surprising understanding of the politics of Cerilia, had punctured Richard's ego while giving his support:

"It is necessary," the half-orog had said. "In the beginning, having a leader recognized by everyone is more important than his wisdom."

Gaelin, Caern and Ruinel were thoroughly enjoying Richard's elevated position. After a week, their unflagging jokes were wearing on his patience.

Richard usually left his bed before dawn. Mother was often up before him, feeding the fires and boiling the first pots of tea. They usually sat in silence, drinking from steaming mugs, thinking their own thoughts and making their own plans for the day.

On the ninth day after Antiet's visit, Richard was just finishing his morning meal of roasted meat and pan fried bread when Caern and Gaelin strolled into the section of the first building they used as a kitchen-dining hall.

Caern paused and raised his right hand, his finger pointing to the ceiling to indicate he had a riddle. Riddling was becoming a popular pastime when the settlers gathered around the fire in the evening.

"It speaks, we listen.

"It rises, we bow.

"We liked it once.

"We revere it now.

"What is it?" he asked Gaelin.

"Why it's Lord Richard," Gaelin replied triumphantly, as if they had not used the riddle six times in the past week.

"Good morning Lord Richard," Caern called out gaily. "May we join you, or is your table reserved only for the higher ranks?"

Richard had awakened with a slight headache, caused by tossing in his bed most of the night. He had been wrestling with the problem of distances between the three stockades and wondering what they could do to alert each other if they were in need of assistance. His failure to find a solution was partly responsible for his headache and his black mood. He glared at Caern, unaccountably resenting the sally.

"My lord looks out of sorts this morning," Gaelin remarked. "Forgive us, Lord Richard, we did not mean to presume—"

Richard slammed his cup on the table, spilling the residue of his tea as he jumped up, knocking over the stool he had been using. He strode out of the room, passing Entiene on the way.

"I'll take your patrol this morning, you find something else to do," he snapped as he passed her. When he reached the corner of the building and turned he saw her, still standing where he had left her. She was staring after him.

In the stable he considered Roomet, his horse for several years and then his newer mount, the ugly, raw-boned Ikki.

"Who wants to go look for goblins?" he asked them.

Roomet stared at his master impassively, but Ikki drew back his lips and his eyes seemed to narrow as if in anger. His expression was only a trick of his ugliness, but that morning it matched Richard's mood and he decided to take his newest mount. Saddled, and with Richard on his back, Ikki was restive, as if ready to charge a company of spider-riders.

"Just slow down," Richard warned him. "We're on patrol, we're not looking for a fight." He was warning himself as well as the horse.

By his own order, the patrol stayed a quarter of a mile from the eaves of the Spiderfell, and as he rode north—Stubby was riding south—he kept the distance he had ordered for the others. Twice he saw moving shadows under the trees. Tal-Qazar's goblins were keeping a close watch, but they remained in the wood and none challenged him.

He continued north though the forest receded to the east more than a mile, and was near the end of his northern trek when he reached an area of thorn bushes where maneuverability was limited because of the thickets of the large, prickly bushes. He turned his horse and was heading south again when a spider stepped out from behind a cluster of bushes and barred his way.

The arachnid stood two feet high and was more than three feet long, but after seeing the spider mounts up close, Richard thought he could kill it without trouble, unless there were more hidden in the bushes.

He was still in the saddle, looking around, wondering if there were more of the creatures when the monster started to shimmer. A sparkling fog developed around it and in seconds dissipated. In front of him stood the elf from the rocky tor.

"We meet again," Richard said as he brought the horse to a halt. "I didn't think you wanted my company."

The elf stared at him for a moment and smiled without a trace of humor.

"Choose, human. Death, or more good fortune than you dreamed. Fight me for your future."

Richard's light headache had disappeared in the crisp cool air, but his bad mood had persisted. His perverse attitude and the irony of the situation caused him to laugh.

"Great rewards or death," he said. "And who are you to offer either one?" He had not pulled his blade, though he felt in the beating of his heart the thud of anticipation.

"If you need a name for your adversary, call me Glencarole."

"That's your name?" For an elven name it rolled strangely on the ear.

"I will answer to it," the elf replied. "Now chose your destiny. Know also that with yours runs Tal-Qazar's."

"Big talk from one elf," Richard scoffed. "If you wanted a fight, you chose the wrong way to start one."

The elf stared at him, eyes wide in surprise. "Speak plainer, *Lord* Richard Endier."

"You found me on a morning when I'm primed for a fight," Richard said. "A simple challenge would have been enough, but you've given yourself too much importance. *You* decide *my* destiny? I laugh at the thought. To fight you now would be to accept your claims, and I don't. You're nothing to me, or my future. I'll give you all the notice you deserve and ignore you."

"Such arrogance in a human is disgusting."

"And so much self-importance in a lone elf is laughable."

"Then both you and Tal-Qazar will die!"

"You're going to kill the awnshegh?" Richard scoffed. "All alone?"

"Any time I choose," the elf replied.

Richard started to grin and then bit back his smile. The elf might be able to do it, he reasoned. Glencarole's ability to change his shape could give him a distinct advantage in a fight with the awnshegh.

"Then why don't you? Tal-Qazar hates elves and kills every one he can find. Why draw me into it? I've never harmed an elf, in fact I have saved three from the goblin patrols." Richard paused when he realized his remark could be mistaken for an attempt at appeasement.

"But don't take that to mean I'm a friend of yours."

"Your friendship is not what I seek," Glencarole sneered. "You are here and you have a quick wit." The elf's face lightened with laughter and his eyes sparkled. "My people will laugh for a millennium at the tale of Tal-Qazar waiting by the magic grass house."

As bright as the elf's joy had been, it was fleeting. His face turned stiff and haughty again.

"It happens that your desires and mine travel the same path for a time. If you best me in battle, I will give you the secret that will hold the awnshegh at bay. If you have sufficient wit, you can settle this land in peace, without trouble from him."

"Why?"

"It would serve my purpose to see him live for a time, chewing always on his rage that he could not destroy you or drive you off this land. He deserves more than just death for the suffering he has caused my people over the centuries. Later, he will die at my hands, but I can wait, to enjoy his frustrations."

Richard gazed at the slender demihuman who faced him. The elf's first haughty statements had seemed impossible, but the more they talked, the less ridiculous he seemed. Glencarole sounded as proud as he had when Richard and Werberan had first met him, but a slight inflection in his voice had the ring of truth. The elf believed what he said, he took his abilities for granted and had no need to boast. Still, if they could be allies against the awnshegh, why should they fight?

"Why not just tell me what to do? If I can manage it, you'll have your revenge. Why would you want to kill me if I could be your instrument? Not that I see any reason to believe in this alliance. I'm not backing away from a fight, but your reasoning has to make sense to me."

"I've seen your wit at work and it will serve. You must fight me to prove your strength. I will not give my secrets to a weakling. If you fail, another human will take your place, one who may prove stronger than Lord Richard Endier."

Richard realized Glencarole had used his name and the title the settlers had given for the second time. The first had not quite registered, but the repetition did— along with the implications.

"You have a talent for spying as well?"

"Nothing passes in this land that I do not know. Now, decide human, do you fight, or die without raising your blade?"

Richard remained in the saddle, staring down at the elf. A secret that would hold off the awnshegh and free his people from danger was worth more than gold. Perhaps even worth a life. Was he willing to risk his life fighting the elf? But didn't he risk it every day, waiting for Tal-Qazar and his spider-riders to attack the settlement?

"We fight," Richard said. He dismounted and removed the heavy cloak he had worn that morning. The wind had remained sharp and he felt its bite as he slung the garment over his saddle.

He had not been concerned about turning his back on the elf, and when he led the horse to a stretch of dried grass surrounded by a cluster of bushes, Glencarole sat on the boulder, waiting. Theirs would be a contest with honor, not the desperate no-holds-barred battle of enemies.

As Richard walked back to meet the elf, he admitted to himself a slight concern. In Aerele, where he had taken his military training, he had been praised for his ability with his blade, but he had never fought an elf and had no idea of the other's skill or tactics.

When Richard approached, the elf stood, drew his blade, and they circled. They touched the tips of their weapons lightly as all fighters do when they want to test their adversary's eye and response.

"It's your challenge," Richard said when he tired of the preliminaries.

Glencarole smiled and his face lit with an almost innocent enjoyment. He pressed the attack and Richard was faced with a strength and speed he had not expected from so slender a creature.

A shower of sunbeams reflected off the two swords as the tip of Glencarole's sword parried Richard's, circling, striking, deflecting the human's weapon. Thrown off his stride by the elf's tactics, Richard gave ground. He took a quick step to the left and distanced himself from Glencarole by putting a thorn bush between them. Over the top of the thorns he could see the elf's face, his mouth curled in a sneer, but Richard was not concerned about the elf's opinion of him.

He was more interested in the wrist and arm movements of his opponent. His mind was panting with the effort to translate what he had seen into muscular movement, but when it finished, he stopped circling the bush and stepped out into the open again.

A closed, almost hopeless expression darkened the elf's face as he moved in for his second attack. He used less skill, as if he had taken Richard's measure and decided no more was needed. When his blade struck the human's weapon, the elf discovered his error. Richard gave a firm twist of his wrist as the two blades came together and succeeded in a ploy that the elf had found unsuccessful. Richard had caught Glencarole's quillon, and while he had not disarmed the elf, Glencarole was forced to step back while he took a firmer grip.

The elf's expression lightened, his eyes sparkled and a small smile escaped his tight mouth.

"You learn quickly, human."

"An advantage of not being all-knowing," Richard replied, moving in, the point of his blade circling slowly.

The elf's eyes danced, his feet moved in a smooth rhythm out of time with his flashing blade. He pressed until Richard backed up, tripped on a branch, and fell. With a dancing step and a leap, Glencarole was at Richard's side, but he had made the mistake of checking the stony ground where he intended to land. He was quick, a flick of gaze nearly as rapid as the strike of a serpent, but Richard had seen it, understood the implication and was ready for him.

The human rolled and kicked. The elf's feet touched the ground to be tangled in Richard's swinging legs. Glencarole fell toward a thorn bush, twisting and throwing himself sideways to miss the hard, sharp points. By the time the elf had scrambled to his knees, Richard was on his feet, sword in hand, waiting.

Glencarole rose beneath the point of Richard's blade, his gaze darting from the human's face to his weapon and back.

"Chivalry from a human?" he asked as he rose to his feet.

"Not chivalry, I'm at a disadvantage," Richard replied. "How can I kill the one who holds the secret to my success?" Richard still did not quite believe the elf could ensure his success, yet the longer he was in

Glencarole's company, the more he respected his opponent. "And once I prove I can destroy you, how can you kill me if my strength suffices for your plan?"

"And you judge the fight to be over?" Glencarole sneered, but Richard thought he caught a glimmer of hesitation.

"That's up to you. What do you consider victory? Perhaps we should set rules before we continue."

Richard had hardly finished the question when a goblin spear whiffed through the air and clanged off his upraised blade, missing his face by inches. Less than a hundred feet away, a group of six spider-riders were emerging out of the brush.

"We have other problems," the elf said. His last words were shouted as Richard turned away, racing for his horse and his bow. Another spear hit the ground a few feet in front of him, but he was away between the bushes and had reached Ikki. He grabbed the bow and his quiver from the saddle and slapped the horse on the rump, sending it back toward the stockade.

He was safer on foot where he could use the brush for cover. As the horse galloped away he slipped from bush to bush, working his way north for a hundred yards. As he suspected, the spider-riders thought he would have moved south or directly east, after the horse. Three passed to the south, two checked the ground for his trail, while the third watched for him to rise above the thorny bushes.

In the distance he heard a cry of pain from a goblin voice and the ear-piercing wail of a giant spider. The elf was keeping some of the enemy occupied.

The goblin rider nearest him spotted a dislodged stone and was just turning its head toward Richard when the human let fly his first arrow. The goblin gurgled as the point entered its chest. Richard's second missile was already on the way. His aim had been faulty and the second goblin, the one watching for him in the distance, screamed as the shaft went through its right arm. The goblin's scream startled its mount, which reared on its four rear legs and unseated its rider.

"Time to move," Richard murmured to himself and scuttled east, toward the Spiderfell, keeping low. Twice he used his hands to help balance his scuttling crawl as he took a second direction unexpected by the spider-riders.

When he reached a thorn bush that was slightly taller than the rest, he risked its thin camouflage to raise his head and look around. A quarter of a mile to the south he saw two spider-riders racing through the brush as if they were after a quarry. Closer, the single uninjured goblin had decided to give up the chase and return to the forest, urging its mount on by hitting it on the cephalothorax with the shaft of its spear.

Thinking the fight was over, Richard carried his bow in his right hand. He kept low, easing through the underbrush as he turned southwest toward the stockade.

He paused as the goblin with the wounded right arm passed him, clicking softly, calling to its spider mount.

Richard pulled his sword and stayed low until the goblin had passed him. Then he jumped, swinging the blade and stabbing with the force of his leap. The humanoid's hardened leather and metal helmet clanged as the severed head hit the ground.

So much for the goblins in the immediate vicinity, Richard thought, and was sheathing his sword when he discovered his mistake.

The injured goblin had been calling to its mount, and the creature had been on its way to join its rider. It loomed up in front of Richard, and behind the first, a second arachnid was following.

ANUIRE

twenty-three

Richard drew his sword and resisted the urge to back away. One step in the wrong direction and the spiders—the first just over three feet tall and five feet long—would leap. The second stood nearly a foot taller than the first, and was longer, but it was blocked by the row of thorn bushes on each side and its companion in the lead.

At close range the huge spiders were more frightening than when seen from a distance. Sparse, coarse hair covered their bodies and legs, six of which were shorter and stouter than normal for the species; a concession to strength, Richard decided. Extending eighteen inches beyond the long-fanged mouth, bone mandibles with serrated edges worked back and forth, shredding air in anticipation of a victim.

The first spider gave a shrill, ear-piercing cry and rose on its four rear legs, scuttling forward with no loss of speed. Its forelegs, six feet long and ending in clawed pedipalps, struck at Richard as it charged. Richard leapt to the side. Too close to a thorn bush, he felt the piercing of the little needles as he hacked at the spider's right leg. The blade skittered down the hard exoskeleton, but he caught the joint of the pedipalp and the monster hissed as it drew back, the eight inch claw dangling uselessly.

The spider raised its head and screamed. The sound seared Richard's hearing though the pitch was too high for him to hear it clearly. Behind the first, the second spider reared, plunged to the right, backed up, and tried the left, but it was trapped by the impenetrable clumps of thorn bushes.

Richard retreated slowly, hoping for an avenue of escape, but the first spider leapt forward, grabbing him with its uninjured left foreleg. The clawed pedipalp dug into the human's back as the creature swept him toward the sawing mandibles. Unable to withstand the strength of the spider, Richard hacked ineffectively with his sword in his right hand. In his left he still held his bow, and he jabbed at the spider with the end of it. The sawing mandibles caught him in the sides and he felt a rib on his left side crack as he thrust with the bow, knowing it would be his last attempt. But he had been successful. The point of the weapon entered one of the spider's many eyes.

The pain caused the monster to lose its grip with the mandibles, and Richard felt the ground under his staggering legs as the spider raised it's head again for another scream. With a desperate swing, Richard hacked through the tough hide of the neck. His waning strength would not have been sufficient to inflict a fatal injury, but the spider, crazed with pain, jerked him toward the mandibles again and the strength of its own left foreleg drove the sword through its neck.

Richard writhed in agony as the serrated mandibles sawed at him one more time before the monster released its hold and collapsed. The human fell, gasping with pain. He half crawled, half scrambled under a thorn bush while the second spider, sensing the death of its companion, climbed over the twitching body.

Richard wriggled on his stomach as he retreated farther back under the bushes. He knew his shelter was only a temporary respite. The spiders disliked the thorn bushes, but when pressed by their riders they had plowed through them, and the remaining spider was unlikely to give up the chase.

When he found an opening in the center of the clump he rose shakily to his feet. Thrusting the point of his sword in the ground, he pulled an arrow and nocked it. The second spider was less than ten feet away, separated from him by three thick bushes. When he stood, the monster arachnid rose on its hind legs in a challenge.

His fighting strength nearly gone, Richard targeted the spider's open mouth. His hopes sank as the weak shot left the bow, but his aim had been true and the missile entered the creature's mouth, going well down its throat. The spider's roar changed pitch. It shut it's mouth and screamed again as the shaft broke.

Richard fitted another arrow to the bow, hoping for a shot in the eye, the only other part of the spider's body that was vulnerable to his decreasing strength. He shifted his aim as the monster twisted its head back and forth too quickly for him to be sure of his shot.

Then, from above his head, Richard heard the rush of wings. He looked up to see a large eagle swoop down and hover. The bird seemed to block out the sunlight with a wingspan of more than fifteen feet. It hung in the air, poised just over the spider. In its claws it held a boulder two feet in diameter. It dropped the boulder on the spider's head and Richard saw the arachnid's skull split. Brains and blood showered out before the spider collapsed.

When he looked up, Richard saw the eagle winging its way back toward the Spiderfell. He raised his right hand in salute and slipped the second arrow back into the quiver. He watched as the bird swooped low over some distant bushes. Too low, he realized, as a spear flew up and caught the bird in the left wing. The giant eagle screamed in pain and defiance and was falling from the sky when it succeeded in pulling the shaft free. Richard had already started working his way in the direction of the falling bird when it regained altitude, staggering through the air as it's right wing out-flew the injured limb. Soon it was out of reach of the goblins, and on its way to the Spiderfell. Slowly, because every movement hurt, Richard sheathed his sword and worked his way out of the clump of thorn bushes.

* * * * *

Three hours later Richard was sitting on his bed while Werberan used a healing spell on his broken ribs.

"I didn't worry about getting back safely," he told the priest-knight. "Glencarole would not have left me if I was in any danger."

"Then, in your opinion, you won the fight?" Werberan asked.

"The object was not to win, it was not to lose," Richard said. "If Glencarole is to achieve his goal, and me mine, neither of us could kill the other."

The warrior-priest of Haelyn nodded.

"I just wish I knew if he's able to keep his promise. I'd hate to think I fought him for nothing." Richard had been making light of his genuine concern for the elf that had both endangered and saved his life. He gazed into Werberan's cool gray eyes and recognized a withholding of thought. Worry that the priest-knight might be keeping back information he needed, made him impatient.

"Anyone who joins our settlement owes it loyalty," he snapped. "If you know anything that would influence my decisions, I have a right to your knowledge."

"It isn't knowledge." Werberan spoke softly, thoughtfully. "It's concern for the elf. He may not be able to do what he promised."

"I have a right to know about him," Richard persisted. His future decisions might be based on the dependability of the elf. He was not asking out of curiosity, and he was determined not to be thwarted.

"No you don't," Werberan growled back. "You have too many conversations with Tal-Qazar to allow you to know." His expression softened slightly. "He might be able to pull information out of your mind, and if he did, you would endanger . . . Glencarole's purpose, and his life."

The priest-knight sighed.

"If I am correct in my thinking, he should be allowed to keep his secrets." Werberan stared off into the distance; his mouth formed a firm line. Then, with a sigh, he turned his attention to Richard again.

"If I'm right, he will never be your friend. Still, because of his hatred of Tal-Qazar, he will keep faith with you if he's able. If legend speaks true he has no need to lie about his abilities."

"I need to know more," Richard said, frustrated that the paladin was not sharing his knowledge.

"His tale is not mine to tell," Werberan said shortly, then turned away, leaving before Richard could press the issue.

* * * * *

For the next three days Richard rode guard patrol, frustrated by Werberan's refusal to divulge Glencarole's true identity and his own inability to find the elf. In his mind, Richard was sure he had won the fight, or at least proved himself strong enough to use the secret the elf promised, but he still did not have the knowledge to hold off the awnshegh.

On the third evening, when Richard returned to the stockade and entered the dining hall, he paused. Tannen Oesole from the Endier settlement had arrived with nine bedraggled and morose strangers. Richard's mind and face closed with his objection to newcomers. None of the three stockades could afford to take in more settlers until the next harvest. Too many mouths to feed could lead, in desperation, to hunting in the Spiderfell, which would endanger all their lives.

"Seems we're handy for river rescues," Tannen grinned, then explained the problem. The Mhorien river men had been sailing down the Maesil River from Shieldhaven, on their way to the City of Anuire. Their boat had been caught in a whirling eddy at the confluence of the Maesil and Tuor rivers. A log, swept down the Tuor by a storm in the mountains, was caught in the same eddy and had punched a hole in their craft.

"Stove in the side of the boat like it was an egg," griped a small, bearded man who seemed to be the leader.

"We would have taken them downstream to Moerel, but our boat is out of the water for repairs," Tannen explained, dropping the onus on Richard.

Several of the settlers were gathered around the tables in the dining hall, and they all nodded as if they saw no reason why the Mhoriens should not be helped.

"I need salt and more spices," Mother said, turning his small eyes on Richard.

"Ruinel says one of my people has a shop in Moerel," Stubby spoke up as he poked at a loose thread on his trousers. "The thorn bushes are hard on my pants."

"Endier has a long list of supplies," Tannen added. "That is, if you wouldn't mind bringing them up the river for us. We won't have our boat back in the water for a month or more."

"Then we go to town," Richard said, giving in. He disliked leaving, losing a chance to find Glencarole and settle the issue of the fight, but the elf had not shown himself. For three days Richard had felt like a fool as he tried to talk to rabbits, birds, and chipmunks, thinking each might be the elf in another shape.

The next morning, Richard, five members of the Rivervale stockade, and the eleven visitors rode down the river to Moerel. They arrived by late afternoon and said goodbye to the river men, who left in search of passage to Anuire City. Entiene had been loaded with lists and coins to shop for the settlers, Ruinel went to visit his family, and Hirge accompanied Tannen on his shopping expedition. Richard and Stubby went with Entiene and had just stepped into the street when a townsman, looking back over his shoulder, bumped into Richard.

"Watch where you're going," he snapped at Richard, more than willing to lay the blame on a bumpkin dressed in shabby farmer's clothing.

"You'd be well off to curb your tongue," Stubby retorted as he glared up at the townsman. The feisty little halfling suggestively put his hand on his sword hilt.

"You are addressing *Lord* Richard Endier—of the province of Endier," Entiene added, her eyes flashing.

"Let's forget it," Richard snapped. He was impatient to finish the shopping trip and return home, but the other two ignored him. The townsman, weaving a little and breathing the fumes of wine into their faces, looked scornfully at Richard.

"A lord, is it?" He laughed, and Entiene took a menacing step toward him, but Richard grabbed her arm and pulled her back. He hustled his companions up the street.

"Trouble will just delay us," he warned. A few yards away, a fashionably dressed stranger had stood listening, then hurried away as soon as the altercation was over.

After only a few steps they began to notice the unusual number of well-dressed men and women on the streets. In the first shop they entered they found the clerk in a state of excitement. Baron Naele Diem and his court were visiting the river city—one of the ruler's rare tours around his domain. Richard considered an attempt to see the baron and ask again for a patrol for the forts, but quickly decided against it.

To expedite the shopping chores, Richard, Entiene, and Stubby divided the long list and spent the afternoon accumulating a load of supplies in the back room of the inn. An hour after dark, Richard returned with his last purchases. He entered the main room with his bundles only to be met by four uniformed soldiers, wearing the insignia of the Baron's personal guard.

"You're to come with us," said the captain.

Richard knew there was no point in questioning the soldiers so he nodded, left his bundles in the care of the wide-eyed innkeeper, and allowed the guard to escort him to the home of Chamis Goerent, Ruinel's father and the mayor of Moerel.

The mayor's house stood well away from the business district and was unusually opulent for such a small city. Richard was led into the main hall, which was filled with tables and chairs, and crowded with the most important residents of Moerel and twenty or more visitors. The room was stifling with the heat of so many people, candles, and a fire in the large hearth.

At one end of the room the baron sat with Mayor Goerent at a table loaded with platters of food and flasks of wine. The baron's face was flushed with the combination of heat, wine, and the unaccustomed rigors of travel. His bottom lip protruded in a pout.

"You again," Baron Diem said, as if he had been unjustly injured. Sitting beside the baron was Master Seone Hamnet, the tall, thin man with the mocking face who always seemed to be at the baron's side.

Master Hamnet gave a soft laugh and said to Richard, "After troops to guard the shacks you've put up in the Spiderfell?"

"I beg your pardon, my lord, but I did not seek this audience," Richard replied calmly. He waited while the baron's gaze darted around the room as if he could find in the faces of the interested onlookers the reason for Richard's presence.

"He's the one calling himself lord of a new province," Master Hamnet prompted the ruler of Diemed.

Before Richard could answer, Ruinel, sitting at a lower table, rose and stepped up beside him.

"I beg pardon, my lord baron, father, Master Hamnet, but he has never done so," Ruinel's voice rang out across the room. "It was the decision of the settlers in the three forts to proclaim him lord of a new province. We have chosen him our leader in a venture that will extend the borders of our land." Ruinel bowed to the baron. "Under our gracious ruler, of course."

Knowing Ruinel well, Richard heard the slight inflection on the word, "gracious" and hoped no one in the room caught it. The compliment was begrudged.

Master Hamnet's face darkened. The baron glanced at him uneasily and fingered his glass.

He's afraid of the Master Trader, Richard thought, half shocked by the idea. The Trader's Guild was jealous of every ruler's control of any trade route, and if the province of Endier succeeded, Diemed would double its claim on the eastern bank of the Maesil River.

The baron took another swallow from his wine goblet and glared at Richard.

"I have given no permission to develop another province," he said. "There will be no province of Endier."

"I beg pardon, Lord Baron, but it doubtless slipped your mind, though your good chamberlain will remember, as he did before."

Baron Diem turned to the chamberlain who nodded, his agreement with Richard as reluctant as it had been in Aerele when Richard had asked for troops.

"He accosted you on the street, my lord, when you were beset by citizens."

"An unfair advantage," the baron objected, with an uneasy eye on Master Hamnet. "When I am importuned by citizens, I get confused, I hardly know what I am saying."

"Nevertheless, Endier exists because you did give us permission," Richard replied, his voice calm but hard. "All the settlers are agreed that we wish to remain loyal to Diemed."

Master Hamnet's face darkened again and the baron shifted under the trader's threatening stare.

"I don't want your loyalty!" The baron shouted at Richard, his face paling with fear while his cheeks were red with rage. "Go back to your hovels and leave me be. I don't want to hear your name again."

"Endier exists," Richard said again. He had not shouted but his determination rang across the hall. "If you lay no claim on the land then we will hold it for ourselves."

"Hold it if you can . . . if the Spider lets you," the baron said. "Build your shacks and live in them with your rag-tag friends. Just be gone and leave me alone!"

Richard bowed, turned on his heel and marched out of the hall without another word. His head reeled with the implications of the baron's last words. He was in the street again before he realized Ruinel had followed him. They had covered two hundred yards more before Ruinel spoke.

"How about a province of Goerent?" he asked.

As they passed beneath a street lamp, Richard glanced at Ruinel, whose face was aglow with a happy excitement Richard found puzzling.

"What are you talking about?"

"The *Province* of Goerent in the *Land* of Endier." The baron said we could keep what we took, so you take the land and I'll settle for a province within it."

"He'll never allow it," Richard said, fighting to keep his hope and ambition under control. "He was drunk and afraid of the master trader. Make no mistake, if we can hold the land and beat back the Spider King, we'll fight the baron sooner or later."

But he felt as if he would burst with excitement. Baron Naele Diem had disclaimed any desire for the land north of the Lanwin freestead. He had said they could keep what they could hold, and he had said it in front of many witnesses.

If they could keep it; if Glencarole did have the secret of holding off Tal-Qazar. . . .

As they walked along the dark street, Richard felt a little dizzy, as if he stood on some great height. He bubbled with the excitement of the rarefied air and warned himself to take care with his future steps. Great heights could lead to great falls.

ANUIRE

TWenTY-FOUR

When the settlers returned, sailing slowly up the
Maesil River, they put in to shore at Farmstead. While
the others rested, Richard and Tannen left the boat
and spent the afternoon with Antiet, the leader of the
third settlement.

"Better news than we'd hoped for," Antiet said as
they sat around a rough-hewn table. "It's no surprise
to us that we'd have to tame the land ourselves, but
we expected the baron to claim it once it was safe."

"He will," Richard warned the farmer. His determination to create the land of Endier had grown stronger
with every hour that passed, but he considered it his
duty to point out all the dangers and pitfalls.

"If we can hold off the Spider King, we can hold
back the baron," Tannen said with a confidence
Richard was not certain he shared.

"Aye, but we'll be the ones facing the brunt of
Naele Diem's attack if he doesn't keep his word,"

Antiet reminded his fellow leader. "Best we put most of the winter into preparing for a battle with one or the other . . . maybe both."

"Right," Richard said. "When we are no longer threatened by the awnshegh, we'll need to reinforce your numbers. I'd like to believe the land is ours, but I cannot trust a promise made in a drunken rage."

He and Tannen inspected the southern fort. Hassan had helped them to construct catapults and ballistae, and their walls bristled with heavy defenses. Like Rivervale, they were roofing their single building with baked tiles, and mud-daubing their walls, protection against fire arrows. They had sacrificed comfort for defense and would soon be ready to hold off all comers. Since they were farmers, not trained hunters or fighters, they had little skill with bows, but practicing under the experienced eye of Werberan, they were improving steadily.

The next morning at dawn the boat continued up the river to Endier, unloaded supplies at the northern fort and stayed the night. The following morning the settlers of Rivervale sailed back down the stream to their own stockade.

Early in the summer, when Richard had learned of Hassan Aghahn's expertise with defensive weapons, he had named the Khinasi his second in command. Richard returned to Rivervale to find the small, bearded man standing guard on the walls, absently curling his beard and hair until both were divided into long curls. Paeghen was keeping watch on the northeast corner of the palisade.

"You may have arrived just in time," Hassan said when Richard joined him.

"Have you had any trouble?" Richard gazed out over the cleared land. At midafternoon on a clear, reasonably warm day, the horses should have been grazing on the remaining grass, but they were all in their stalls. More than half the settlers were scurrying to bring the supplies up from the boat. They were dropping their loads just inside the doors of the two buildings. The rest were at work splitting timbers into rough spear lengths, sharpening points and notching them for the ballistae.

Mother was hardening the points of ballista shafts in the three fires he tended. Oil jars hung over the flames, heated and ready to be used in the catapults.

"Yesterday Gaelin and Anders reported a massing of goblins just inside the eaves of the Spiderfell." Hassan continued to curl his beard with his fingers. "Early this morning I rode out to take a look. That haze is the smoke from their campfires. There are hundreds, maybe thousands of goblins out there."

"How did you get away from them?"

"They just stared at me, they didn't even throw a spear."

"Then they're waiting for Tal-Qazar," Richard muttered. "We knew he'd come sooner or later."

"We should give some thought to protecting the path to the river," Hassan suggested. It was obvious that the Khinasi did not believe they would be able to hold off the awnshegh's forces. Richard also had his doubts.

"We'll put Entiene and Paeghen on the southwest corner," Richard said. The women were experts with their bows and their voices, with the naturally higher pitch of females, could carry further through the noise of battle if they needed to shout an alarm. "Anders and Borg can take the—"

"Farmstead!" Paeghen shouted, pointing south. Richard was just in time to see a flash and a smoking arc as it sailed out over the river.

"What was that?" Richard asked. In the late morning sunlight he should not have been able to see a fire arrow three miles away.

"The priestess Daire put a spell on a pair of fire shafts to be shot from the ballistae, to signal an attack," Hassan said. "We should keep a watch to the north as well."

Richard gazed to the south and back toward the east again, torn between ordering his people south to help defend Farmstead and keeping them in Rivervale to defend their own fort. When the farmers asked for permission to set up their own settlement, Richard had warned them they could expect little or no help from Rivervale if they were attacked.

They had made the choice and accepted the risk, but they were farmers. The trained fighters were all at Rivervale and Endier. He was still wrestling with his decision when the choice was taken from him. The dark line of the Spiderfell had begun to spread and approach. The awnshegh's army was marching toward Rivervale.

"Did you finish the trenches?" Richard asked, suddenly remembering their first line of defense.

"By the goodness of Avani!" Hassan slapped his head with his hand. "I had forgotten. The trenches are dug and filled with dry grass and wood, but we still need to spread the oil."

While Hassan shouted for Gaelin, Caern, Anders and Ruinel, Richard scrambled halfway down a ladder and jumped to the ground. He sprinted toward the smokehouse, where the oil jugs had been stored, and grabbed two. The four fastest runners in the settlement joined him and they all raced through the small eastern gate.

From the walls of the palisade, the approach of the goblins and spider-riders had been visible, but once on the ground, a low hill prevented Richard and the four who raced to pour oil on the dry grass from knowing how close the enemy had approached.

Ignoring the first trenches, Richard ran for the farthest from the fort. He threaded his way through the narrow passages between the trenches, working his way north. At the extreme end of the first defensive line he unstopped one large oil jug and ran along the inside of the trench, spilling the oil as he went. The jug was nearly empty when he reached the first break and sprinted across it to spill the rest in the next trench in line. When the first jug was empty he dropped it and opened the next. He was more sparing of the second jug as he ran down the line. He crossed the second break and was a hundred yards from the end of the line when four spider-riders came in sight over the low hill and bounded toward him.

Every sense warned him to drop the oil jug and sprint for the fort, but the ballistae were trained on specific points along the trenches. Their flaming shafts would set the dry grass afire, but the oil would help spread the flames faster. He had not yet reached the center of the southern section of the outermost trench.

Forty feet away, Gaelin was shouting to him, but fear and fatigue had sent the blood pounding in Richard's ears until he could not understand the words.

He gritted his teeth and dropped his eyes to the path in front of him, refusing to acknowledge the approach of the spider-riders. He held the large jug in both hands as he ran down the line of the trench until he was sure he had at least passed the area targeted by the ballistae. With a heave he threw the thin-walled jug onto the dry grass and grunted in disgust as it bounced, rolled out of the trench and broke against a stone.

He whirled and started back toward the break in the second space when a giant spider leapt across the first trench and landed in his path. He heard a scrambling sound and a second appeared less than ten feet behind him. The spider mount was just turning toward him when an arrow pierced one of its eyes. The giant arachnid gave a scream of pain and rose on its rear legs, unbalanced itself, and fell over backward onto its goblin rider. Richard pulled his sword and charged the first rider, hacking at the foreleg of its mount and when the spider drew back, the head of the goblin fell from its shoulders.

Surprise stopped Richard for a moment before he realized a ballista spear had taken off the humanoid's head and sailed on beyond. He lifted his hand, signaling his thanks, though so accurate a shot had to have been the result of half hope, half accident.

Before the huge spider mount sorted out its confusion over being attacked and the jerking of the reigns still gripped by the headless body of the dead goblin rider, Richard had passed it and was sprinting back toward the fort. Out of the corner of his eye he saw Gaelin shoot another arrow, but he did not stop to see if the missile found its mark, or even what his cousin's target had been.

"Follow me and let's get inside," he called to the others. A glance over his shoulder warned him they had no time to lose. The spider-riders formed the vanguard of the attack, but they were not alone. The ground was black with smaller spiders, crawling and jumping as they kept pace with their larger companions. Farther back, between the crawling mass of arachnids came goblins, and towering above them were trolls.

The spider-riders were gaining on the sprinting humans when they reached the door of the stockade and slipped through. Richard paused, holding the gate slightly ajar and looking back until the black mass of crawling spiders was less than a hundred feet from the door. He closed it and climbed the ladder to the catwalk, his mind and will outdistancing his body

as he slowed, a concession to a stitch in his side. He
pressed his hand against it as he joined Hassan. The
Khinasi gave him a mournful look.

"I wanted to fire the last trench, but I was afraid
you'd be caught in the flames," he said, apologizing
for not helping when Richard was in danger.

"No," Richard shook his head, still a bit too breathless to say all he wanted. "We wait as long as we can
before we set the trenches aflame, but we need to oil
the walls now."

"Oil the . . . ?" Hassan stared uncomprehending for
a moment and then understood. Because Richard was
still breathless and gasping, the Khinasi shouted
orders down the line. The defenders grabbed the oil
jugs and sloshed oil down the adobe-coated outer
sides of the stockade. Moments later, Caern was
ready with a torch.

"Hold until I give the word," Richard shouted,
stopping the lord's son from setting the blaze too
soon.

Around the walls the defenders stood waiting.
Richard felt his skin crawl as the spider-riders
slowed. From behind and around them, flowing over
the ground like some slow and evil flood, a black
mass undulated over the ground as hundreds, thousands, millions of smaller spiders moved toward the
stockade.

He looked over the faces of his people to see how
they were being affected by the mass of crawling spiders, and he realized that two of them were missing.

"Where are Werberan and Daire?" he asked
Hassan.

Beside Richard, Hassan shivered and plucked at
his curling beard, tugging the curls into disarray.
Richard realized the Khinasi, so efficient in building
war machines and complicated lifting equipment,
had no head in a fight. He stared at Richard with

blank eyes for a moment before comprehension cleared his eyes.

"They went out behind you, but I didn't see them after that."

Richard knew the two clerics had rings of invisibility, and he hoped they would be safe. He called out to them but no one answered. The scrape of heavy leather boots on the catwalk was the only sound, until the Vos, unable to remain silent, raised his head and bellowed to his god.

"Kriesha, give me an enemy I can fight," Pyotr called, his voice shaking with fear and frustration. "No honorable warrior should fall to those things."

Gaelin's nerve broke. He gave a sob and grabbed for a torch, ready to fire the oil-soaked adobe wall.

"No!" Richard shouted at his cousin, but he knew he would not be in time to stop him. Fortunately, Mother, who had just climbed to the catwalk, grabbed the torch from Gaelin's hand.

"Not yet," Richard called, resisting his own panic. Like the Vos he was willing to meet an enemy his own size, but the thought of being covered by a mass of spiders had set him to trembling also. Still, for his plan to be effective they must give no hint of it until the greater portion of Tal-Qazar's army had gathered around the fort.

Behind the flowing black mass, the spider-riders, and the goblins and trolls on foot were closing in. Many were within the ring of trenches, but Richard gripped the bow in his hand as he forced himself to wait.

The first of the spider-riders began to howl and pat their mounts who set up an eerie cry of their own. The sound hit the ears of the defenders like sonic shafts. Mother, with his orog hearing, shook his head and slapped at his ears as if beating off some pesky insect.

Along with the terrible noise came a shower of goblin spears, almost a relief after the wait.

"Bows!" Richard shouted, knowing they had to make some response or the goblins might realize they were being led into a trap.

All along the walls, the settlers shot out into the massing goblins. The attackers were so closely packed that nearly every arrow found a target, but the numbers seemed hardly diminished. There were not enough arrows in the settlers' arsenal to kill more than a quarter of the approaching force.

"Space your shots," Richard called. "Don't use all your arrows!"

"We need to do more," Hassan said, and Richard knew the Khinasi was right. The goblins knew the walls were defended with heavier weapons.

"Let go the north, center, and south catapults," Richard ordered.

"They're coming up the walls!" Caern shouted, his voice trembling.

Richard risked thrusting his head out through one of the arrow slots. The black mass was creeping up. Some of the smaller spiders were nearly at the top of the oil-soaked adobe.

"Now we find out if our walls are as fireproof as we hoped," he muttered to Hassan. He raised his head. "Fire the walls!"

Out in the fields, more than two thousand goblins, spider-riders, and trolls were advancing. A few had passed the closest trench. The smoke roiling up from the flames licking at the adobe walls prevented the settlers from seeing much of the field. There was no point in waiting longer to spring their trap.

"Light the fire shafts and let go the ballistae!" Richard shouted. "Oil catapults—let go!"

Stubby, in charge of the smaller oil catapults that sat on the ground inside the stockade, ran from one to the other, hacking at the hide thongs. Thin-walled jugs of oil flew up, arcing over the walls and out onto the massed army.

Hassan had put many hours into individually blocking each of the four shafts of the ballistae so, when fired, each missile would take a slightly different elevation.

Each shaft found its mark. Some plowed their way through spider-riders, goblins, and trolls as the burning missiles hit the trenches and set them ablaze. Richard blinked and rubbed his eyes as he peered through the smoke rising from the oil-soaked walls and the burning spiders that had been climbing them. Out on the field he saw the fire, racing along the trail of the oil he and the others had spilled on the dry grass that would ignite the dry wood underneath.

Hundreds of goblins and trolls, and many of the last of the smaller spiders were standing directly in the path of the racing fire, unable to escape because of the crowds around them. The nine foot tall trolls, whose dry, leathery skins were highly flammable, were the first to catch fire. They staggered among the goblins like huge burning torches. The oil jugs had broken against goblins and spider mounts, and on the ground where the oil had spilled, the fire spread with a deadly vengeance.

The light wind, blowing from the west, carried away most of the stench of burning flesh, but the defenders on the walls nearly gagged at the smell. Not even a gale could have lessened the horror of dying screams.

"Not all places burn," Mother said, shaking his head. Usually concerned with the cooking and mending, he had not taken part in the plans for the defense of the settlement. His interest, such as it was, had totally disappeared when he learned there was to be no hand-to-hand combat and he could not use his spiked bolos. He had no intention of throwing them off the walls where some goblin might carry them off.

"We wanted passages through the fire," Richard explained, pointing to Gaelin, who was re-targeting one of the four-shaft ballistae. "If they have no way through the fire, they'll wait until it dies out. If they can get through, they'll be enraged enough to use the clear passages in limited numbers—numbers we can manage."

"It is good, I think," Mother said. "I will have a use for my arrows." He patted the bundle of shafts he had brought up to the catwalk. The half-orog's thick arms could pull a bow Richard's human strength could not even string. Mother was not an expert with the weapon but he could hardly miss a target in the packed horde on the field.

"Get them ready," Richard said, peering through the smoke.

More than thirty spider-riders and at least fifty of the goblin infantry had passed the inner trench before the fires had started. At first they were confused, sidling about, fearing they too would be caught in the flames. It had not taken them long to realize they were beyond the blazing defenses. The deaths of their companions had enraged them beyond sanity.

With screams and shouts they charged the walls.

TWENTY-FIVE

Richard picked up his bow, then spared a last look around the palisade catwalk to check the positions of its defenders. They lacked the numbers to defend the wall that faced the river so they had decided to leave it unmanned. If the Spider's forces attempted to surround the fort, the battle would soon be lost, and the settlers would have to evacuate the fort before they were cut off. Borg and Paeghen stood waiting on the northwest and southwest corners. On the north and south walls, Anders and Entiene, the youngest members of the settlement, also watched. The four would not take part in the first battle, but would deter any forays the goblins might make on the sides of the fort, and could give the alarm if any major force circled around to the river.

The other sixteen defenders were spread evenly along the east wall. The best bowmen were placed between the four catapults and the four ballistae. The other eight manned the heavy missile throwers.

Screaming and roaring their challenges, half the fifty-goblin infantry rushed toward the walls. The other half had the wit to take advantage of the fires behind them and had stopped to pull up the dry grass, wrap it around their arrow tips and light them from the defensive fires. A flaming arrow flew over Richard's head and he glanced over his shoulder to see where it landed.

"Your stew might burn," he shouted to Mother. The fire arrow had struck Mother's banked cookfire and set it ablaze again. The half-orog looked around, growled, and sent an arrow flying toward the offender. He struck the goblin in the arm, not a fatal blow, but the force of the arrow knocked the human-oid back into the fiery trench.

"Burn *my* stew," Mother muttered, nocking another arrow.

More fire arrows arced over the walls, but Richard was busy finding targets among the spider-riders. He missed with his first arrow because the huge arachnid mount sidled. His next two shots dropped two spi-der-riders, but he had to draw back to blink his eyes, allowing his tears to wash away the smoke that rose from the burning, dying spiders at the base of the walls.

As he rubbed his stinging eyes, a stray arrow, obvi-ously misdirected, dropped down from the sky and nicked his left hand. Though it barely cut the skin, it clipped one of the veins on the back of his hand. Mother paused, saw the bleeding and whipped out a strip of clean cloth.

"It's not bad," Richard objected, but Mother grabbed his hand and started wrapping a tight ban-dage around it.

"Too much blood," Mother announced. "You'll be no good if it all leaks out."

In the seconds it took for Mother to complete the rough and ready bandage, Richard had been looking south, down the line of defenders. A dark column of smoke in the distance caught his attention. It was not a part of the fiery defenses of Rivervale, it was too large and too far away. His heart sank. It could only be the southern fort, Farmstead, burning. He wondered if any of the farmers had lived through their battle.

But trapped as they were in their own fort, he could do nothing for the settlers in the south. He gazed down the line of his own fighters. A few feet away, Pyotr had been loading a catapult scoop with heavy rocks. As Mother wrapped the cloth around Richard's hand, the big Vos turned the crank with amazing speed and stood with one hand on the release nut. He raised the other to the sky.

"Behold, great Kriesha, the number that die under your servant's hand!"

Fascinated, Richard watched the stones fly from the catapult. The six stones all found targets. Four struck a group of spider-riders charging through a gap in the flames. Two crushed the skulls of their riders' mounts.

Perhaps the Ice Lady *was* assisting the Vos. Richard cast an uneasy glance toward the afternoon sky.

"Best that if you can," Pyotr shouted to Droene, who was sighting a ballista a short distance away.

"With Avani's help I will," the youngest of the Endiers shouted back.

"Not a bad wound, you can fight," the half-orog said as he tied the bandage and picked up his bow. His combination of solicitous care for the settlers and his orog pragmatism caused Richard to smile.

"Sarimie assist me!" Torele, one of the three who had arrived with Brosen, but had stayed in Rivervale after the rebellion, stood between the right center catapult and the ballista next to it. His arrow found an easy target in the neck of a charging goblin.

"Is this a battle among the gods?" Mother asked. "I shall call on Haelyn." He missed his target and growled. "I shall call on another god."

Richard tested his hand, found it painful, but still strong enough to pull his bow and was reaching for another arrow when he caught a whiff of smoke blown by the western breeze. He looked around. The back and side walls inside the fort had been covered with adobe to prevent fire arrows from burning them, but one blazing missile had fallen among the cured wood the settlers were using to make furniture. Only a few pieces remained, but what had been left was blazing furiously. Since it had been left near a catwalk support, the entire walk was in danger.

Paeghen, seeing the trouble, had left her post and was drawing water from the well, carrying two dripping buckets as she raced for the fire. Entiene had moved to cover both their positions.

"Mother! Help Paeghen," Richard ordered. The half-orog drew a strong bow but was the least accurate of the defenders.

Leaving them to handle the fire, Richard shot two arrows, but he had lost his accuracy. His second arrow brought down a goblin, but not the one he had targeted. He was glaring at his wounded hand when Stubby, ducking under the left center catapult, came running down the catwalk.

"Werberan," he panted. "I heard his voice, but I couldn't see him. He wants us to open the gate."

"I thought Werberan and Daire had stayed outside," Richard grunted. "Stay up here and watch. Tell me when it's safe to open the gate." He hurried across the roof of the newest building and down the ladder. He waited impatiently while Stubby watched and then gave him the word.

How would he know when the paladin had entered, he wondered as he removed the bar and opened the small door a few inches. He didn't have to worry. He felt it pushed from the other side, cloth brushed his arm and another's strength, added to his own, helped him to close it. As he replaced the two heavy bars, the paladin appeared beside him. The priest-knight's clothing was ripped in several places and his armor showed bright streaks where weapons had scarred it.

"I thought you would have stayed invisible," Richard said.

"I was, but they came up around me so thick I was stuck several times by accident." Werberan looked beyond Richard to where Mother and Paeghen were battling the fire inside the fort.

"I wasted my time. My intention was to attack Tal-Qazar but I couldn't find him," Werberan explained, then he saw the smoke rising from the fire inside the fort. "I'll give them a hand," he said, trotting off.

Richard turned and quickly reached the ladder to the catwalk. Back at his chosen position, he looked up and down the walls. Mourde gripped his shoulder. Between his fingers protruded a goblin arrow. At the northeast corner, Caern Tier used the northern catapult to throw a volley of oil jars out into an open area where another group of trolls were massing for a charge. Beside him, Vaesil, a friend and companion of Torele, used his tinder box to set fire to a scrap of cloth tied around an arrow.

Gaelin freed the nut on his ballista and brought down two spider mounts. Their riders would have to fight on foot. Closer to Richard, Hirge was re-targeting his heavy weapon, but the single shaft he fired fell harmlessly into one of the fire trenches. He shook his head and reset his alignment. Wise, Richard thought. He had not wasted four shafts on an uncertain alignment.

Out in the recently tilled fields, the ground was black and smoking, but the grass had burned away, leaving well-defined concentric circles of blazing fires as the wood in the trenches burned. On the smoking ground lay hundreds of blackened bodies: huge spiders, goblins, a few orogs, and more than a hundred trolls. Some still burned. Others were just charred piles, twisted into grotesque shapes.

Richard and Hassan had been correct in their belief that the passages between the fires would draw the enraged survivors, but they were soon blocked by piles of their dead comrades. The catapults and ballistae, carefully targeted on the narrow isles, had killed many more than Richard had dared hope.

Beyond the fire trenches more than two hundred goblin infantry and less than fifty spider-riders seemed to waver, appearing and disappearing as the waves of heat from the trenches distorted clear sight. Richard had no idea how large a force Tal-Qazar might command, but not even the awnshegh could afford to lose so many fighters.

And where *was* the Spider King? Had he attacked Farmstead? Somehow Richard doubted it. He expected the awnshegh would be more interested in destroying Rivervale.

Screams and shouts from the western side of the fort drew his attention. He turned to see Paeghen climbing the ladder to the catwalk, calling her sister's name as she ascended. Anders was sprinting down the long western wall and Borg was moving west to cover both their positions. Werberan and Mother were scrambling up the ladder behind Paeghen. Entiene was no longer at her station.

Richard leapt from the catwalk to the roof of the first building. He risked dislodging the newly laid roof tiles as he raced along the roof of the building, onto the kitchen and dining wing. Paeghen, Mother, and Werberan had reached the walk, and were pelting the southern fields with arrows. When Richard leapt up on the catwalk he saw the reason. Four spider-riders were rapidly retreating. Two lay dead on the ground, but the others were out of range. With them was Tal-Qazar. He was dragging a thick strand of webbing, and entangled in it, Entiene struggled impotently.

Two arrows were buried in the awnshegh's cephalothorax, but neither seemed to slow him. Safely out of range, he looked back over his shoulder and roared at the defenders on the walls.

Paeghen, distraught over the loss of her sister, was trying to climb over the wall, held back by Mother and the priest-knight.

"He's got my sister," she sobbed, giving way in her grief when fear could not have broken her spirit.

"How did they get so close?" Richard demanded, blaming himself for overlooking some obvious omission in his plan of defense.

"They used those uprooted bushes, working their way up from the river," Werberan said, pointing to the discarded camouflage near the walls. The settlers had cleared away the foliage around the path to the river, but they had not bared the rocky ground near the southwestern corner of the fort.

"She could not look everywhere at once," Paeghen said, defending Entiene's lapse while pulling herself together with an effort. "We can't let him take her."

"We won't," Richard said, wondering what they could do. They had to try something. But even as he spoke, he saw a group of more than fifty spider-riders coming from the south, joining the awnshegh.

Paeghen saw them too and leaned against the wall, knowing they had no hope of rescuing her sister.

"They're falling back!" Droene shouted.

From the western wall, a cheer of victory went up from the defenders who did not know about Entiene.

The four settlers who stood staring after the retreating awnshegh could not join in the victory shout. The end of the battle, which freed the rest of Tal-Qazar's army to rally around him, had sealed Entiene's fate.

ANUIRE

twenty-six

When news of Entiene's loss passed through the
group they silently gathered on the western wall.
Everyone stared out over the blazing trenches, watching the retreat of the Spider King's army. The merry
young woman had been well-liked by all the settlers.

"There has to be something we can do." Droene, his
blue eyes dark with misery, looked to Richard.

"No," Paeghen, most closely concerned, answered
him. "The remainder of the monster's army has
drawn back and will defend him. "Entiene would not
want you to give up all your lives in a foolhardy
attempt to free her."

"We can defend the fort, but twenty would never
stand a chance in the open," Hassan said softly, his
voice heavy with regret.

"Not even twenty," Werberan said as he looked
around. "Mourde's wounds have to be attended to.
Goblins sometimes poison their arrows."

Six of the defenders had been wounded. Most, like Richard's hand, were small wounds that needed to be cleaned, but were not fatal in themselves. Werberan gave Mother a handful of herbs to boil to make poultices that would draw out any poison or infection.

Since Gaelin and Caern had escaped injury, Richard ordered them to stay on watch. Oervel and Pyotr went to work reloading the ballistae and catapults. Richard warned them to keep an eye on the gate. Daire, the priestess of Sarimie, had not returned. She would have to pick her way between the still-burning trenches and the dead on the field. The others were helping the wounded or sorting out and counting the remaining arrows, shafts, and oil jugs when Oervel gave the alarm and raised his bow.

"One of Tal-Qazar's spies," he called down.

Richard stared into the sky.

"No! Don't shoot it!" he shouted as he watched the eagle laboriously flying toward the fort. It's right wing beat furiously, trying to overcome the limited use of the left. An eagle with a wounded left wing was too uncommon for the bird to be anything but Glencarole in disguise.

"Werberan!" Richard shouted for the paladin.

The bird tried to hover, but with one injured wing it made an undignified landing directly in front of Richard. On its clawed feet it stood nearly four feet tall. It stared at the human with sharp yellow eyes and from deep within its throat it gave a low chirp, almost a growl. The others backed away, understanding they were not to kill it, yet not trusting the fierce eyes and beak.

Werberan appeared in the doorway of the second building and with a sigh he walked over to join Richard.

"It's Glencarole," Richard said. "I don't understand why he's still in eagle form."

"I don't think he can change his shape until his injury's healed," the paladin replied. The eagle seemed to understand. He gave another low, growling chirp.

"He risked something coming here," Richard said, "Can you help him? Turn him back into an elf and heal his wound?" He knew the bird had risked being killed before anyone understood who he was, and Glencarole would hate asking for help from humans. He would not have come if his mission had not been important.

Werberan sighed and shook his head. "Tomorrow or the next day, perhaps."

The eagle shook his head and screamed: his objection nearly deafened the onlookers.

"There's nothing left of my healing powers and very little else." Werberan held out his hands palms up, indicating his helplessness. "The fight, healing Mourde, and there was poison in Raenwe's wound . . . I never pretended to be all-powerful. I might be able to return him to his elf form, but—"

"No!" Borg spoke up. "I have no healing spells for humans, but I have some for birds, and I have more than one."

Though Glencarole seemed unable to speak in his avian shape he clearly understood human speech. He turned immediately to the druid and gave a low trill.

"Do you need privacy?" Richard asked, not really even sure what druidic magic was, let alone what it required.

"I'm fatigued. Quiet would help my concentration," Borg told him. "I'll use the smokehouse if you've no objection."

Richard thought the druid could have picked a more comfortable, less crowded place, but he nodded and watched as the eagle followed the druid into the little building. The smokehouse was crammed with sides of venison, wild boar, smoked rabbit, and fish, but the fire had been out for a week.

While Werberan went back to tend to the two most seriously wounded settlers, Richard strolled over to sit at the outside tables by Mother's cookfire. The half-orog grumbled as he divided his attention between the boiling pot of herbs the warrior-priest of Haelyn needed and the half-orog's large pot of scorched stew. That evening they would eat a less than satisfactory meal, courtesy of the goblin arrow that had restarted the cookfire. Mother took the accident as a personal insult. He muttered imprecations upon all goblins and recited a litany of tortures he planned for the first one he met. Listening to him, Richard's shivered as he realized just how much orog bloodlust remained in Rivervale's cook.

When Werberan was satisfied with the progress of his patients, he left them and took a seat at the table where Richard waited. The boiling medicine was ready and along with it a pot of steaming red-root tea. The paladin's gray face took on color as he drank his heavily sweetened tea. He watched and gave advice as Droene, helping Mother, tied a poultice around Richard's hand.

"It's taking Borg a long time to heal Glencarole," Richard said, looking over his shoulder at the partially opened door of the smokehouse.

"He may not find it easy," Werberan replied. "He's not working with a real bird."

Another half hour passed before Borg stepped out of the smokehouse and gestured to Richard. When Werberan rose to accompany Rivervale's leader, the druid shook his head. Borg headed for the tables, and the two men met in the open, out of hearing of the others.

"Were you successful?" Richard asked.

Borg nodded. "After two only partially successful

tries. He wants to speak with you in private."

Rightly guessing the elf had been able to return to his true state, Richard entered the smokehouse to find Glencarole leaning against the wall just inside the door. He wrinkled his nose in distaste.

"I'll never understand a human's desire for flesh."

Richard looked pointedly at what had been a haunch of smoked venison, but was now little more than bare bones lying on the floor. The elf caught the direction of his gaze.

"Your druid suggested I should gorge myself while still in my eagle form. He believed the meat would aid in regaining my strength. I find he was right, but I could not have eaten it as an elf."

"I searched for you," Richard said.

"As your follower of Haelyn suggested, I could not change shape while I was wounded. The poison from the arrow kept me from healing. I would not risk approaching this place until necessity drove me to it."

"Necessity?"

"The fate of humans seldom interests me, but all elves honor the six gods of the humans who fought the evil Azrai at Mount Deismaar. We do not worship them, but we honor those who absorbed their power and continue their work. Also, the gods' servants. . . ." He paused, allowing Richard time to grasp the significance.

"Daire!" Richard blurted, the hair rising on the back of his neck. "The priestess of Sarimie?"

Glencarole nodded. "I watched the battle from the small patch of wood you decimate and replant. A wounded spider mount charged into her, knocking her down, I think. It inflicted a wound on her shoulder when it stepped on her with its clawed pedipalp. The pain must have negated the spell she was using—if it was a spell . . . I know nothing about the magic of clerics. She became visible and was captured."

"Another one," Richard said, his heart sinking. His first impulse when Entiene was captured was to go charging after the Spider King. The others had the same desire. Since everyone was fond of Daire, their need to rescue the women would double and he was not sure he could hold them back.

"Time is short if you wish to save her," the elf said.

Hope flared, died, and flared again.

"How?" Richard asked. "Do you know a way for eighteen humans to attack an army, save two women and escape alive?"

"No, but I do know a way for *one* human to attack Tal-Qazar and escape with two women—and everything he desires."

"You judge it time to give me the secret you spoke of. . . ."

"I will give it, since you indeed proved your strength—in our battle as well as your defense of this fort." In a few words Glencarole described what he saw as the impending battle between Richard and the awnshegh.

"He would never agree," Richard said, his heart sinking. The elf's eyes flashed.

"Do you then spurn my help? It is the only chance for the priestess of Sarimie and the other you spoke of. Tal-Qazar will not kill them immediately. They will suffer . . . horrors before they die." Despite his bravado, the elf shuddered, his eyes dark with memories Richard could not imagine.

"How do I get to him?" Richard had been shaken by what he had seen in the eyes of the elf. Still, if there was a chance to save the two women he had to try.

"How do I reach Tal-Qazar?" Richard asked.

"I will take you."

ANUIRE

twenty-seven

Richard stood staring at the elf. Was insanity contagious? he wondered. Did the "blood of darkness", the power absorbed by the awnsheghlien, reach out to taint their enemies as well as their allies? Tal-Qazar was insane. Glencarole had to be mad to suggest Richard enter the Spiderfell alone to confront the awnshegh. Richard had to be crazy to consider it.

Dimly, through the partially open door, he heard Caern calling to Pyotr.

"Sails coming up the river!"

"It's the settlers from Farmstead!" Stubby, who had the sharpest eyes, shouted. "So many the raft is ready to sink."

A cheer for the survivors echoed through the fort.

"We'll need more weapons if they go with us," Gaelin called out.

"We could take the rest of the ballista shafts," Droene shouted to his brother. "They would serve as spears."

And his settlers were crazy as well, Richard thought as he realized they were making plans to go after Entiene. They would die in the attempt to rescue her, and he would die along with them, since he could not let them go alone. It didn't take long for Richard to realize that if he had to go, it was better to go with the elf. He might at least save the lives of the other settlers, if not the two women. He might even have a better chance of surviving the attempt, since Tal-Qazar would see a lone human as less a threat than forty.

Glencarole, who had been watching him through narrowed eyes, twisted his mouth in a sneer.

"Mayhap your heart is not as strong as your arm."

"Stronger than my reason, I think. You would not want to give your secret to a fool, and only the witless would confront an awnshegh without careful consideration, at least."

"I accept the wisdom of thought, yet you cannot delay too long, else you will meet him in the forest."

"But he's already in the forest," Richard objected.

"Now he is, but a score of miles and half again the distance, the forest gives way to barren hills and rocky tors. He will have to cross them on his way to the Web. I can take you there."

"I won't have to confront him in the forest, where his spiders can fall on me out of the trees?" Like Pyotr, Richard had less horror of dying at the point of a sword or a spear than being attacked by hundreds of tiny enemies he could not fight.

"It is so."

His decision made, Richard opened his mouth to speak it. His mouth was dry, his throat felt parched and his chest seemed unwilling to push out the air to sound the words. He overcame the reluctance that infected his entire body.

"I will go."

Once the words were spoken, he walked zombie-like out of the smokehouse. Without a word he returned to the table, picked up his cup of red-root tea, by then cold, and drank it down. He picked up a score of arrows gathered by Gaelin and filled his quiver before picking up his bow. His cousin stared at him.

"What are you doing?"

"I have an errand. I leave you in charge of the clean-up detail and Hassan in charge of the defenses until I return. Mother will see to bedding down the farmers."

"Where are you going?" Gaelin's bright green eyes sparkled with the residual anger of battle and concern for his cousin. "You're not leaving this fort alone."

"You chose me leader, and I will do my job," Richard retorted. "You can take my orders or leave."

His cousin was ready to argue but paused as gasps and yelps of wonder came from the settlers and everyone stopped their work. They were all staring at the smokehouse doors. Richard and Gaelin turned to see Glencarole emerge from the building.

The elf was in his eagle form again, but as he came through the door, his head, shoulders, breast, body, and wings enlarged until the bird that hopped to the center of the palisade stood twenty feet tall. Glencarole had been speaking literally when he said he would take Richard to meet Tal-Qazar. The settlers watched in silence as Richard walked over to the giant bird. As one they started to shout their objections when their leader climbed up on the giant eagle's back, but a warning scream from the wickedly hooked, two-foot long beak was enough to drive them back.

Richard clutched at the feathers of the monster bird as it leapt into the sky, clearing the walls of the fort before it opened its giant wings. They spread fifty feet on each side of him, partially obscuring its rider's view of the ground below. Five beats of those giant wings carried them across the still-burning trenches, the tilled fields, the little copse of trees, nearly decimated by the woodcutting required to build the fort. Another two brought them to the eaves of the Spiderfell.

Below them the thick woods shut out the view for two miles or more. They occasionally saw open areas that could have been meadows or bogs. They were too high for Richard to see clearly and he did not bother to ask Glencarole, who could not speak in his eagle shape.

Their destination was not yet in sight when Richard noticed how far ahead Glencarole's shadow had advanced. He looked back to see the sun sitting on the horizon. Below them the dark wood was rapidly losing all color in the deepening twilight.

They came to a wide break in the forest, an area of low hills and tall, rock outcroppings. In almost total darkness the giant eagle circled and dropped through the late evening. He hovered, looking about until he had chosen his landing spot near a rough, rocky tor, too tall to be called a hill, not tall enough to be called a mountain.

When Richard took advantage of the rocks to step off the bird's back, the giant eagle shimmered and shrank until Glencarole, the elf, stood on the ground below him.

"Wait here," the elf said. "You will need torches." Glencarole blended with the night and disappeared.

Richard paced on the rock, cursing himself again for his madness. He had made his decision and, once made, he had no thought of going back on it. His real irritation came from his feeling like he was under the elf's control, powerless, a position that rankled him.

Time passed slowly, but in less than half an hour

the elf returned with eight reasonably straight poles, each seven or more feet long. At one end Glencarole had tied dried moss and grass to make a large torch head. He propped six against the bottom of the tor and brought the others with him as he climbed.

"Now we wait," he said, taking a seat on a rock. "One other thing I will say to you. Remember, with Tal-Qazar, you win all you bargain for or die. Only a fool would wager his life with little to gain."

Richard wanted to ask what the elf meant, but after he had spoken the elf drew his knees up against his chest and wrapped his arms around them. A wall seemed to develop between them. Richard had been shut out of the elf's thoughts.

An hour later the moon rose and Richard looked about him. In the pale illumination he could see to the east the dense forest, less than a mile away. A row of rocky tors ran away to the northeast and southwest. He and the elf waited on the eastern-most point of a wide arrowhead of heights.

A second hour was giving way to a third when he saw a column of torches winding their way through the hill country to the west. They moved slowly, but before long he could hear on the wind the grumbling of the goblins and the moans of the wounded. When the head of the column was less than a quarter mile away, Glencarole came out of his trance and rose from his seat.

"I will light the first torch for you," he said. "Curiosity will bring Tal-Qazar to the head of the column. Remain on the heights until he recognizes you. By that time his lieutenants and his best fighters will be close enough to hear your challenge. With them as witnesses, he'll have no choice but to accept it."

Richard blinked at the sudden brightness of the torch and by the time his eyes adjusted, he saw in the illumination a small mouse that wrinkled its nose at him and zipped into a crack in the rocks.

Richard stood beneath the light of the torch and waited. The first of the column approached and he could see it was made up entirely of spider-riders. More than a hundred led the march, but they slowed, hesitating to approach the lone human who confidently stood on the tor.

In the light from a cluster of torches he saw Entiene and Daire, each bound to spider mounts. They were sitting upright and struggling—they were alive.

Tal-Qazar, who had been farther back in the column, came forward and the riders followed him closely. The awnshegh stopped fifty feet from the base of the tor and glared up at Richard. He stood staring as a murmur ran down the column. Behind it the silence of the night was absolute.

ANUIRE

twenty-eight

Richard waited, almost frozen with his own anxiety, yet knowing his presence was throwing fear into the goblins who would be uncomfortable and unhappy with the unusual situation. He let the fear grow until he thought it had reached its peak.

"Mighty Tal-Qazar!" He shouted and his voice echoed off the stony heights. "All powerful awnshegh, immortal in whose veins flows the power of the blood of Azrai! Brave King of the Spiderfell—so brave he must send armies against one man! A single human he fears to face one-on-one in contest."

His challenge caught Tal-Qazar by surprise. Stunned by the human's daring, the awnshegh's jaw dropped and his eyes widened. Behind him his spider-riders were just as shocked, and the muttering began softly, as if they could not contain themselves, yet did not want their leader to hear them.

Tal-Qazar twisted to look back over his shoulder.

Small stones clattered beneath his clawed pedipalps as he half turned to face his forces. He roared at their insolence and whirled back to face Richard.

"You, Richard Endier, a puny human, would challenge *me?*" he shouted.

"I, Richard Endier challenge you, Tal-Qazar, Goblin King, Spider King, who is mighty in the blood of darkness! I challenge you to a contest of wit."

"Say on!" The awnshegh roared a laugh—a forced laugh. "I will hear you out before I destroy you. I will drink your blood. I will devour your body while you still live—"

"Is that a promise that you will do those things?" Richard demanded at the top of his voice.

"It is a promise," Tal-Qazar replied. "It is known by all that Tal-Qazar, Goblin King, through whose veins passes the powerful bloodlust of the god Azrai, always keeps his word."

"But only if you win the contest," Richard shouted down. "I offer my life. What are you willing to wager?"

"What do you want? Not that it matters, because no puny human can stand against me."

"My life, the lives of those two human females, and all the land from the Maesil River to this stretch of hills following their line to Ghieste in the north and to the settled lands of Diemed in the south. You will cede it to me and your armies will never again cross that border."

"You don't want much for your life, human."

"I am wagering the life of Richard Endier, what did you expect?"

Tal-Qazar stood glaring at Richard, thinking, until the growing muttering within the ranks behind him forced him to a decision.

"You have your wager, human. Now what is your contest?"

"One of wit," Richard replied. "I will riddle you for that which I have named."

"Riddles?" Tal-Qazar threw back his head and laughed. "You did not know, human, that I have the greatest store of riddles on Cerilia."

"This I have heard," Richard said. He picked up the second torch and started to climb down the tor. He stopped on a ledge five feet off the ground with his back to a stone wall. He was in reach of the other six torches Glencarole had made for him.

When the awnshegh realized Richard did not intend to descend to ground level he approached within ten feet of the ledge. Behind him his spider-riders closed in. With them were Daire and Entiene. A filthy cloth had been used to gag the priestess of Sarimie. Both of the women stared at him, fear and hope warring their eyes.

Richard turned to prop his second torch, still unlit, against the wall behind him, then casually turned back to face the awnshegh. His apparent lack of fear started the spider-riders to muttering again.

"You are wasting my time," Tal-Qazar snarled. Two spider-riders had ridden forward to flank the awnshegh, and the light of the torches they carried reflected off the spittle dripping from the angry king's mouth.

"It was my challenge, so you deserve the first turn," Richard said.

This set off another wave of muttering, but Tal-Qazar roared for silence before he asked his first riddle.

"Huge, tiny, wet and dry,
"Bare, covered, low and high,
"Always used and not depleted,
"Downtrodden but not defeated.
"What is it?"
The goblins cheered until their master snarled for

quiet. Richard waited for the noise to die down so he could be heard. He glanced at the two women and saw the fear in their eyes because he had not answered. In the light of the torches Richard seemed to be looking down on nothing but blackness, speckled with the flashing of eyes and fangs that reflected the torchlight. Then he realized the ground around the tor was black with spiders, hundreds of thousands that had escaped the fires and traveled with the army.

He could not prevent the shudder that went through him and resolved to keep his eyes on the Spider King before the image of being devoured bit by bit by the tiny, crawling creatures paralyzed his mind. He forced himself to answer the riddle.

"The land. Cerilia, all of Aebrynis," Richard replied. "The game is hampered by the noise of your troops." The riddle was an old one. Richard took his turn.

"If you have it, you lack it:

"If you don't lack it, you don't have it."

The goblins muttered, but Tal-Qazar's eight clawed feet scuffled on the stones as he laughed.

"Need," he said. "Is that the best you can do, human?"

"I didn't find your first one any harder," Richard replied. "Do you have another, or have you used your store already?"

"I have many, human.

The riddles continued through the night. Both Richard and Tal-Qazar continued to ask the simpler ones, testing each other. At dawn, Tal-Qazar shifted, glared up at the sun and back at Richard.

"I must eat," the awnshegh announced. "I do not call a halt to the contest, but I must eat."

"I have no argument with that if you provide food for the prisoners and for me—but it must be food we can eat—fresh meat and wood to cook it," Richard cautioned. "And allow the women to join me here. They cannot escape."

"It will be so," the awnshegh said. He shouted commands to his minions in the uncouth goblin tongue. A group of goblins shifted as Tal-Qazar turned toward the forest. A spider-rider freed Entiene and Daire. A path in the blackness parted as the two females stumbled toward the rocks were Richard waited.

"Are you injured?" he asked as Entiene climbed the rocks, still trembling in fear of the millions of little spiders.

"No, just terrified," she said.

"You should rest," Daire cautioned. "Leave it to us to make the fire and cook the meat . . . if they bring meat."

Richard agreed. He knew the women were exhausted, but their lives depended on his contest. He was unable to sleep, but he lay down on the rock, willing his mind into a stupor of non-thought.

Within half an hour three spider-riders brought two freshly killed and cleaned rabbits and a stack of firewood. While the women cooked the food, Richard dozed. They had finished their meal, during which he had questioned them to learn any new riddles they might know, and he was dozing again when Tal-Qazar returned. The contest began again. Richard had asked the last riddle so it was the awnshegh's turn.

"Everyone wants it
"It belongs to a few
"Fewer still can use it
"Harm comes to those who do.
"Answer that one."

Richard heard the half-hidden tinge of regret in the awnshegh's voice when he spoke the last line, and knew the answer, though he had never suspected Tal-

Qazar of disliking his shape.

"Power," Richard said and waited for the muttering of the awnshegh's minions to die away before he asked his next riddle. The rhyme puzzles flew back and forth. The day passed and as a second night darkened the sky the spider mounts became restless. The goblins came and went into the wood, taking turns as they foraged for food. Some of the riders dismounted and sat on the ground. The spiders crouched with their bellies resting on the rocky soil, their long, jointed legs arching up over their bodies.

Two of the torches made by the elf had lasted through the first night. Two lasted through the second night. Dawn of the second day of riddling was breaking when Richard spared a thought for the other eight. Would the game go on for two more nights?

Again they paused at dawn while the awnshegh returned to the deep forest to eat and the women cooked strips of fresh deer meat the goblins provided.

"I wouldn't have thought we'd be fed so well," Entiene said, her voice drifting into Richard's dozing stupor.

"He would not skimp on our food," Richard mumbled. "His honor, and the contest, demand too much."

Richard was still eating when the awnshegh returned, but Tal-Qazar bade him take his time, as though the Spider King could afford to be magnanimous, knowing he would win the contest.

After a day of fighting and two nights and a day of riddling Richard's fatigue washed over him in waves, so he sat on a boulder as he listened to Tal-Qazar's next riddle.

"We dream of it,

"We work for it,

"We know its just ahead

"No one can lay a hand on it

"Neither the living nor the dead."

"Tomorrow," Richard replied quickly.

One of the spider-riders rose, urged its mount to its feet and charged toward the human, but Tal-Qazar roared and stepped forward, knocking the goblin off the back of the huge spider.

"Think you I cannot win?" he demanded. "Your lack of faith in me will be suitably rewarded."

The goblin drew back, pulling its mount with him.

"Ask your next riddle," the awnshegh snarled, glaring at the human.

"A game for children
"Is the bane of men,
"Where loss is greater
"Than the win."

Tal-Qazar's mouth dripped spittle as he moved restlessly. His eyes, red with anger, turned from Richard to the troops around him. He looked at the sky, already growing light in the east, and back at the ground before he chuckled softly.

"War, human, war. Now it is my turn. . . ."

The second day passed and the sun set. Daire and Entiene slept in snatches. Tal-Qazar's army was taking turns sleeping on the ground, but Richard and the awnshegh still faced each other.

Fatigue slurred Tal-Qazar's voice.

"Tiny . . . helpless . . . buried as dead,
"It feeds us . . . and shades us . . . and
"Glows green and red."

A child's riddle, one known to every five-year-old on Cerilia. The awnshegh was as tired as Richard.

"An apple seed," he said.

Tal-Qazar glared at his opponent, but with his new awareness Richard realized the fire in the Spider King's eyes had dimmed. The awnshegh was as wit-worn as the human.

"If I could put it in a cup
"And give everyone a taste

"My cup would still be full

"And I'd have it still to waste."

Tal-Qazar grimaced. He flexed his muscles and clenched his fists as he struggled for an answer. More than five minutes passed. The goblins traded speculative looks, for once too fearful even to mutter. The two young women, who had been drooping in fatigue, raised their heads. They seemed to be holding their breath.

"Knowledge?" Tal-Qazar asked, his voice tentative.

Richard nodded, not happily. He waited for the awnshegh to ask his next one.

"I cannot touch it, but it supports me.

"I cannot taste it, but it sustains me.

"I cannot feel it, but it is my armor."

Another simple one. One used less as a riddle than as an encouragement in the training barracks in Aerele, but Richard was so tired he had to fight to bring out the answer. He knew it, it lurked in the forefront of his mind—his exhausted mind.

Minutes passed and the goblins were chattering in triumph when Richard held up his hand for silence.

"Courage."

Tal-Qazar had been smiling, salivating at the thought of Richard's death. He snarled, raked the rocky ground with his clawed pedipalps and waited.

But Richard had run out of riddles. His tired mind was blank. The goblins were howling with glee and closing in on him. In the light of his third dawn on the rock, he saw the tears streaming down Entiene's face.

His reeling mind sorted the words, forming a rhyme as he made up his own riddle.

"No vessel have I.

"I'm days from the sea,

"Yet it's in my hand

"And part of it's me."

Tal-Qazar stood frozen as he thought. The goblins

were trading looks again. The awnshegh searched Richard's face, looking for a clue, but the human dropped his eyes, not daring to look at the woman who had given him his idea. Realizing their leader was searching for the answer, the goblins held their breath until they could stand it no longer. They gave a nearly unanimous collective gasp, but they were still afraid to speak.

Time dragged on, the sun rose above the woods. The warmth of its rays were drugging Richard, and he stood up, afraid he would go to sleep. An hour passed, and then two, and still Tal-Qazar did not answer. Finally, his eyes met Richard's and the human saw the defeat reflected in them.

Tal-Qazar raised his head and screamed. The frustration in his voice carried across the forest and echoed back from the rocky tors. Then his eyes lit with an unholy light.

"We put no time limit on answering the riddles," he said with a grotesque, fanged grin.

No, they had not. Richard cursed himself for a fool.

"But you have no answer, so our lives are safe from you. The land is mine until you can solve the riddle."

"You are a puny, short-lived human, and could die before I do," the awnshegh argued.

"The answer will be a legacy of my descendants. As you honor your word, they will honor mine."

Tal-Qazar continued to stare at Richard. He scraped his pedipalps against the hard ground, tearing small boulders from their anchors in his frustration. When a goblin raised a bow, pointing his arrow at Richard, the awnshegh shouted at his soldier, then turned back to face the winner of the contest.

"It has been said. It will be so." He issued a spate of orders in the goblin tongue and turned away, plowing through his army toward the forest. Three hundred feet from the foot of the tor, he stopped, roared his frustration and thrashed, killing two goblins and one of the huge spider mounts.

His two lieutenants eased away, taking up stations as if they were point guards, dutifully protecting their master while staying out of the immediate range of his anger.

Tal-Qazar was nearly a quarter of a mile away when he gave another sudden roar and the screams of more goblins echoed off the rocks.

The last of the goblins were leaving the field when the mouse crept out of the crack. The little rodent blurred its shape and enlarged. Both women drew back suddenly as the misty shape sharpened into a large spider. Entiene grabbed a large rock and would have crushed the arachnid's skull if Richard had not grabbed her arm.

In his arachnid shape, Glencarole simply ignored the humans. He detoured around the bodies of the goblins and the spider the awnshegh had killed and followed Tal-Qazar's army into the Spiderfell. Richard grinned, knowing the elf was seeking his own reward, the enjoyment of the awnshegh's frustration.

"What was that?" Entiene asked.

"A secret we are not allowed to share," Richard replied. The elf had kept his word. "A friend, though he would be the last to admit it."

Daire nodded as if she understood. When the spider was out of sight she asked for news of the settlers.

"I don't know if the northern fort was attacked." Richard said. "Farmstead was burned, I believe, but most, if not all of the farmers fled in time. They were arriving at Rivervale when I left. We had no losses, but several wounds."

"The poor farmers will have to begin again," Entiene said.

"But not in a fort," Richard replied. "We have the land for farms, all we need, and it is safe from the awnshegh." Probably safe for all time, he thought. Tal-Qazar was on the verge of complete madness. As time passed the awnshegh's thoughts would become more and more jumbled and he would be less likely to be able to answer the last riddle.

"Lord Richard Endier," Daire smiled at him. "Lord of his land."

"When can we return to Rivervale?" Entiene asked. "This contest has taken a week and a day."

"Three nights and two days, but legend may agree with you, though our lord has no need for his tales to be exaggerated." Daire gave Richard a teasing glance.

Richard did not reply. Instead, he climbed the tor to look out over the forest. He could not even dimly make out the river, the western border of his new domain.

His land!

His, he decided, though the rest of the world, particularly Baron Naele Diem, might not agree with him. But if he could hold it in the face of Tal-Qazar, he would hold it in the face of the baron when the time came. He thought of the settlers and what winning this contest would mean to all of them. He was reminded of the Vos, Pyotr.

He raised his arms, stretching his hands toward the sky.

"Haelyn and Sarimie! All you gods! Look upon and bless the dawn of a nation! *A new history begins!*"

Appendix

Tal-Qazar

Tal-Qazar squared his shoulders in an attempt at bravado. As the leader and most powerful sorcerer of the goblins of the Spiderfell, he had marched south to fight on the side of the Shadow, Azrai, whose messengers had promised glory, spoils beyond any goblin's wildest dreams, and an end to their enemies.

The great god Azrai was determined to destroy the humans that had fled his dominion in Aduria, and had brought vast armies north across the land bridge that connected the two continents. Thousands of humans marched alongside thousands of gnolls, goblins, orogs, and ogres, as well as beastmen the likes of which Tal-Qazar had never seen. Most of the humanoids of the Cerilian continent had traveled south to stand with Azrai.

Only one thing had kept Tal-Qazar from feeling total joy in the anticipation of the battle; before the fight began most of the Cerilian elves were allied with Azrai. The goblins hated the idea of fighting beside their traditional enemies, but in the end they had not had to suffer the indignity. The elves, miserable demi-humans that they were, changed sides, and Tal-Qazar's people had killed many that day. The elves killed many goblins too.

At dawn the battle lines had stretched as far as Tal-Qazar could see on both sides. He waited impatiently while the foolish humans went through the motions of what they called chivalry, dipping their flags and blowing their horns. Well they might ask the favor of their gods, he thought, but he knew Azrai asked nothing so silly of his fighters. Azrai waited to feed on blood, terror, and death.

And he *had* fed on it, Tal-Qazar remembered, rubbing his long-fingered hands together with glee. The goblins had been deafened by the first clash of weapons and the screams of the wounded and dying. The slopes of the mountain ran red with blood. Tal-Qazar could not even hear his own battle cries.

He and his followers climbed over piles of the dead and dying as they chased the humans. With them retreated the miserable elves. The battle swelled back and forth. Several companies of elves had broken through the southern line a quarter of a mile to Tal-Qazar's left. He raged at the necessity of turning aside to stop them, but he had retreated to reinforce the wavering line of Adurian ogres.

The elves had been fighting in a phalanx, archers and spearmen striking from within a moving wall of shields, and even the goblins had been pushed back with the ogres. Some of his people had made the mistake of mingling with the huge ogres, who towered over them, two and three times their height, and were trampled by the panicked primitives who were unused to the discipline of the more intelligent elves.

Tal-Qazar had been exhorting his people to gather together and use their own shields. Having cast all his spells, he drew the twin curved, serrated swords that had become his trademark. He blinked against the growing darkness, thinking it merely a dust cloud raised by the hordes of fighters when Demargog, his trusted lieutenant, grabbed his arm and directed his attention to the northeast.

"Wh-wh-what—who?" Demargog stammered. Tal-Qazar often swore at his lieutenant for his stammering, but this time the sorcerer ignored it. He was too busy staring in numb disbelief.

In the sky above Mount Deismaar, giant fighters had appeared in the sky. They were covered with ornate armor and helms and armed with swords and spears. Their huge shields cast shadows across the battlefield. Their panoply glowed with a terrible light. It struck the top of the mountain, blinding Azrai's forces that had fought their way up the slope. Screams of terror from ogre, troll, goblin, and even human voices rode the wind.

Tal-Qazar's people, more than two miles from the foot of the steep incline, were protected from it by the shadow of another giant warrior in the sky. His armor was black and his black shield stood between them and the blinding light of the gods on the mountain. His presence ate the light from the day.

"The gods themselves fight—and Azrai protects us!" Tal-Qazar cried out to his people, but the elven leaders were also shouting, urging their numbers on. There were six glowing gods while Azrai stood alone in his darkness.

The gods met, their blades clashed with a roar that deafened both armies. The battle was fierce, and as they fought the gods descended toward the top of the mountain, shrinking in size.

One great shield tumbled out of the sky. The goblins and ogres raced south to avoid being struck. The elves had fled north. Tal-Qazar and his people were still fleeing the giant shield when he felt the power of the descending gods.

The oxygen seemed to be sucked from the air; he could hardly breathe. The smell of lighting overpowered all other odors, even the stink of the ogres. He risked one glance back to see light and darkness collide at the top of the mountain and then the world seemed to dissolve around him.

The mountain exploded.

Death rained all around them. Falling earth, rocks, arms, legs, bodies and weapons fell from the sky. If the shield of the unknown god had struck the ground it was buried under the debris along with the elves Tal-Qazar's goblins had been fighting. All thought of battle was forgotten as they sheltered where they could. Tal-Qazar barely dodged a boulder that came hurtling out of the sky. An ogre, trusting to the goblin's sharper eye, had been following the sorcerer, hoping for safety, but had not been quick enough to avoid the huge rock.

In dodging the boulder, Tal-Qazar stepped into the path of another bit of debris. He was struck on the shoulder by a severed human hand.

Tal-Qazar and his goblins had reveled in the killing, their bloodlust high as they destroyed their enemies, but the magnitude of the destruction caused by the mountain's exploding terrified them. Even Tal-Qazar had to fight himself to keep from fleeing. He trembled, his entire body shook. Fear and a strange exultation washed through him, each controlling him in turn, like waves on a beach pushing and pulling at a piece of flotsam.

To hide his shaking, he braced himself against a

fallen tree limb. He made it appear as if he were resting his twin serrated blades on a thick branch. In fact, he gripped them tightly and pressed hard, using the tension to cover the signs of his fear. When the huge boulder fell, Demargog had taken shelter behind it, and ten other goblins followed him. When the fallout was over, and only the dust drifting on the wind was still settling, they crept out to join Tal-Qazar.

Demargog looked around. The surviving ogres were backing away, moving south, toward the land bridge. Their small eyes were stretched wide and they spoke in whispers. The goblins could not understand their language, but by their gestures they were all for fleeing back to their homes.

Tal-Qazar gazed up at the sky and decided it would be safe to climb the large boulder that had barely missed him and killed his ogre companion. The monster rock was shaped like a large, rough teardrop and the top rose nearly twenty feet above the plain. He ordered Demargog and the rest of the goblins to pull the large tree limb over and he used it as a ladder to climb the first ten feet. Then he scaled the rough surface and squatted on the top, looking out over the plain.

Where there had been a mountain, only a low mound of broken rock remained. The plain stretched as far as he could see, and the only movement was a battle standard. The ornately carved truck at the top of the pole was buried in the ground and the broken shaft rose and dipped like a splintered elbow. The red and gold cloth, ripped until he could not make out the design, still waved bravely in the breeze.

To the south he could see bugbears, ogres, beastmen, and humans as they left the field, heading south, toward the land bridge that would take them home.

"The stinking cowards are leaving us," he growled. They could afford to leave the battle. South of where

Tal-Qazar stood there were no enemy forces to stop their flight. He and his people would be traveling north, through the site of the battle. They could be facing hordes of enemies.

Logic told him he and his people had little chance of reaching the Spiderfell again, but once the waves of fear and euphoria had stopped, he found he had no fear of the numbers they might face. He was surprised by his own courage. Below him, the eleven goblins looked up fearfully, their eyes on him just for a fraction of the time as they gazed at the sky and back again.

"There is no battle for miles," he called down. "First we will search for survivors—and then for our enemies!"

His followers were still terrified, but as he looked into the eyes of each, they straightened, lost their fear, and grinned, the battle-lust building in them again.

For the rest of the day they roamed the battlefield, searching for survivors. They killed six elves and three humans. They looted the dead, gathering all the food pouches, waterskins, and any likely weapons they could find. They found another forty-two goblins, eight had to be dug out from under the fallen debris, and thirteen were injured, but still able to walk.

They found seven trolls and two gnolls that were too badly injured to travel south with their people. The trolls were slowly regenerating and the two gnolls would live if their wounds were covered with heal-mold and bandaged. Tal-Qazar, greedy for followers, took them into his small army and they began their trek north. The goblin leader had no fear of what he would meet, his courage was growing greater with every hour, but he was not devoid of common sense. At first they traveled by night, watching for campfires and listening for the rattle of armor and weapons. Traveling was slow over the rough ground and on the first night one of his point guards growled an oath, then gave a scream. He had tripped in the darkness and fallen on the point of a partially-buried spear. Tal-Qazar kicked the hapless, dying goblin for being so careless.

Just before dawn they were challenged when they suddenly came upon a camp that had no fire. They encountered a hundred goblins, wearing the markings of a tribe from the Stone Crown Mountains. They had lost their king, and Tal-Qazar immediately conscripted them into his own group. Leaderless, they were willing enough. Many were walking wounded.

The growing band continued to travel by night. Three times they passed large camps with hundreds of humans or elves, whose tracks showed that they were also leaving the battlefield. Tal-Qazar suspected few of the remaining humans and elves were capable of fighting. They probably remained behind to take care of the injured, but he was not willing to risk his small force of able fighters if he proved to be wrong.

They traveled through three nights, pulling the gnolls on a makeshift travois. He found several groups of gnolls, trolls and goblins who were fleeing north and commanded them to join with his people. Before long Tal-Qazar was leading nearly four hundred humanoids, but his appetite for more followers grew with each new fighter.

On the fourth dawn after the battle, the gnolls could walk, the trolls had regenerated, and they walked during the daylight. They had been traveling for four hours and the sun was high when out of a small copse of trees stepped a human knight in full body armor. He carried a spear and a large shield with the device of an Anuirean order, one Tal-Qazar had seen in battle. From his belt hung an ornate sword. His plumed helmet was open. He sniffed the air as if scenting more than goblins, gnolls, and trolls.

Tal-Qazar understood. Emanating from the human

was that strange odor similar to the smell of lightning, the one he had noticed when the human gods joined in battle.

Behind the goblin leader, his troops muttered. The few who had bows were fitting arrows to the strings, but Tal-Qazar raised his hand, challenging his own four hundred followers.

"He is mine! You shall not have him!"

No thought was quick enough or powerful enough to have given such force to his words. Tal-Qazar could not have said what caused him to hunger for battle with the fully armored human that towered over him by two feet. He only knew he had to fight the challenger, that all his being was called to that battle, and any goblin that attempted to deprive him of it would die.

He rushed forward, away from his troops. The knight seemed equally anxious. They met in a clash of the goblin's blades against the point of the human's spear. The force of the weapons threw out sparks on the dry ground, but neither the goblin nor the human noticed. When strangers met in single combat, they usually spent a few moments testing each other's skills, seeking weak points, but the lust for battle was too great in Tal-Qazar to spend the time. He fended off the first thrust of the spear and set himself for a second.

The second thrust came as he expected, and he moved to the side with an agility he had not known he had. He whipped his serrated swords and hacked at the shaft of the spear from above and below with super-humanoid strength, cutting cleanly through the shaft.

The human stepped back and drew his sword. Tal-Qazar allowed him the time. He was so certain of the outcome his apparent generosity was in fact a sign of his contempt for his enemy.

They met again. The knight, in his helmet, six and a

half feet tall, and the goblin, shorter by a full two feet. Tal-Qazar had lost his helmet in the battle, and the rest of his panoply was being carried by one of the trolls. He had disdained it in his new bravado.

The knight stepped forward and swung his mighty sword, but Tal-Qazar ducked the first two swings and sprang into the air, leaping over the third, lower slash. He ducked and wove, leaping forward, backward, meeting the heavy blade of the human with quick, ringing blows of his imposing weapons.

Behind Tal-Qazar, his goblins howled. Some were laughing at the spectacle of the goblin hopping around the iron-clad knight. Humor was no part of their howls, laughs and giggles; they were giving voice to their amazement that one goblin was able not only to hold off his opponent, but so sure of his victory that he could toy with an armored knight like a wood cat with a chipmunk.

Tal-Qazar's fatigue had fled with the appearance of the knight. From deep within him had come a strength and energy he had never known. It seemed inexhaustible and he reveled in it.

The human's next blow was quicker than Tal-Qazar expected. The tip of the sword cut through the heavy cloth sleeve of the goblin's left shoulder and dug into the flesh. Blood streamed down Tal-Qazar's arm. With a hiss of in-drawn breath and a mental withdrawing, the goblin was able to hold off the pain.

As the knight's sword slashed at him he leapt again, bringing his right sword down on the human's blade with a ringing clang. The human had been swinging at him for more than five minutes, but the goblin had not even tried for a blow against his enemy. He was still just hacking occasionally at the blade when he felt the first drops of rain.

"Be done," Omistag called out. "The wounded need shelter!" Omistag was a minor goblin sorcerer who had a few healing spells and considered himself the new clan's healer.

Tal-Qazar knew Omistag cared nothing about the wounded. He used his position as healer to give himself importance. Tal-Qazar did care about them, not as individuals, but as the numbers he led. He would not let one die if he could help it; to reduce the number of his followers would be a personal affront.

The knight kept thrusting with his sword while Tal-Qazar nimbly ducked aside. The goblin waited and when the knight tired of missing with his thrusts, he used his blade to slash back and forth. Tal-Qazar waited for his chance, leaping in and out until the knight slashed left and then brought his blade back to the right. When he did, the goblin let the blade whiz by, struck at it with both of his own swords, knocking it further to the right and slightly unbalancing the fully-armored human.

Tal-Qazar leapt four feet into the air and kicked hard at the shield, slamming it back into the knight's chest with his left foot, but his right followed with even more force. Off-balance, the knight fell backward and Tal-Qazar was on him in a flash, hacking first at the hand that held the sword, severing it at the wrist. His next blow was to the knight's neck, where the helmet and breast plate met. His two scimitars came together and severed the human's head from his shoulders.

Behind him the goblins, trolls and gnolls howled, hooted, and cheered.

Tal-Qazar barely heard the triumphant shouts of his followers. Something strange was happening to him as he stood over the body of his adversary. That bizarre, euphoric feeling that had so confused him after the explosion of Mount Deismaar was overwhelming him again.

On the battlefield it had washed over him along with the terror caused by the exploding mountain and the falling debris, until he could no longer isolate the two feelings. As he stood over the body of the human knight he felt the waves of power flowing into him. He stood still, unwilling to move lest he disturb the sensation. When it passed, he turned to his cheering followers.

Most of them seemed to think Tal-Qazar had remained standing by the human's body, savoring his victory or simply resting after the heated duel, but Demargog was watching him with narrowed eyes, as if he knew what the victor had experienced.

Not even Tal-Qazar was sure of what happened after the death of the knight. At first he just reveled in his renewed and growing strength; then he explored himself with mental fingers, probing and testing the newness inside. The battle had been long and hard, but when it was over he was not even breathing hard. On the march he had been impatient with his followers who were tired, some in pain and many grumbling because they were hungry. The food they had looted had been finished the day before.

Before the mountain exploded, Tal-Qazar had felt the fatigue of a hard morning's battle, but since the waves of fear and euphoria, he had not been tired or hungry. He had been filled with ambition and a need to increase his followers. He realized he had been automatically crushing a sense that he was all-powerful, that he could do anything.

Logic, the caution of a lifetime had been holding down the feeling of god-like powers. He knew he needed to continue trying to hold it down. The human knight acted as if he also had the power of a god, but it had done him little good. . . .

God-like powers—and the gods had been destroyed.

They had fought and died with the smell of lightning in the air, and the knight had smelled of it. Did everyone who was on the field carry the stink of lightning? Tal-Qazar raised his hand, brushing back his hair as an excuse to sniff his skin. The smell of it was stronger than it had been right after the explosion.

The gods had been destroyed, but power was indestructible, only waiting for another user, and he had absorbed that power!

Some of that power, he admonished himself, unwilling to risk too much bravado, even to himself. The human knight had held a part of it, and when he died at the goblin's hands, Tal-Qazar felt the warrior's strength flow into him. It had been more than a human's strength. It had been a *god's* strength.

The idea left him breathless. His quick, sly mind warned him of a vulnerability. Had any of his followers absorbed any of the gods' powers? He had to be sure, but he was not ready to question anyone. He walked over to Demargog. The odor was on him too, but not as strong.

"Start the march," Tal-Qazar ordered. "I'll remain here and see that the stragglers keep up."

Demargog nodded and led the way. Tal-Qazar checked each goblin, troll and gnoll as they passed. None had the smell. When he was sure, he hurried past the marching column and joined Demargog at the front of the troop.

"It was a great battle while it lasted," Tal-Qazar said, trying to draw his lieutenant out.

"Augh, that it was, after the tree vermin changed sides," Demargog replied. "It would've been shame on us if we fight 'side 'em."

"I smell their stink on the trail," the goblin leader said. "Many lived to travel north."

"Mayhaps we catch up w'some," Demargog turned his head to grin at Tal-Qazar. His eyes sparkled with bloodlust. "You want I should take some troops 'head an' see what we find?"

Tal-Qazar thought about the suggestion and felt his own lust for killing rise. He was caught between wanting to scout and raid himself and the need to keep his small band together. Demargog could do the scouting, possibly destroy a few elves, and at the same time find other humanoids to join their group. But what if the lieutenant found another warrior who had absorbed the godly power? He would either be killed or return strong enough to challenge Tal-Qazar.

The goblin king warned himself that his thinking was pre-explosion, when he had been an ordinary mortal. What if Demargog did increase his strength? He would be a stronger arm for his king. Tal-Qazar had no doubt he could best Demargog if the need arose.

"Yes, go," Tal-Qazar agreed. "Let no elf live and send back any goblins and gnolls you find. We will build an army that will conquer Cerilia."

Demargog chose twenty followers and trotted away to the west, having agreed that many leaving the battle would be traveling closer to the banks of the Maesil River.

Left to his own inclinations, the goblin king would have marched well into the night without a break, but many of his followers were walking wounded. Others were pulling hastily constructed travois with the more severely injured. If he was to build a great army, he needed to preserve the lives of his followers. They stopped early in the afternoon and he sent out hunters.

He remembered the wound on his shoulder and pulled away the torn sleeve where the dried blood had glued it to his skin. He stared at his arm in disbelief. The knight's blade had cut into his arm, the blood on the ripped tunic bore testimony to a wound, but he could not find the injury, not even a scar where it had healed.

Was this too a gift of the godly power?

When the others slept he did not feel the need, but he warned himself not to push his new strengths too far.

After checking to be sure the patrols were guarding the perimeter, he dozed off, to be awakened before dawn by the sound of hoof beats passing to the east.

He sat up to see the night guards gathered on the eastern side of the camp. They were muttering, clutching their spears, and peering into the darkness, but the sound died away as the unseen riders continued north. He tried to lie down again, but a clump of earth or a rock made him uncomfortable. He twisted, reached beneath him to remove the obstruction and found nothing on the ground.

It was inside his clothing! He slipped a hand inside his pants and felt a short, stubby shape with a soft claw on the end.

"What in—?"

He tugged at it and felt the pull on his muscles as if he had been trying to pull off his own leg. It was attached to him!

"Golid!" He shook the gnoll who slept next to him. "Get up. Light a torch and come with me!" He led the way into the darkness with the gnoll stumbling along behind. Within a clump of bushes, and with the torch as illumination, he pulled down the back of his trousers and stared with horror at the thick, two-inch appendage growing out of his right hip.

"What that be?" Golid asked, his small eyes stretched wide, his dog-like nose wrinkled in a disgust he could not hide.

Tal-Qazar stared at the gnoll and cursed himself for a fool. He had allowed the gnoll to see, and the creature would spread the word. Tal-Qazar was growing a deformity.

No! He could not allow anyone to know. With super-humanoid speed he pulled his knife and cut the startled gnoll's throat before Golid realized what was happening. He caught the torch as the gnoll dropped it and held it in one hand while he adjusted his trousers with the other.

As he walked back toward the camp, his mind was in a turmoil, but he had the presence of mind to tell the guards the gnoll would be returning after it finished its business in the bushes. The next morning the guards would find Golid and think some enemy, lurking in the dark, had killed him. The incident would help to keep the night guards alert. Tal-Qazar returned to the spot where he had been sleeping and stretched out, staring into the darkness for the rest of the night.

What was happening to him?

For the next two days he periodically left the group and, under the cover of the underbrush, checked the strange growth. It had not enlarged, but it remained.

Demargog sent messengers four times. Twice to report on attacking and killing small groups of elves, and twice to lead small groups of gnolls or goblins back to Tal-Qazar. True to his mission, he was gathering in the leaderless humanoids and had increased Tal-Qazar's band by another forty members.

The sun had not cleared the horizon the next morning when a gnoll came trotting into camp. It was panting from its run, its long tongue hanging out of its canine mouth.

"Muchly goblins, going north, with a new king goblin. Him plenty strong," the gnoll panted. "Demargog say they join us, but goblin king he say no, he take Demargog and us with him or you come fight."

"Then we'll fight," Tal-Qazar said, his blood rising. He called for the troll who had the responsibility of carrying his armor. He called two of his people to help him, but they had not finished strapping on his pauldrons before he was shouting for their removal. He felt stifled and confined. He did not understand his own feelings, but he knew he could no longer fight encased in metal.

Since the gnoll reported the camp of new goblins was not more than two miles away, he ordered the entire troop to follow as he led the way west. They topped a low rise and saw more than three hundred humanoids milling about at the edge of a stream. Demargog and his people were in the middle of a large group, guarded by spears. As Tal-Qazar descended the slope he saw more than fifty of his own people that he had thought dead. They grinned at him, but the spears of the strangers prevented them from joining the column coming down the slope.

The strange goblins sweated under the heavy furs worn in the north country and their shields carried the insignia of the tribes of the Silverhead Mountains.

The humanoids following Tal-Qazar stopped on the gentle hillside, most only visible from the waist up as they stood behind the low bushes. At the bottom of the hill, half the Silverhead group were on the opposite side of the small stream. Some still squatted around the numerous cookfires within the shade of six trees. They were roasting several horses.

A quick estimate of the numbers convinced Tal-Qazar that if his people, captured by the leader from the north, fought on his side, the odds of winning a pitched battle were with him, but many would die, many that he wanted for his own army. He knew he would win if he faced the Silverhead goblin king. The bloodlust and the strength surging through him told him he could not lose.

The cluster of fifty goblins parted and one—no, two—stepped out and swaggered toward the stream. Tal-Qazar stared, and behind him the humanoids muttered, as they realized the king from Silverhead was two goblins, joined together at the side. Their two bodies were connected at the hip and halfway up the chest. Their four legs moved in perfect step as they splashed through the four foot wide, ankle-deep stream.

Tal-Qazar had heard of twins that were linked as these, but the occurrence was rare and almost all died shortly after birth. He had never heard of any becoming warriors. He had not thought it possible that any could hold the leadership, which was usually decided by a test of arms.

By the swagger of the twin goblins, they had no fear of facing a single opponent.

"These armies will be joined," the right head of the king from the Silverheads shouted.

"Under my leadership," Tal-Qazar shouted back, surprised at his foe, but undaunted at the prospect of meeting them in battle.

By the weapons the northern king carried, all four of his arms were capable of independent action. The two outer hands held long spears and right inner one carried a shield while the left inner hand gripped a sword.

Tal-Qazar had intended to rely on his long, serrated blades, but seeing the weapons carried by his opponent, he called for a spear and a morning star from one of the trolls. The handle of the morning star was as long as he was tall. The chain was weighty and the iron ball of the weapon was as large as his head—even without the spikes. The goblin who brought it to him could hardly lift it, but Tal-Qazar reached inside himself for that newly gained strength and hefted it as if it had been a long, finger-thick branch from a tree.

He strode down the hill to meet his opponents. The twin kings of Silverhead jumped forward to meet him, their two spears out-thrust, but he fended one with his own shaft while he whipped the morning star around, aiming for the right head of the twins.

They ducked as one and pulled back, holding him off with the long spears and he paused, considering them. He sniffed, but caught no whiff of the odor he had come to associate with the god's power and knew he was not facing another who had absorbed the strength of Azrai. The twins each had a head—and, he supposed, a brain—but they moved and acted as one. He was really fighting one creature with four arms. The four legs did not seem to lessen its considerable agility.

A part of his mind warned him he would not have considered meeting this pair alone before the battle of Mount Deismaar, but he could not draw back. His ambition swept away all thought of failing. He carried a god's power and would *be* a god.

Tal-Qazar whipped the morning star around his head, the long shaft, the chain, and the spiked ball gave him a longer reach than the spears of his opponent. He spun the weapon over his head. Even for him the weight of it nearly pulled his shoulder out of joint.

With open disdain for the spear he still held in his left hand—an inferior weapon to the morning star in his right—Tal-Qazar threw the spear with all his strength. It struck the shield of the twins and the point penetrated the metal. The jagged point stuck in the shield, leaving the twins with the choice of either dropping it altogether, or attempting to use it with a long shaft sticking out of it.

The twin kings turned sideways, the one on the left acting as protection to the other, who was trying to pull Tal-Qazar's spear out of the shield. Both groups of goblins roared their reactions. Behind Tal-Qazar, his people were leaping about and shouting, urging him on. On the other side of the creek the fire tenders left the roasting horses to watch the fight. They muttered and moaned when the spear penetrated the shield.

Tal-Qazar gripped the morning star with both hands and continued to whirl it, setting the rotation and following its movement so when it swung high over his head when behind him, he stepped back out of the reach of the spears, and when it dipped to nearly shoulder height as the arc brought it around in front of him, he took a step forward, risking the twins' spears to bring the spiked ball into play.

He saw the weakness of his ploy and abruptly changed tactics, dropping the ball lower on its forward pass, he caught the left spear with the chain and jerked it out of the left twin's grip. The right twin was quicker than he had thought it could be, throwing the shield aside and whipping out a knife.

Tal-Qazar felt a grin rising. A knife against that whirling ball of death? These fools were not warriors, he thought, just before the knife whipped through the air and caught him in the left shoulder. The blade buried deep into the joint, leaving his left arm useless. He faltered and the morning star lost momentum, nearly swinging back on him before he suppressed the stunning pain in his shoulder and set it swinging again.

The twins had seen him falter and stepped forward to take advantage of his vulnerability. The right twin thrust at Tal-Qazar with his spear point while the left pulled his sword.

The spear point caught Tal-Qazar in the left thigh, throwing him slightly off balance, but the ball of the morning star was coming around again. In one all-out effort to destroy his enemies, Tal-Qazar pulled on all of his newly gained power and leapt on his one good leg. He threw himself forward, knowing he would fall, but he brought the ball against the head of the left twin.

The left twin's head disintegrated with the blow. Bones, brains and blood showered the other, as well as drenching Tal-Qazar and the ground around them. Tal-Qazar fell on his face in the dirt, driving the knife deeper into his shoulder. He rolled, as much to keep the knife from doing further injury than to escape the still living twin.

But the battle was over. The living twin had

stepped back, lugging the now limp half of his body. He stared at it with horror. If Tal-Qazar did not kill him, he would be attached to the dead and soon decaying half that would. His eyes said as much.

"I leave you your life for as long as you can keep it," Tal-Qazar told him, shouting the words so the hundreds of goblins gathered around could hear him. His generosity was a necessity. The knife in his shoulder and the gaping wound in his leg would make an attempt on the living twin a foolishly risky act. Remembering the knight and the power he had gleaned from the dead human, he would have made the effort if he had sensed any of the god's power in the twins.

At Tal-Qazar's orders, the living twin staggered west, away from the camp. The goblins and other humanoids who had followed the king of the Spider-fell hurried down the hill and to the campfires, demanding most of the cooked meat as their due, since their leader had won the fight. The Silverhead goblins had caught a number of horses, and Tal-Qazar decided to suspend travel until the animals had been slaughtered, cooked, and eaten. He was still unsure of his new abilities and was not sure even he could keep the loyalty of a starving army.

During the night he was awakened by a new discomfort. He had expected the wound in his shoulder—Omistag had removed the knife—and the gash in his leg to bother him, but remembering the cut on his arm he had reached within himself for that regenerating power and within minutes after the fight the wounds had closed. When he awoke he felt his shoulder and leg and found them completely healed. No, the problem was—he reached back, fearing, but half expecting what he found.

The stub of another leg had grown, this time on his left hip.

He lay trembling with fear and horror. What was happening to him? What caused the mutations? At first his mind, caught up in panic, raced in circles of terror. If the growths continued, what would he become? Disgusting visions of deformities raced through his mind until a chilling sweat soaked his clothes, his stomach roiled and gorge rose in his throat.

Why had they sprouted?

A small part of his mind, still clinging to logic, changed the "why" to "when." He had discovered the first growth after the fight with the human knight. The second had appeared after his battle with the goblin king from the Silverhead Mountains.

After battles. But why now, when he had been fighting all his life? After Mount Deismaar and the gods had been destroyed. After he had answered the "when," the "why" answered itself. The deformities had grown after he had used the power. His new strengths were exacting a terrible price.

The next morning he led the march north, toward the Spiderfell, telling himself he would not use his new gift. Nothing he could gain was worth losing himself. He had become king of the goblins in the Spiderfell without Azrai's gifts, he could live without them in the future. When he topped a small rise he paused and looked back at the straggling line that followed him.

More than seven hundred humanoids stretched out in a half-mile line. They numbered less than a quarter of the warriors that had followed him south, but after the battle, and the destruction of the mountain, he could have gathered the largest force on Cerilia. Others would come, he reasoned. More of his people might have survived.

The greed for more power and a larger army, those feelings that had been growing in him since the battle, warred with reason and caution because of what had been happening to him.

"I will not use the power," he muttered to himself as he continued the march, striding along well in front of his army, where his audible ramblings would not be heard.

"I am a goblin, I will remain a goblin, even if it means not using my strength." The decision needed reinforcement. "I am a goblin. I am a goblin. I will stay a goblin."

As he crossed the next hill, he saw a group of his people, nearly a hundred, gathered around several campfires. They shouted with joy as he came down the hill, laughing and dancing about as they hurried forward to greet him.

Their racket was cut short as from the far side of the group, came a shout.

"Tal-Qazar! I challenge! " Uchlig, one of his lieutenants, spoke the words Tal-Qazar had been dreading.

The goblins in front of him parted, sidling back to give Uchlig passage and to get out of the way of the fight. Uchlig strode toward Tal-Qazar, his steps firm and his eyes glowing with bloodlust. As he approached, the king of the Spiderfell smelled the stink of power.

Tal-Qazar howled in rage and frustration, knowing he had to meet Uchlig in combat. He had no fear of losing, only what would happen after, knowing that in the night he would awaken to some new mutation.

He was momentarily weakened by unwanted and horrible images of what he would become. He forced them from his mind and gathered his strengths. No matter what happened he was Tal-Qazar, and he would remain king of the goblins.

He pulled his blades and stepped forward to do battle.

If you enjoyed *The Spider's Test*, read these other great **BIRTHRIGHT**™ books from TSR . . .

WAR
Simon Hawke
   Now available in hardcover! An epic tale of passion, betrayal and war set against the backdrop of the disintegrating Empire of Anuire.

THE HAG'S CONTRACT
John Gregory Betancourt
   Richard Endier isn't the only human to face the terror of the awnsheghlien! What is pirate king Ulrich willing to sacrifice to free his kingdom from savage humanoids?

GREATHEART
Dixie Lee McKeone
   A human orphan raised by elves is caught between an invasion from the Shadow World and the evil ambition of a powerful awnshegh.

THE IRON THRONE
Simon Hawke
   The first BIRTHRIGHT™ novel brings the Emperor Michael Roele himself face-to-face with the most terrifying awnshegh of all—the Gorgon!

BIRTHRIGHT™

BOOKS

Threescore generations have passed since that impossible day when six gods sacrificed themselves to destroy one of their own and the bloodlines were born.

Mount Deismaar
Cerilia, Year Zero

The human tribes—my ancestors—moved up into the wilderness of Cerilia from the southern continent of Aduria, dragging their gods with them. Crossing a land bridge now hidden deep under the waves of the Straits of Aerele, they found seemingly limitless land in which to grow and prosper. So, too, did they find desperate enemies and the evil agents of the very god from whom they fled—the Shadow, Azrai.

Years of war and bloodshed followed, and Azrai gained in followers among those seeking to protect their ancestral lands. The Shadow made converts even among the reclusive elves, who first welcomed the newcomers to Cerilia, but soon grew wary of their expansion. As dark forces grew to both the north and south, the human tribes were forced together and went to war as allies in the War of Shadow.

Like their human followers, Anduiras, god of war and nobility; Reynir, goddess of the woods and streams; Brenna, goddess of commerce and fortune; Vorynn, lord of the moon and magic; Masela, the lady of the seas; and Basaïa, queen of the sun, joined the fight against the Shadow. Lines were drawn, champions chosen . . . blood spilled.

Until they all came to face each other at the foot of Mount Deismaar. Those who survived did not have words to describe the explosive burst of energy—the power no mortal should ever have been exposed to—and the mountain was gone. With it, to oblivion, went Azrai and the other gods—all of them. Six destroyed themselves to destroy one, for the sake of millions of suffering mortals and the future of Cerilia.

But what happens when man and elf, goblin and dwarf are showered with the essence of the gods? This instant of destruction became an instant of creation, and the bloodlines of Cerilia were born. Some, bathed in the glory of the likes of Anduiras, became great heroes, champions of justice. Others, corrupted by the malignant power of Azrai, became hideous monsters, abominations—*awnsheghlien.*

The champions of the dead gods, now possessed of supernatural powers of their own, fed on the empowered blood of the other survivors in the brutal practice of *bloodtheft.* From this chaos, the Empire of Anuire was born and some measure of peace came to Cerilia.

Then, like all things, the Anuirean Empire came to an end. Some say the true spirit of the empire never really survived the death of its founder, Michael Roele, less than half a century after his rise to power. On the ruins of the empire grew the beginnings of the Cerilian kingdoms of today, our own among them. Led by the descendants of the survivors of Deismaar, these kingdoms hold the future of Cerilia in their unsteady hands.

Who will be the next Roele?

What will be the next Anuire . . . the next Deismaar?

We, the people of Cerilia, tempered by our unimaginable past, look toward our future with fear . . . and with hope.

—Rhobher Nichaleir
Archprelate of the Western Imperial Temple, Tuornen